The Athenaeum

NORTHWESTERN WORLD CLASSICS

Northwestern World Classics brings readers
the world's greatest literature. The series features
essential new editions of well-known works,
lesser-known books that merit reconsideration,
and lost classics of fiction, drama, and poetry.
Insightful commentary and compelling new translations
help readers discover the joy of outstanding writing
from all regions of the world.

Raul Pompeia

The Athenaeum

A Novel

Translated from the Portuguese
by Renata R. M. Wasserman

Introduction by César Braga-Pinto

Northwestern University Press ✦ *Evanston, Illinois*

Northwestern University Press
www.nupress.northwestern.edu

Printed in the United States of America

10 9 8 7 6 5 4 3 2 1

Library of Congress Cataloging-in-Publication Data

Pompeia, Raul, 1863–1895, author.
    [Ateneu. English]
    The athenaeum : a novel / Raul Pompeia ; translated from the Portuguese by Renata R. M. Wasserman ; introduction by Cesar Braga-Pinto.
        pages cm. — (Northwestern world classics)
    Includes bibliographical references.
    ISBN 978-0-8101-3079-1 (pbk. : alk. paper) —
ISBN 978-0-8101-3106-4 (e-book)
    I. Wasserman, Renata R. Mautner (Renata Ruth Mautner), 1941–
translator. II. Title. III. Series: Northwestern world classics.
    PQ9697.P655A813 2015
    869.33—dc23

                                                            2014050147

CONTENTS

Darwinism, Max Nordau, and Raul Pompeia's Struggle for Existence

César Braga-Pinto

> What would be my fate, in that society that Rebelo
> had described with horror, his half-words of
> mystery raising undefined fears, his exhortations
> to energy making friendship sound like hostility?
> —*The Athenaeum*

Raul d'Ávila Pompeia (1863–1895) is one of nineteenth-century Brazil's most intriguing literary figures. The dramatic narrative of his life and death, with its hidden or inscrutable aspects, continues to fascinate contemporary readers.[1] Born into a family of plantation owners in Angra dos Reis (a small town neighboring Rio de Janeiro, then the capital of the Brazilian monarchy), Pompeia moved to Rio in 1873, where he studied first at the prestigious boarding school Colégio Abílio, and then at the equally prestigious Imperial Colégio D. Pedro II. He studied law in São Paulo from 1881 to 1884, and it was during this time that he became a passionate abolitionist, inspired by the ideas of the journalist and former slave Luiz Gama (1830–1882). He began collaborating with another activist, Antônio Bento (1843–1898), in arranging the systematic escape of slaves.[2] After failing his final exams, he moved to the northeastern city of Recife and managed to graduate. He returned to Rio in 1885 to become a fervent polemicist and prolific contributor to numerous newspapers. He regularly published articles on art, literature, politics, and daily life in Rio de Janeiro, as well as novellas, poetic prose, and short stories, though only two of his works appeared in book form during his lifetime.[3] He also drafted political cartoons, caricatures, and other illustrations for books and newspapers, and even tried his hand as a sculptor.

Pompeia was widely known in the intellectual and bohemian circles of Rio de Janeiro, where he made both friends and enemies. Rumors circulated about his eccentric and supposedly "morbid" temperament and his allegedly deficient sexuality: one of his contemporaries, the writer Coelho Neto (1864–1934), maliciously commented that Pompeia shied away from "women's skirts" during their college years in São Paulo like the devil from the cross.[4] Highly concerned with the harmful effects of the press and public opinion, Pompeia tried to take control of his reputation without sacrificing his opinions or integrity. In March 1892, a newspaper printed a nasty exchange of insults between Pompeia and the poet Olavo Bilac (1865–1918) that began when an article attributed to Bilac accused Pompeia of engaging in masturbation (associated with degeneration at the time), and Pompeia responded that Bilac had committed incest. When Pompeia ran into Bilac on Ouvidor Street, the two writers engaged in a fistfight, and then Pompeia—who had written against dueling as a practice—challenged Bilac to a duel.[5] It is said that the duel was aborted by friends and the police on the so-called field of honor, but it seems Pompeia was unsatisfied with the resolution of the humiliating dispute.

Pompeia faced further hostility when he declared his support for the authoritarian and militaristic government of Floriano Peixoto (1839–1895), who came to power in 1889 at the end of the monarchic regime. Pompeia defended Peixoto's stated goal of consolidating the republic at all costs, even through the use of force and censorship, a position that increasingly isolated him from his contemporaries. His eulogy of President Peixoto in June 1895 was interpreted as an insult to incoming President Prudente de Morais (1841–1902) and earned him the scorn of many. An article signed by Luiz Murat (1861–1929), a friend of Pompeia's since his college years, referred to his Lusophobic nationalism as a notable case of "morbidity."[6] Murat further insinuated that a cowardly Pompeia had avoided the duel with Bilac three years earlier. The controversial eulogy also led to Pompeia's dismissal from his position as the director of the National Library in October 1895.

Two months later, on Christmas Day, at one o'clock in the afternoon—the thirteenth hour, which he had once called "the hour of death"[7]—Raul Pompeia committed suicide with a gunshot to his chest.[8] The thirty-two-year-old writer had written extensively on the subject of suicide (including a comment that shooting oneself in the head was messy and therefore in bad taste), and he ended his life with a well-rehearsed performance. His melodramatic suicide note was immediately reproduced in the major Brazilian newspapers: "To the NOTICIA newspaper and to Brazil, I declare that I am a man of honor."

Natural Selection

Pompeia's *The Athenaeum* (1888) is a classic boarding-school narrative, in which the educational institution is a microcosm of social and political life in a Brazil characterized by antiquated values and institutions. Published the same year as the abolition of slavery and one year before the proclamation of the republic, the novel can be read as an explicit critique of outdated monarchic institutions, and perhaps also (though less obviously) the institution of slavery.[9] At the same time, and despite its author's efforts to dissociate his life from his work, the novel has largely been read as autobiographical, inflected with Pompeia's resentful and vengeful recollections of his years in boarding school and his disdain for the pedagogical methods and capitalist ambitions of the school's headmaster, reconceived in the novel as the caricature Aristarco.[10] By no means a typical naturalist work in the style of Émile Zola, *The Athenaeum* is clearly informed by Darwinist thought, in part by way of the works of Max Nordau (1849–1923).

The novel's opening lines allude to the then-familiar Darwinian notion of the struggle for life: "'You are about to enter the real world,' my father told me, at the gates of the Athenaeum. 'Be brave; it will be a struggle.'" The expression "struggle for life," which Brazilian newspapers often quoted in English in the second half of the nineteenth century, derives from the title of Charles Darwin's *On the Origin of Species by Means of Natural Selection, or the Preservation of Favored Races in the Struggle for Life* (1858). In chapter 3 ("Struggle for Existence"), Darwin stresses that he uses the metaphor "struggle for life" to emphasize the interdependence of all beings and the even more important idea of "success in leaving progeny." Rather than simple competition, the struggle involves what he called "a web of complex relations": "The dependency of one organic being on another, as of a parasite on its prey, lies generally between beings remote in the scale of nature. . . . But the struggle almost invariably will be most severe between the individuals of the same species, for they frequent the same districts, require the same food, and are exposed to the same dangers."[11] Although it had circulated in French editions since the early 1860s, Darwin's work was not widely discussed in Brazil until the mid-1870s. It was subject to a variety of (often disparate) interpretations, from monogenism to polygenism, from the justification of slavery to its condemnation, from readings that emphasized conflict and competition to those that stressed solidarity and collaboration. The resulting view of Brazilian society could be triumphant or pessimistic, with different degrees of racial determinism. Neither optimistic nor overly pessimistic, Pompeia's approach to social life can be called critical social Darwinism.

The Athenaeum was published at a moment when the various iterations of Darwinist thought were already well established in Brazil. The Darwinian intentions of the novel's opening sentences are unequivocal, and have to do with whether or how a boy entering the school world will adapt, survive, and evolve once immersed in the competitive reality of the educational institution and social convention.[12] But Pompeia was critical of the kind of ruthless doctrine that promised the survival of the *strongest.* While the terms in which Pompeia understood evolution may not be entirely clear (for example, whether or to what extent he saw any escape from his contemporaries' fatalistic view of scientific laws), the novel was likely informed by the strain of social Darwinism propagated by Nordau. Particularly influential was Nordau's early *The Conventional Lies of Our Civilization* (1883), an extremely popular book at the time. Pompeia admired and praised it in a review less than one year before *The Athenaeum* began to appear in the pages of *Gazeta de Notícias.*[13]

Nordau's book examines and critiques modern society's religious, political, economic, and sexual institutions. According to his version of Darwinism, "man has two powerful instincts which govern his whole life and give the first impulse to all his actions: the instinct of self-preservation and the instinct of race-preservation. The former reveals itself in its simplest form as hunger, the latter as love."[14] Modern pessimism, he claims, derives from the failure of institutions to act in accordance with the evolutionary principles of natural selection and the struggle for existence, which he believes constitute the foundation of all political and social facts:

> We believe that the development of the human as well as of all other races, was perhaps first made possible by sexual selection, and certainly promoted by it; and that the struggle for existence, using the term in its most comprehensive sense, shapes the destinies of nations as well as of the most obscure individual and is the foundation for all forms of political and social life.[15]

For Nordau, who calls pessimism the disease of the civilized world, *fin-de-siècle* man is so pathologically pessimistic and skeptical because he must abide by institutions that he perceives as false, antiquated, and contrary to his most basic instincts:

> We believe in the powerful and beneficent effect of sexual selection, and yet we defend the modern conventional marriage, which, in its present form, directly excludes it. We acknowledge the struggle for existence as the inevitable foundation for all law and morality, and yet, every day we pass laws to uphold and perpetuate conditions which absolutely prevent the free exercise of our powers, and deny to the strong and those worthy of the fullest life, the right to make use of their strength, and we stigmatize their inevitable victory over the feeble, as a capital crime. Thus our whole system of life is based upon false principles which we inherited from former ages.[16]

Thus, according to Nordau, the modern individual is trapped in the intolerable situation of leading two distinct and contradictory lives—an exterior life imposed by conventions, and an interior one driven by the instincts of love and hunger. The resulting tension causes an excessive expenditure of moral force: "In this insupportable contradiction we lose all enjoyment of life and all inclination for effort."[17] He further argues that civilized man has grown selfish and that all social intercourse is based on lies and hypocrisy, making men grumpy, bitter, and unhappy. Nordau derives a principle of solidarity from Darwin's notion of the interconnectedness of all living beings. He believes that solidarity, which he calls "nature's morality," is the only principle that can create conditions favorable to the existence of the species, and that morality and institutions should both be based on solidarity: "Nature's morality is the only one which mankind has ever really recognized—all other systems of morality are and always have been external hypocrisy, self-deception and the deception of others."[18] Ultimately, Nordau accepts that inequality is as natural as liberty: "the struggle for existence, that inexhaustible source of the beautiful variety and wealth of form and appearance in nature, is nothing else than a perpetual demonstration of inequality."[19]

Pompeia reads Nordau's work somewhat selectively, emphasizing solidarity, popular participation, and his revolutionary defense of communism. For Pompeia, "in [Nordau's] transparent language there shines the great soul of European socialism in incendiary bolts of lightning." Somewhat contradictorily, Pompeia seems to find in Nordau a democratic, egalitarian, social-reformist ideal that runs counter to the laws that would dictate a strict doctrine of struggle for life and natural selection. *The Athenaeum*, which narrates the struggles of an eleven-year-old boy as he selects his friends and associates with others as a way to adapt to a hostile environment and overcome the obstacles that it presents, can be read as a Nordauian critique of hypocrisy and a lament for the solidarity lacking in modern society. One of the boarding school's teachers summarizes its ruthless laws: "the weak are sacrificed; they do not prevail." In this perverse form of education, the mere *survival* of the fittest, or rather the *strongest*, is at stake.

And yet diversity ultimately prevails in *The Athenaeum.* Although Aristarco's boarding school represents a microcosm of Brazilian elite society, it is unlike elite society in the relative diversity of its student-citizens. In one of the novel's most self-reflective moments, the eloquent Dr. Claudio describes the boarding school as an "encounter and confusion of classes and fortunes" whose mission is "the training of the fighter as he engages in the fight," away from his family's protection. In contrast to the majority of authors publishing in Brazil in the late nineteenth century, Pompeia never translates struggle for life, natural selection, or survival of the fittest into class or racial hierarchies. The society of the boarding school includes "superior," "strong," and "fit" blacks, as well as "inferior," "weak," and "unfit" whites. Among the teachers is Venancio, an eloquent and "bronze-colored mulatto [mestiço]";[20] among the students are the *moreno* (dark-skinned) Álvares; the black Maurílio, who excels in math; the mulatto Negrão; and Batista Carlos, "of Indian blood, robust, an evil mug, scratching himself nonstop as if his clothes bothered him." White students like Almeidinha and Candido are identified by their "girlish face[s], sickly pink cheeks," and "feminine ways." And at the end of the third year, the dark-skinned students Negrão and Álvares pass with distinction, while pale and sickly Franco from rural Mato Grosso, who suffers constant humiliation while confined in (and within) the boarding school, receives poor grades and ultimately fails to endure the struggle. Interestingly, Franco is described as "a penitent expiating the guilt of an entire race," a clear reference to slavery and the so-called curse of Ham (or Canaan). His demise should be read less as a biological result of natural selection than as a consequence of injustices suffered by slaves as well as other outcasts of modern society. In this cruel and unjust hierarchy, Aristarco occupies the highest rank, and Franco the lowest.

A number of critics have pointed out that Sérgio, the narrator-protagonist, initially identifies with the outcast Franco; indeed, he repeatedly sees himself reflected in the figure of the underdog, sometimes with sympathy and compassion, sometimes with anxious disgust. As Brazilian critic Alfredo Bosi has suggested, "like Sérgio, the boy [Franco] knows himself to be the 'other' in the barbarism that threatens the institution. In him the universal desire for a scapegoat is cultivated. . . . He is the oppressed in its pure state."[21] Sérgio ironically describes Franco as "a perfect example of depravation offered to the holy horror of the pure." The unforgiving power of public opinion stigmatizes the less-fit student as a way to assert its own superiority. But Sérgio mocks this presumptuous judgment, ironically stating: "None of us is as bad as he is!"

The struggle for life in Pompeia's novel—and arguably in his professional career and personal life as well—requires defending one's reputation, but even more, protecting one's honor from shame. The novel teaches that an individual should strive to command the respect of public opinion, but must maintain an unrelenting commitment to moral rectitude in doing so: "as of old promises to myself, promises to walk the straight and narrow—I don't quite know how to say it, old reasons of vertebrate vanity; aversion to subterfuges." The novel acknowledges that personal integrity and self-respect do not always coincide with demands for social recognition, particularly those imposed by arbitrary conventions and antiquated institutions, such as the boarding school and the press:

> Capricious and unreliable queen, this opinion tyrannized
> us beyond any appeal, final as a judgment from the high-
> est court. The fearful newscast, compiled at the whim
> of the unreliable justice of the teachers, often violent,
> ignorant, hateful, immoral, reared itself up as an irre-
> deemable attack on reputations. A judge could be driven
> from the bench by conclusive evidence of his defects; the
> written defamation was irrevocable.

The ability to adapt to the social milieu, and especially the forces of opinion, is at the core of this *fin-de-siècle* version of evolutionary thinking in which "natural" selection can lead to exclusion from society and even life. Pompeia's famous description of society as an inverted hedgehog (*ouriço*) captures his bitter view of a struggle for life that encompasses both institutionalized power and environmental influences: "The middle, let us say, is a reversed hedgehog: instead of the centrifugal explosion of darts, we have a convergence of spines toward the center. Caught in the stinging mass of spines, it is necessary either to find a duct toward the exit or accept the unequal contest between the skin and the quills. Generally, one chooses the duct." Pompeia thus suggests two options for surviving the miniature world of the boarding school: the attempt to preserve one's integrity and the corresponding struggle to reconcile it with the demands of the environment, or resignation and acceptance of the inevitable inequality of the struggle. While resistance may (seek to) lead to some form of transgression of social norms and conventions, resignation may have different meanings and consequences. It may signify total acceptance of social conventions, as in the case of those whom the narrator calls "victims of their uniforms." Or it may mean acknowledging defeat and accepting one's status as a "loser" or eternal scapegoat, as Franco does when he withdraws from society and, ultimately, from life, losing even his sense of honor and ability to feel shame: "The worst case in this system of justice by pillory was when the student became hardened by habit, his sense of shame murdered, as in the case of Franco," who went about life at the boarding school "with the stony insensibility he used as his armor against humiliation."[22] Survival in the Athenaeum (like survival in Pompeia's moral world) depends largely on having the strength to endure the scrutiny and judgment of others, and the ability to withstand harsh words and public shaming: "Public opinion is a devilish opponent that can count on the ultimate complicity of the victim himself."

But how can a member of this society keep his integrity and not be crushed by the power of public opinion? How can he learn to resist and react in face of slander and defamation? If scrutiny and the gaze, with their potent power to discipline, are central to the pedagogical machine of the boarding school, they are also always associated with the imminent violence of a venomous tongue.[23] Throughout the novel, the struggles of individuals are recorded as linguistic battles, in which insults, comments, insinuations, opinions, and slander threaten to expose the boys to shame and dishonor. For Sérgio as an adult narrator, the romantic nostalgia of the childhood years is fundamentally euphemistic, as it conceals the wounds and damage caused by this linguistic violence. Even time cannot erase the traumatic marks of past insults, injuries, and obscenities. Sérgio's earliest memories, of a time before boarding school, are already tainted by competition and cruelty toward outcasts like the laughingstock or effeminate boy. Rather than retaining sweetly nostalgic childhood memories, Sérgio is left with the obscene effects of an unpronounceable insult: "I remember hearing there for the first time a crude insult, a swear word viewed with such terror at the establishment that when the class tattletale went with it to the teachers, they referred to it just by its two initials."

And as the twentieth century approached, those subjects most vulnerable to the violence of the insult were the members of a race considered inferior or individuals whose sexuality deemed deviant.

Sexual Selection

The three public speeches that Dr. Claudio gives in the novel have long been read as a reflection, at least in part, of Pompeia's philosophical opinions. Taking this reading as valid, it appears that he did not subscribe to the strictly competitive version of natural selection or the struggle for existence.[24] On the one hand, Dr. Claudio (or the "subversive" master, as the narrator calls him), defines evolution in Darwinian and, more specifically, Nordau-ian language: "There are two elementary representations of realized pleasure: nutrition and love." On the other hand, he seems opposed to the institutional appropriation of the pleasure principles:

> The fatal necessity of nutrition was made into a principle: it was called industry; it was called political economy; it was called militarism. Death to the Franks! Reaching for the black flag of Spartan Darwinism, civilization marched toward the future, fearless, undaunted, crushing underfoot the artistic prejudices of religion and morality.[25]

The Athenaeum thus critically evokes not only the law of natural selection as proposed in Darwin's *On the Origin of Species* but also the notion of sexual selection that Darwin further developed in *The Descent of Man, and Selection in Relation to Sex* (1871). It is not difficult to understand why Darwin's language, once decontextualized, could be used to explain and justify social exclusion and enforce the control of sexualities. *On the Origin of Species* calls natural selection "preservation of favorable variations and the rejection of injurious variations." For Darwin, "it may metaphorically be said that natural selection is daily and hourly scrutinizing, throughout the world, every variation, even the slightest; rejecting that which is bad, preserving and adding up all that is good."[26]

Darwin defines sexual selection as "the struggle between the males for the possession of the female" in order to secure the preservation of the race—that is, to reproduce. As Leela Gandhi has suggested, one may read "the entire field of late-nineteenth-century homosexual polemics as a mediated reaction" to *The Descent of Man*. Gandhi explains that, if evolution depends on reproduction, then "the tasks of successful reproduction demand an acute sexual dimorphism in nature, sharply distinguishing the secondary sexual characteristics of males and females as romantic (or aesthetic) inducement to the grisly business of productive mating." According to evolutionary theory, such sexual differentiation becomes more pronounced among more developed groups: "only in the 'civilised world' do we witness the comprehensive implementation of the sex or gender divide, which in turn holds the key to successful (monogamous) reproduction." Ultimately, "the principles of sexual selection . . . were thus instrumental in producing the nonheterosexual or homosexual as a 'civilizational' aberration." Darwin's *Descent* would eventually be translated into "a manifesto for heteronormativity."[27]

Sérgio's education can be read as a fundamentally sexual education presented in an evolutionary, normative, emasculating (straight) line of sexual differentiation from effeminacy to heteronormative virility. Not surprisingly, gender differentiation is understood in the binary terms of weakness/strength, as in the following warning from one of his classmates:

> The geniuses create two sexes here, as if it were a coed school. The timid, innocent, bloodless kids are smoothly pushed into the weak sex: they are dominated, coddled, perverted like unprotected girls. When, behind their parents' backs, they believe that school offers the best of lives, well received as they are by the older students, half-naughty and half-affectionate, they are lost. Be a man, my friend!

When, in one of his first speeches, the school's director tells students to "watch the dark corners; supervise friendships," he makes the institution's nature as a vigilant panopticon explicit, as well as the disciplinary and heteronormative project that it carries out. However, the master's disciplinary gaze is only one of those exchanged within the boarding school. In the same way that the novel does not subscribe to the vulgar, draconian Darwinism that promotes death to the weak, sexual differentiation is never complete, and the identification between masculinity and strength is not total. The response to the mandate "be a man" is necessarily ambiguous and unstable.

The novel can be, and has been, read primarily as a narration of the protagonist's struggle to build moral (heteronormative) character, or "moral energy," as Sérgio often calls it. One of Pompeia's contemporaries, for example, described Sérgio as driven by "a lack of force to resist."[28] Thus, to survive the hostile and masculinist world constructed by the school's disciplinary order, Sérgio must ignore Rebelo's advice to "be a man" and accept the feminized role of protégée or "girlfriend," assuming a "voluntary subjection, the feminine vanity of dominating through weakness." The young protagonist then passes through several evolutionary "phases" of sexual differentiation, engaging in a number of real or phantasmatic relationships: with Sanches (through sexual inversion), Bento Alves (sexual perversion), Egbert (sexual sublimation), the "prostitute" (sexual corruption), and finally, separation from the father and sublimation of love for the maternal woman. The adult narrator retrospectively acknowledges, without any sign of shame or remorse, that "there can be a certain effeminacy as a phase in the development of one's character."

Critics have tended to emphasize this linear and teleological interpretation, thus accepting and reproducing the straight evolutionary line of the narrator's trajectory from juvenile experimentation to a fixed and immutable heterosexuality. This reading is supported by Pompeia's drawings, which were included as illustrations in the second (1905) edition of *The Athenaeum*. The Brazilian critic José Paulo Paes, for example, restates the first-person narrator's opinions and affirms that repeated "traumatic" experiences are necessary to the development of normal sexuality: "escaping the homosexual violations and searching to improve himself in the platonic friendship, until he finds his elective heterosexual objective."[29] I believe this normalizing reading is flawed in that it identifies the entire novel with either Aristarco's disciplinary project or Sérgio's guilty, dissimulated conscience.

Rather than following the linear interpretation that critics have favored, we should pay closer attention to the novel's counternarratives, which reinterpret the doctrines of "hunger" and "love." An example is the scene (and corresponding illustration) of public shaming that represents the punishment of a same-sex couple. After finding a romantic letter signed with the woman's name "Candida," Aristarco assembles the student body—all of whom know that their classmate Candido wrote the letter ("there was nobody, one can truly say, who was not implicated in the school comedy of the sexes")—so that the boys can denounce the author. The criminal couple (who are ironically named for two classic works on education, Jean Jacques Rousseau's *Emile* and Voltaire's *Candide*) and twelve accomplices are exposed in a spectacle of public humiliation. However, the gaze that disciplines, objectifies, and subjects the other gives way to a new gaze that turns shame into complicity among the damned: "Candido [Lima] and [Emilio] Tourinho, arms shielding their eyes, stole glances at each other, taking comfort in the shared disgrace like Francesca and Paolo in Dante's *Inferno*." Once again, it is clear that Aristarco's disciplinary gaze is not the only gaze in *The Athenaeum*, and it cannot take away the power of gazes that flirt, conspire, and defy. At the end of the novel, the lovers are punished, but not expelled.

This scene, which sympathetically depicts the powers of love, is immediately followed by one in which Pompeia recasts the power of hunger. In that episode, Sérgio defies the headmaster in an act of insolence, and the fight against authority and the institution escalates. Right after the two lovers are punished, a riot breaks out among the students. The headmaster summons twenty students for interrogation and public shaming, but manages only to build support for the homosexual couple among the subversive group: "in our quality of *political prisoners*, victims of our generous sedition, we were not vexed by our penance." Finally, the remaining students also riot: "It was an indescribable tumult, the voices of a populace in revolt, whistles, shouts, insults, in which the high-pitched screams of the younger ones pierced the confused clamor. . . . It was the revolution of the guava paste! An old complaint."

Hunger and love: these were the real motivations behind the "guava paste revolution" and the scandal around the homosexual couple, respectively. This single sequence of events includes infliction of harm on the father, public humiliation of the homosexual couple, and social and economic rebellion against the group's inadequate nutrition. And yet, nobody is punished, ostensibly because the school has to preserve its image. In the meantime, the narrator introduces what he calls his only "true" friendship, separate from any sense of dependency and in accord with classic models of equitable friendship:

> But to Egbert I was a true friend. For no better reason
> than that one does not argue with affection. We impro-
> vised on the theme of collaboration; we exchanged mean-
> ings; neither owed the other. Nevertheless I experienced
> the delightful need for dedication. I thought myself
> strong for being able to love and show it.

This ideal friendship is defined as the capacity and willingness to share guilt and shame. When the headmaster summons Egbert, Sérgio confesses that he is "crushed by not being able to find a way to share in his shame." By the end of the novel, this friendship has faded into mere cordiality, leaving room for Sérgio's erotic and then filial love for Ema, the headmaster's wife. Again, a strictly teleological reading of *The Athenaeum* would view the evolutionary heteronormalization of Sérgio's sexuality as the true meaning of the novel. But if the principles of hunger and love, as elaborated by Nordau, are the central motifs of Pompeia's narrative, then transgression, complicity, political organization, and defiance seem to be its meaning and motivating forces, along with the promise that a feeling of shame can be turned into a sense of honor.

In both Pompeia's life and work, concern for issues of honor and shame forms the consistent core of his personal, political, and intellectual trajectories. They determine his political ideals, practices, and moral principles. While the notion of individual honor necessarily involves regard for public opinion, shame can be a response to a situation that threatens an individual's integrity or features values and conventions that an individual is unable or unwilling to abide. In *The Athenaeum*, the inflexible subject (Franco) degenerates and dies, but so do social conventions and institutions that no longer correspond to the desires and demands of the community of students. Acts of public shaming that the institution intends as a form of discipline inadvertently provoke a moral revolution. In the case of Pompeia's own dramatic demise, it seems that his individual (inflexible?) integrity could not or would not adjust to the pressures of social, political, sexual, and gender conventions. In a situation that caused him intense shame, suicide appeared to be the only remaining way to demonstrate honor. As Pompeia once stated: "as drama of honor, the suicide is most accomplished."[30]

Notes

1. I base this description of Pompeia's life on two biographies of the writer: Eloy Pontes, *A Vida Inquieta de Raul Pompéia* (Rio de Janeiro:

José Olympio, 1935); and Camil Capaz, *Raul Pompéia: Biografia* (Rio de Janeiro: Gryphus, 2001).

2. On Pompeia's abolitionism, see César Braga-Pinto, "The Honor of the Abolitionist and the Shamefulness of Slavery: Raul Pompeia, Luís Gama, and Joaquim Nabuco," *Luso-Brazilian Review* 51, no. 2 (December 2014).

3. *Uma Tragédia no Amazonas* (A Tragedy in the Amazon) was first published in 1880, when Pompeia was only seventeen. *The Athenaeum*, here translated into English for the first time, was published in 1888 in both serial and book form. The second edition, published in 1905, included illustrations by the author. The novel has previously been translated into Czech, French, and Spanish: *Atheneum*, trans. Jarmila Vojtíková (Prague: SNKLU, 1963); *L'Athénée: Chronique d'une nostalgie*, trans. Françoise Duprat and Luiz Dantas (Toulouse: Ombres, 1989); and *El Ateneo: Crónica de Nostalgias*, trans. Paula Abramo (Mexico City: Universidad Nacional Autónoma de México, 2014). The Spanish edition contains one of the most complete introductions to Pompeia's work in any language. Because there is practically no critical bibliography on Pompeia in English, I shall refer to most of the important criticism in Portuguese. Unless otherwise indicated, all translations from critical works in the introduction are mine.

4. Coelho Neto, *Revista da Academia Brasileira de Letras* 49 (January 1926): 62–64.

5. Dueling, a fashionable new import from France, had become popular in Brazil. Local bohemians performed rituals of honor reparation to amuse themselves, and many wrote articles defending the practice, calling it a civil way to solve disputes and create a sense of fraternity among the members of Brazil's emerging lettered elite. But it was seldom taken seriously in Brazil, and newspapers of the period joked about the ridiculousness of duelists and the cowardice of occasional combatants. By 1890, the new Republican Criminal Code had outlawed dueling. César Braga-Pinto, "Journalists, *Capoeiras*, and the Duel in Nineteenth-Century Rio de Janeiro," *Hispanic American Historical Review* 94, no. 4 (November 2014): 581–614.

6. Luiz Murat, "Um Louco no Cemitério," *Comércio de São Paulo*, October 16, 1895.

7. Capaz, *Raul Pompéia*, 245.

8. Pontes, *A Vida Inquieta de Raul Pompéia*, 316.

9. *The Athenaeum* was published as a serialized novel in the newspaper *Gazeta de Notícias* between March and May 1888, and as a book later

that year. Publication of the last installment was delayed due to the abolition of slavery on May 13, 1888, and the radical, iconoclastic closing chapter was not published until the following Friday, May 18.

10. Mário de Andrade's 1941 study of the novel was the first critical piece to explore the theme of revenge in *The Athenaeum*. See "O Ateneu," in *Aspectos da Literatura Brasileira* (São Paulo: Martins, 1972), 173–95.

11. Charles Darwin, *On the Origin of Species* (Oxford: Oxford University Press, 2008), 60.

12. Pompeia's struggle for life does not have the social Darwinist connotation associated with the "arrivisme" of other writers of his time. In fact, less than a month after publication of the last installment of the serialized novel, Pompeia's peer João Pardal Mallet (1864–1894) noted that "Aristarco . . . represents this desire to shine which today assaults all men . . . it represents the tendency of a society that substitutes the Darwinian formula *struggle for life* for this other one: *struggle for high life*" (*Diário de Noticias*, June 7, 1888). *The Athenaeum* was published one year before Alphonse Daudet's *La Lutte pour la vie* was performed in Paris for the first time. Valérie Stiénon, "Penser la querelle par la sélection naturelle," *COnTEXTES: Revue de sociologie de la littérature* 10 (2012): 1–14.

13. *A Semana*, July 9, 1887. Nordau's book, translated by Manuel Coelho da Rocha and published by Laemmert in 1887, was in its second edition as early as 1889, and its third in 1896. Pompeia also reviewed the Portuguese translation of Nordau's *Paradoxes* a few months after he finished the novel. *Gazeta de Notícias*, August 6, 1888. In contrast, Darwin's *On the Origin of Species* was not translated into Portuguese until 1913, when Joaquim Dá Mesquita Paul's translation was published (Porto: Livraria Chardron, de Lelo, and Irmãos, 1913).

14. Max Nordau, *The Conventional Lies of Our Civilization* (Chicago: Laird and Lee, 1895), 269. This notion is derived from the last lines of Friedrich von Schiller's 1795 poem "Die Weltweisen" (known in English as "The Philosophers"). These lines, which declare that hunger and love are the driving forces in the world, later informed Freud's theories of drive, which he included in the third chapter of *The Interpretation of Dreams* (1898) and *Civilization and Its Discontents* (1929). Graham Frankland, *Freud's Literary Culture* (Cambridge: Cambridge University Press, 2006), 39–40.

15. Nordau, *The Conventional Lies of Our Civilization*, 26.

16. Nordau, *The Conventional Lies of Our Civilization*, 28.

17. Nordau, *The Conventional Lies of Our Civilization*, 30.

18. Nordau, *The Conventional Lies of Our Civilization*, 363.

19. Inequality, for Nordau, serves to improve the average man: "The oppressed inferiors revolt, the oppressor overpowers them. In this struggle the powers of the weak grow stronger and the faculties of the strong attain to their highest possibility. . . . The average type becomes continually nobler and better . . . the result, a constant progress toward the realization of the ideal" (119).

20. According to Angela Alonso, Pompeia's teachers at the Imperial Colégio D. Pedro II included the Afro-Brazilian Vicente Ferreira de Souza, who hailed from the northeastern province of Bahia and taught Latin and philosophy. Along with José do Patrocínio and André Rebouças, he was one of Brazil's most prominent antislavery activists. "Flores, Votos e Balas," diss., Universidade de São Paulo, 2012, 119.

21. Alfredo Bosi, "*O Ateneu*, opacidade e destruição," in *Céu, Inferno: Ensaios de Crítica Literária e Ideológica* (São Paulo: Ed. 34/Duas Cidades, 2003), 74.

22. The end of the novel reveals that Franco, although he had grown used to public humiliation, felt at least enough shame to forge his grades in order to impress his father (192).

23. Alfredo Bosi's discussion of the centrality of seeing and being seen in the novel is illuminating on this point. "*O Ateneu*, opacidade e destruição," 61–68.

24. Ledo Ivo called these speeches "essay islands" that reproduce some of Pompeia's main philosophical and aesthetic ideas. *O universo poético de Raul Pompéia* (Rio de Janeiro: Livraria São José, 1963), 45. For further discussion of whether Dr. Claudio's speeches express Pompeia's views, see Leyla Perrone Moisés, ed., *O Ateneu: Retórica e Paixão* (São Paulo: Brasiliense/Edusp, 1988), 227–54.

25. As Bosi has noted, Pompeia's response to the determinism of the scientific ideas of his time is better characterized as extremely ambivalent than as passively accepting: "The prestige of the laws of Darwinism cohabits with an anarchism without chains, resentful and incendiary" ("*O Ateneu*, opacidade e destruição," 52).

26. Darwin, *On the Origin of Species*, 64–68.

27. Leela Gandhi, *Affective Communities: Anticolonial Thought, Fin-de-Siècle Radicalism, and the Politics of Friendship* (Durham, N.C.: Duke University Press, 2006), 48–49.

28. Araripe Júnior, "Raul Pompéia: *O Ateneu* e o romance psicológico," in *Obra Crítica* (Rio de Janeiro: MEC/Fund Rio Barbosa,

1980), vol. 2, 150. This series of critical articles was first published between December 1888 and February 1889, just a few months after the novel's release.

29. José Paulo Paes, "Sobre as ilustrações do *Ateneu*," in *Gregos e Baianos: Ensaios* (São Paulo: Brasiliense, 1985), 60. For less heterocentric readings of the novel, see Marco Antonio Yonamine, "O reverso especular: Sexualidade e (homo)erotismo na literatura brasileira finissecular," diss., Universidade de São Paulo, 1997; Leyla Perrone Moysés, "Lautréamont e Raul Pompéia," in *O Ateneu: Retórica e paixão* (São Paulo: Brasiliense/Edusp, 1988), 15–40; and especially Silviano Santiago, "*O Ateneu*: Contradições e perquirições," in *Uma Literatura nos Trópicos* (São Paulo: Brasiliense, 2000), 66–102. Richard Mikolski and Fernando Figueiredo Baliero analyze both *The Athenaeum* and the events of Pompeia's biography from a Foucauldian point of view in order to understand how "the specter of degeneration" (85) among the Brazilian elite in the late nineteenth century called for a "pedagogy of sexuality" that associated race and sexuality with the political project of constructing a viable nation and the ideal of virile nationality (76). Richard Mikolski and Fernando Figueiredo Baliero, "O drama público de Raul Pompéia: Sexualidade e política no Brasil finissecular," *Revista Brasileira de Ciências Sociais* 26, no. 75 (February 2011): 73–88.

30. *Jornal do Comércio*, December 1, 1890.

The Athenaeum

Chapter 1

"You are about to enter the real world," my father told me, at the gates of the Athenaeum. "Be brave; it will be a struggle." I often thought, afterward, about the truth contained in that warning, which stripped me, with one swift gesture, of the illusions I carried as a child nurtured, like an exotic plant, in the loving hothouse of domestic affection, so different from what one finds outside, that any poem about mother love seems but a sentimental artifice, and whose only advantage is that the creature so cultivated becomes more sensitive to the jolts of its first life lessons, to having its soul painfully tempered in that new, harsh climate. Let us remember, then, with hypocritical nostalgia, those happy school years, as if the same uncertainties that now stalk us had not stalked us then, under a different guise, and as if we had not been subject, from those earliest years, to disappointments that still offend us.

"Happy school years" is a euphemism, like all that nourishes our longing for old days said to have been better. If one thinks of it, it is always the present that assaults one. With different desires, different, ever-changing aspirations, always fired by the same fervor, built on the same fantastic foundation of hope, the present is always the same. Under the changing colors of the hours, with a touch more gold in the morning, a touch more red at dawn—the landscape is always the same along either side of life's path.

I was eleven.

For a few months I had attended a day school on the New Road, where several English ladies, under the direction of their father, dispensed education to the local children as they thought best. I would arrive at nine, shyly, ignore the lessons with great regularity, and yawn till two, writhing with boredom on the chipped and worn pine benches that the school had bought used, shiny from being rubbed by generations of little scamps. At noon they gave us bread and butter. That taste was what remained with me of those months, and also the memory of some of my schoolmates. One of them liked to make the class laugh, an interesting, disheveled little blond monkey, who had the habit of gnawing at a callus on the back of his left hand; another, foppish, elegant, kept himself apart, and came to school all starched and radiant in white, his shirt closed on the diagonal, from shoulder to waist, with mother-of-pearl buttons. Also, I remember hearing there for the first time a crude insult, a swear word viewed with such terror at the establishment that when the class tattletale went with it to the teachers, they referred to it just by its two initials.

Later, I was tutored at home.

Despite these attempts at a school life, to which my family subjected me before I met with the real trial, I was perfectly virginal as to the new sensations of the next phase. A boarding school! Soon my individuality would be freed from the placentary coziness of home, and I would have to define myself. I suffered by anticipation my farewell to the early joys of my life; I looked with sadness at my toys, so old already, the dear platoons of lead soldiers, a military museum of all the uniforms, all the flags, miniature samples of the power of states that I arranged in formation and sent into combat like a dark threat to the balance of the world, or that I forced onto the battlefield in a disordered crowd—a tempestuous massing of geographic hostilities, definitive, boiling encounters of race and border hatreds that I eventually calmed with the ease of a Divine Providence, making and imposing wise decisions sealed in the promiscuous harmony of the wooden boxes to which they retired. It would be hard to leave behind, a prey to rust, the elegant ship that plied the pond in the garden; it might never again break, with the beat of its wheels, the sleepy peace of the red,

silver, and gold fish, thoughtful in the shade of the wide cala-
dium leaves, in the diamond transparency of the water . . .

But there was something attractive in the prospect as well, a
first serious stirring of youthful vanity: I would distance myself
from my family, like a man and, on my very own, engage in a
struggle where merit counted; I was full of confidence in my
own strength. When they told me they had chosen the educational establishment that would receive me, the news found
me fully armed for the brave conquest of the unknown.

Then, one day, my father took my hand, my mother kissed
me on the forehead, bedewing my hair with her tears, and I left.

I had visited the Athenaeum twice before my installation.

At that time, the Athenaeum was the top boarding school
in the country. Its fame was supported by steady advertising,
kept up by its owner and headmaster who, from time to time,
reorganized the establishment, announcing it as new and improved, like merchants who close out their shops so they can
start over with the latest shipments from the fashion centers.
Thus the Athenaeum had its credit solidly established with the
parents, to say nothing of the good will of the offspring, all of
whom listened with enthusiasm to the booming drumbeat of
the ads.

Dr. Aristarco Argolo de Ramos, of the well-known family of
the Viscount of Ramos, from the north of the country, filled
the Brazilian empire with his fame as a pedagogue. There were
commercials for the school in all the provinces, invited talks
at different venues in the towns, and piles of gift boxes for the
local press, mostly books for teaching the early grades, thrown
together hastily with the breathless cooperation of prudently
anonymous professors—boxes and boxes of volumes bound in
Leipzig, flooding the public schools everywhere, an invasion
of blue, pink, and yellow covers, where the name of Aristarco,
sonorous and in full, offered itself to the astonished veneration of those who thirsted for the alphabet in even the most

remote corners of the fatherland. Even places that did not search them out were surprised some beautiful day by a flood of those books, all free, spontaneous, irresistible! And what could they do but accept the grain with which to make the bread for their minds? And their letters gained weight, perforce, from that bread. A benefactor. No wonder that, on feast days, personal or national, at school ceremonies or receptions at the imperial palace, the broad chest of the great educator disappeared under constellations of ribbons, medals, jewels, all of his opulent honorific trinkets.

Pomp brought out the real man. It was not just that decorations chirped from his chest like a breastplate made of crickets: Athenaeum! Athenaeum! The entire Aristarco was an advertisement. His gestures, calm and solemn, were those of royalty, the exalted autocrat of the syllabary; the hieratic slowness of his walk evidenced the effort with which, at each step, he pressed public education forward; the blinding beam of his eyes, under the hirsute roughness of his Japanese monster's brow, piercing with light the surrounding souls, represented the education of the intelligence; his chin, severely shaved from ear to ear, was smooth like a clean conscience and represented the education of the moral sense. Even his stature—in the immobility of his posture, the repose of his figure—the stature, one could say, by itself said of him: here is a great man . . . can you not see *Goliath's cubits*?! Entwist over it all a huge moustache—massive twin volutes of snowy threads, carefully shaped, covering his lips like a silver lock over golden silence, beautifully paraded like the fruitful seclusion of his spirit—and we will have sketched out, morally and materially, the profile of the illustrious headmaster. In sum, a notable who, at first sight, also gave the impression of a sick man, sick with this strange and grievous illness that is the obsession with turning the self into statuary. Meanwhile, waiting for that consecration, Aristarco made do with the influx of rich students to his institute. In fact, the students at the Athenaeum represented the flower of Brazilian youth.

The tentacles of his publicity machine reached so far into the land that there was no moneyed family, whether enriched by the equatorial rubber boom in the Amazon or by southern cattle ranches, that did not think it a debt of honor toward posterity to send, from their younger buds, one, two, or three representatives to drink from the spiritual springs of the Athenaeum.

Trusting this criterion of selection, based on the reasonable mistake of thinking the richest families were also the best, many, though smiling at the school's noise machine, sent their children to it. And this is how I was enrolled.

The first time I saw the establishment was on the occasion of an end-of-year ceremony.

One of the great halls at the front of the building had been turned into an amphitheater, specifically, the one that served as the school's chapel. The walls were covered with sumptuous plaster-relief sculptures, and a vast, magisterially painted medallion gave depth to the ceiling, sky-blue, from which clusters of delicious cherubs poured down, displaying daring expanses of rosy flesh, waving their tiny hands and feet, unfurling gauzy ribbons in the air. The altar had been taken down, and in its place there were circular stands of seats, covering up the luxury of the walls. The students sat in these bleachers. Since most of the public always preferred the gymnastics show, presented a few days after classes ended, the accommodations left for the outsiders were scant, and parents and friends, generally more numerous than expected, overflowed from the main theater to an adjacent room. From there, perched on a chair, I watched. My father whispered explanations. Before the bleachers stood a long table covered in thick green cloth, with gold tassels. There sat the headmaster, the imperial minister, and the prize committee. I watched and listened.

There was a moving speech by Aristarco; there were speeches by students and teachers; there was singing, and poetry read in various languages. The spectacle filled us with a certain respectful pleasure. The large headmaster, sitting beside the scrawny minister, obliterated him, with the brutal incivility of a scandalous contrast. In the full dress of grand occasions, he sat, his pride like a throne. The gorgeous black garb of the students, with its gold buttons, put me in mind, timidly, of a brilliant militarism, ready to take the field on behalf of science and virtue. The lyrics of the songs, sung in the undisciplined falsetto of puberty; the speeches, vetted by the headmaster, paunchy with the seriousness of middle age on the irreverent lips of adolescents, like an ill-staged pageant of the conservative bourgeoisie, delivered with the mechanical monotony of a barrel organ and wide overplayed gestures, in a cavernous voice and with inappropriate facial contortions as in masks of tragedy: I drank it all in, as if it were the text of a bible of duties; banalities fell into the audience like wise maxims of redemptive teaching. It seemed to me I was watching a legion of the friends of knowledge, the teachers at its head, leading a heroic onslaught against obscurantism, grabbing by the hair and stomping under their feet Ignorance and Vice, who kicked and screamed, miserable encumbrances that they were.

One speech in particular impressed me. To the right of the prize committee stood the orators' rostrum. Firmly and stiffly, Venancio, one of the teachers, climbed its steps; he made forty *mil-réis* per course, but felt important, his voice deep with the ring of independence, a bronze-colored mulatto, small and tenacious, who would later make a career for himself. The speech was boilerplate, medieval tourney compared to modern battle that used the weapons of intelligence; then a pedagogical lecture, its rhetorical flourishes added with hammer blows, and an apologia of school life, followed by an exaltation of masters in general and Aristarco and the Athenaeum in particular. In the peroration, Venancio declaimed: "The Master is the extension of fatherly love, the complement of motherly tenderness, the careful guide of the pupils' first steps on the scabrous trail that leads to the conquest of knowledge and morality. He is experienced in the daily labor of his sacred profession; his arm sustains us like Providence on earth; he follows us attentively like a guardian angel; his prudent lessons enlighten our journey into the future. We owe our father the existence of our bodies; the Master creates in us the spirit,"—attention here to the sensational sorites—"and the spirit is the force that impels, the impulse that triumphs, the triumph that ennobles, the ennobling that glorifies, and glory is the ideal of life, the warrior's laurel, the artist's oak, the palm leaf of the believer! The family is love in the home; the state is the custodian of the citizen's safety; the Master, who teaches and corrects us with his strong love, prepares us for the priceless inner safety of the will. Above Aristarco—God! only God; below God, Aristarco." With a wide gesture, like signing his name with a flourish in space, he tied up that last burst of eloquence.

I was impressed, not so much because I understood all that was going on as because of my blind faith in it all, so easily granted, given my disposition. The walls of the lobby were painted in imitation of green porphyry; before the portico opened over the garden, an ample stairway rose to the second floor. On either side of the majestic portal to that stairway were two works in high-relief: on the right, an allegory of the arts and of learning; on the left, human industry, with naked young boys, just like those in the murals by Kaulbach, smiling and holding symbolic tools—the pure psychology of labor, ideally represented by clean plaster and childish innocence. Those were my brethren! I almost expected one of them to stretch out an inviting hand and lead me into their happy dance. Oh, how wonderful school would be, translation of the allegory into real life, a heavenly circle of hearts at the gates of a temple, in permanent worship—what I had learned as the dulia, the veneration of the saints—by young souls performing the austere ritual of virtue!

I went back to the school for the gymnastics performance.

The Athenaeum was situated by the Rio Comprido—the "long river," as it was called—at the foot of hills whose tall rocky slopes, covered with jungle-like vegetation, threw over its building a melancholy twilight that did not yield even to the high sun of a November noon. This melancholy was plagiarized from the detestable monkish dread of that other educational institution, the Caraça Institute in the province of Minas Gerais. Aristarco took pride in this nature-given sadness, which provided the moral atmosphere of meditation and study, as if chosen especially to bring out the greater luxury of the building, as if it were a small addendum to its architecture.

On the day of the physical education festival, as the program informed us (a top-notch program, because the director's secretary had a talent for putting those together), I did not notice the sensation of solitude, so strong in mountainous areas, I would become aware of later. The gala of the moment made the landscape smile. The trees in the huge garden, made festive by a thousand streamers, glittered in the vivid sunlight with the splendor of a strange gaiety; the colorful strips of fabric looked like huge flowers amid the foliage in an extravagant caricature of spring; the branches bore, like fruit, Venetian lanterns, huge paper apples of a carnivalesque harvest. I was carried along by the crowds. My father held me tightly by the wrist so I would not get lost.

Submerged in the wave, I had to look up in order to breathe. The closest person before me made me laugh: his shirttail was hanging out. But no, it was not a shirttail, it was a handkerchief. From the soil rose a strong aroma of trampled cinnamon; through the trees, at intervals, came gusts of music, as if from a philharmonic storm.

One last, stronger crush, cracking my ribs, squeezed me, through a narrow opening in a wall, into the open space. Before me, an expansive lawn; surrounding it, a line of pennants, happy in the open space, the picturesque and bright colors singing clear over the green bass harmony of the mountains. People stood everywhere in knots. I turned and saw, along the wall, two tiers of stands with chairs occupied almost exclusively by the ladies, their dresses gleaming in a violent confusion of colors. Some were protecting their eyes with gloved hands, or with fans raised to their foreheads against the brightness of a bank of clouds rising in the sky. Above the stands little clumps of bamboo swayed languidly, murmuring softly and casting long trains of shadow on the lawn.

Some of the ladies held binoculars. In the direction they pointed one could see a whitish movement. Those were the boys. "There they come!" said my father. "They will parade before the princess." The imperial princess, who was the regent at that time, sat on the right, on a graceful wooden podium.

Moments later, the students of the Athenaeum were marching toward me. There were about three hundred of them, but they looked countless to me. All in white, wide red belts cinched tight around their waists, iron loops hanging over their hips, and on their heads, small bonnets circled by a braid, its loose ends hanging down. On their left shoulders they bore the ribbons corresponding to their grade. They stepped past us to the sound of trumpets, carrying their props. The first year carried the dumbbells; the second, the maces; the third, the bars. Closing the parade, unarmed, were those who just participated in the general exercises.

After a long round, in formation of four across, they organized themselves into platoons, invaded the lawn, and, to the rhythm of the band made up by fellow students waiting for them in the middle of the field, performed with disciplined assurance the perfect evolutions of an army under the command of the rarest instructor.

In front of the rows of students, Bataillard, the gymnastics teacher, exulted, wearing his success in the high elegance of his posture, glowing in the replicas of his professional skill ad infinitum, in rows on the lawn. It was hard to decide what to admire most, the masculine handsomeness and swelling muscles straining against the crisp denim of the uniform that he wore—white, like those of his students—or the nervous swiftness of the movements, as if viewed in a magic lantern, combining prodigious variety and the unity of supreme accuracy.

On Bataillard's chest jingled the aglets of his command, at the end of crimson braids. He gave his orders in a strong voice that resounded like a trumpet, commanding at a distance, and smiled at the mechanical docility of the youngsters. Like petty officers, the class leaders helped him, placed where they belonged, with their platoons, jouncing the distinctive green embroidered ribbons on their sleeves.

After the parade came the exercises. Arm muscles, pectorals, tendons at the joints, the entire theory of *corpore sano* practiced valiantly on that field with the precise and exact simultaneity of a vast machine. After that, a rush to the apparatuses, lined up on one side of the field, starting at the regent's podium. I cannot describe how dazzled I was by that part of the proceedings. There was a tumult of daring and loose-jointed contortions, a vertigo of turns around the fixed bar; acrobatic temerities on the trapeze, the high bars, the ropes, the ladders; human pyramids on the parallel bars, spilling toward the sides in bent arms and vigorous thoraxes; living statues, trembling with the effort, whose joints we could imagine cracking; transfigurations on invisible support; here and there a small blond head, mussed curly hair plastered on its forehead, the face reddened by the inversion of the body, half-opened lips panting, eyes half closed to avoid the sand falling from shoes; shirts pasted to sweating backs, ownerless caps falling and bestrewing the field; movement everywhere and the sun, white-hot on the uniforms, burning off the last fires of its daily glory over that spectacular triumph of health, strength, youth.

Professor Bataillard, red with agitation, hoarse from shouting, wept with pleasure. He was hugging the boys indiscriminately. Two military bands took turns, drawing the mass of spectators into the excitement of the moment. My heart leaped in my chest in an uproar, dragging me into the crowd of students in a surge of brotherhood. I clapped my hands; shouts escaped me that I regretted when people looked at me.

At the end of the spectacle came the high jumps, races, Roman wrestling, and the distribution of prizes pinned to the winners' young chests by the exalted hands of Her Most Serene Highness and the somewhat less exalted ones of the August Spouse. It was a sight to see the young athletes clinging to each other in pairs, pushing each other, pressing, turning, rolling on the grass with happy shouts and groaning with their efforts, or the runners: some rigid, measuring their breath, lips pressed together, fists clenched against their bodies, their steps small and vertiginous; others, irregular, waving their arms and stepping out, tearing the air with their feet, throwing themselves forward with the awkward eagerness of ostriches, gasping as they arrived, faces plastered with dust, at the end post.

Aristarco was bursting with joy. He had put aside the sovereign self-restraint I had admired in him on the occasion of the previous festivities. All in white, like the students, and wearing a hat of Chilean fiber, he was impossibly ubiquitous. He could be spotted capering around, fawning over the Princely Couple with his nasal little laugh, between flattery and irony, and deploying all the formalities due from a reverent subject and courtier; at the same time he could be seen shouting to the gymnastics teacher, waving his hat, held by its crown; one could see him formidable, with his leonine profile, roaring at a student who seemed to be shirking his duties or another whose knees were muddy from fighting on the wet grass, so vehement in his scolding that it came across as affectionate.

The sporting attire had rejuvenated him. He felt light on his legs and tripped swift-footed before the bleachers, overflowing with compliments for the special guests and friendly exclamations for everyone else. He wafted by like a vision in light denim, snuffed here only to reappear further on, more vivid still. That expansiveness overcame us; he irradiated himself over students, spectators, over the magnetism of the battle pennants. He stole from us two-thirds of the attention demanded by the exercises and compensated us with the equivalent in the astonishing vivacity that gushed out of him profusely, rising in streamers and pinwheels to the clouds, then floating down serenely, attenuated in the afternoon breeze our lungs were drinking in. A consummate actor, he embodied, almost literally, the diaphanous, subtle, metaphysical role of spirit of the feast and soul of his institute.

One thing saddened him, one small scandal. His son George, unlike all the other youths, refused to kiss the princess's hand when he received his prize. The scamp was a republican! At fifteen his opinions had already hardened into convictions ossified in the inflexible spine of his character! Nobody gave a sign of having noticed the exploit. Aristarco, however, took the boy aside. He looked at him in silence and—nothing else. And no one saw the republican again! The unfortunate young man had been consumed, naturally, cremated in the fire of that look! At that moment the band played the anthem of our legitimate monarchy, the last item on the program.

Night was falling when the school formed ranks to the sound of curfew being announced. They marched along the path opened among the spectators, and left the field, singing a happy school song.

In the evening there was dancing in the three lower-floor ballrooms of the main building, and a display of lights on the grounds.

As I left, they were setting off the Bengal lights before the house. With its forty windows lit up by gas from the inside, the Athenaeum became a fairy palace when also lit from the outside. It rose from the darkness of the night like a huge wall of flaming coral, like a living backdrop in sapphire with frightening ghostly shadows, like a phantasmal castle battered by green moonlight borrowed from the intense jungle of romance, woken at the hour of a dead legend for an interview with specters and memories. A jet of electric lights, coming from some invisible source, inscribed in gold lettering A T H E N A E U M in an arc over the middle windows at the top floor of the building. At one of them, on the balcony, stood Aristarco. The Olympian expression of his face showed the beatitude of superior contentment. He was enjoying the sensation of being bathed in light, of the immortality to which he thought he was consecrated. That was how it must be: the benevolent and cold light shining on the eternal busts and the glorious surroundings of the Pantheon. And the pleasure of contemplating posterity at his feet.

Aristarco had those moments, and they were sincere. He lived his own publicity, which replaced him, and he enjoyed it as if he were a billboard enjoying its own redness. At that moment, he was not just the soul of his institute, but its palpable embodiment, the stark synthesis of its title, its countenance, its façade, the material prestige of his school; he was identical with the letters that glowed like an aureole over his head. The letters golden; he himself, immortal: that, the only difference between them.

In my childish imagination I kept a picture of this apotheosis, dazzled into giddiness like one who at midnight left a theater where, thanks to some pious magic, God the Father had personally agreed to contribute to the grandeur of the last scene with his presence. I had seen Aristarco solemn at the first feast, jovial at the second; I got better acquainted with him later, in a thousand situations, under a thousand guises. But the picture that stayed with me of the great headmaster of my school was that one: the magnificent white moustache, the shaved chin, the gaze lost in the night, an ecstatic snapshot in a bolt of lightning.

It is easy to conceive the attraction that pulled me to what I thought was that most interesting world. Imagine, then, my pleasure when my father said that I would be presented to the headmaster of the Athenaeum and matriculated in the college. What moved me then was no longer vanity, but a legitimate and proud desire for greater responsibility, a passionate consequence of the seduction exercised by the spectacle, a rapture of solidarity that seemed to attach me to the fraternal communion reigning at the school. It was an honorable mistake, this candid desire to engage in an idealized task demanding energy and dedication, envisioned in a confused way by limited calculations based on a life experience of ten years.

The director received us in his residence, with grand manifestations of affection. He made himself captivating, paternal; he opened before us specimens of the best patterns lodged in his soul, and placed before us the accounts he ran in his heart. He was a good sort, no doubt: despite the silk jacket and the pumps he wore to receive us, despite the kind familiarity with which he inclined himself to us, not for one second did I divest him of the pinnacle of divinity with which my stupefied sense of discrimination had accepted him.

Truth is, it was not easy to recognize there, tangible and in the flesh, an entity that belonged to the mythology of my first anthropomorphic images: second only to Our Lord, whom I visualized as old, unsightly, bearded, impertinent, hunchbacked, rebuking sinners with thunder, charring boys with lightning. I had learned to read in the beginners' books by Aristarco, and had thought him old like God the Father, though clean-shaven, with a thin, pedagogical face, apocalyptic eyeglasses, a black tasseled hood—scrawny, omnipotent, and evil, one of his hands held behind him to hide the ferule and stuffing the ABCs down humanity's throat.

The more recent impressions overtook my original Aristarco, but that essentially primitive hyperbole colored its successor like a persistent hereditary trait. I watched with pleasure the fierce combat between the two images, and that complication of the silk jacket and the pumps allied itself with Aristarco II against Aristarco I for a place in the kingdom of my fantasies. At that point someone caressed my head. It was Him! I shivered.

"What is my little friend's name?" asked the director.

"Sérgio . . ." I said, and gave him my whole name, without forgetting "your servant," the form of strictest courtesy.

"Well, then, my dear Master Sérgio, you will have the kindness to go to the barber's and get rid of these curls . . ."

I was still wearing my hair long, a loving caprice of my mother's. The advice was clearly seasoned with censure. Explaining himself to my father, the headmaster added, with that little nasal laugh of his: "Indeed, dear sir, pretty boys don't do so well in my school . . ."

"I ask leave to defend pretty boys," objected someone, entering the room.

Surprising us with this sentence, issued smoothly from a smile, there appeared the headmaster's wife, Dona Ema. She was a beautiful woman, in the full bloom of Balzac's "woman at thirty," her shape elongated and gracefully slim but her trunk rising over ample hips, strong as motherhood; her eyes were black, with even darker pupils, filling with darkness the large space between the lids; her skin was of the roseate brown borne by some beauties, which was also the color of the rose apple, if the rose apple were indeed the forbidden fruit. She walked in, with sinuous movements, in the cadence of a harmonious and soft minuet. Her black satin dress followed her curves, shining wetly—the satin showed, boldly transparent, the hidden life of her flesh. The sight fascinated me.

There were formal introductions, and the lady sat on the sofa beside me, with just a touch of excessive self-assurance.

"How old are you?" she asked.

"Eleven . . ."

"You look like six, with that pretty hair."

I wasn't big for my age. The lady curled my hair around her fingers.

"Have it cut and make a gift of it to your mother," she suggested, with a caress. "It is your childhood you will be leaving there, with those blond curls . . . After that, sons have nothing more to give their mothers."

The little poem about mother love delighted me like divine music. I glanced at the lady. She kept her large, black pupils on me, shining in an expression of infinite kindness! What a good mother for the boys, I thought. Then, turning to my father, she spoke sensitively about the solitude of children at a boarding school.

"But Sérgio is one of the strong ones," said Aristarco, recovering his hold on the conversation. "Furthermore, my school is only larger than a home. The love we offer is not exactly the same, but the care and the vigilance are more active. I love children best. My most diligent efforts are directed toward the younger ones. If they fall ill and the family is absent, I don't send them to a surrogate, but care for them here, in my home. My wife is their nurse. I wish my detractors could see her . . ."

And once he had started on his favorite subject, praise of himself and of the Athenaeum, no one else was allowed to speak.

Aristarco—seated, standing, pacing with terrible steps, stopping suddenly to emphasize a rant, gesticulating like a politician at a rally, shouting as if at an auditorium holding ten thousand, always majestic, praising the points of his admirable product like an auctioneer—unfolded, as if in a speech perfectly remembered from his latest presentation, the narrative of his service to the holy cause of teaching. Thirty years of experiments and results, bathing in brightness, like a lighthouse, generations now influential in the destiny of the country! And what about future reforms? It was not enough to abolish corporal punishment, which in itself would be a passable act of benevolence. It was necessary to introduce new methodologies, to suppress absolutely the humiliations of punishment, perfect the system of rewards, arrange work and tasks so that the school would be a paradise, adopt norms as yet unknown, whose efficacy he could feel glimmering just ahead, farsighted as he was, like an eagle. He would bring about . . . horrors, the moral transformation of society!

For one hour he thundered, in sanguine eloquence, the genius of prophecy. We contemplated him, as we had during the festivities, in full oral panoply, in the plenitude of his practical animation. We were looking (me, with terrified wonder) at one outspread in epic grandeur—as if, pressed between two monstrous posters, he were carrying, on a sandwich board, an advertisement for national education. On his back, the record of his indescribable labors; on his front, over his stomach, the future, the announcement of his immortal projects.

Chapter 2

School started on February 15.

In the morning, at the prescribed time, I presented myself. The headmaster, in the main office of the establishment, occupied a swivel chair by his worktable. On the table, a large book was open, showing accounts in massive rows of numbers between red lines.

Aristarco, who dedicated his mornings to the financial management of the school, checked and analyzed the bookkeeper's entries. Students were coming in one at a time. Some came alone, some with an attendant.

At every arrival, the headmaster would slowly close his book, marking the page with a small ivory saber; he swiveled his chair around and made welcoming noises, with an episcopal offer of his hairy hand to be kissed by the boys, filially and contritely. The older ones usually refused to participate in the ceremony and contented themselves with a simple handshake.

Then the boy would disappear, with a pale smile, missing already the happy idleness of the summer vacation. The father, agent, or attendant would then take leave with some complimentary banality, or some words about the student, soothed by Aristarco's little jokes and superior bonhomie as he skillfully floated the man out the door with his little nasal laugh and the light push with which he squeezed his fingers in dismissal.

The chair swiveled back to its initial position; the account ledger again opened its huge pages, and the paternal figure of the great educator dissolved into the simplified, dry, attentive slyness of the manager.

Our headmaster was so accustomed to this alternation of stances, this double face of the same individual, a customary contingency of his priesthood, that he achieved it without any effort. The speculator and the miser inhabited him in an intimate camaraderie, arm in arm. They knew how to turn up, depending on the occasion, simultaneously or in alternation, like twin souls inside the same body. In him the educator and the manager were soldered together in perfect accord, two sides of the same coin, opposed but juxtaposed.

When my father entered with me, Aristarco's face showed a touch of irritation. Maybe he was disappointed by some statistics; perhaps the number of new students did not make up for the number he had lost, or the latest income did not balance the year-end expenses. But that shadow of disappointment vanished in a flash, like the tip of a tunic you barely glimpse in a change of garment, and it was with an explosion of contentment that the headmaster greeted us.

His diplomacy was carefully organized in cubbyholes corresponding to the category of the reception he wanted to dispense. His manners came in a series of degrees, in accordance with the social standing of the recipient. Only rarely was he sincere in his effusions. At the bottom of each smile there was a secret coldness, fairly easy to detect. And the differences were clearly marked, according to politics, finance, scholarly achievement of the student, and based on the differences etched in the bookkeeper's notes. Sometimes one of the children felt the pinprick in the way the hand was held out to be kissed, and walked away wondering about the reason, which was not evident from his report card . . . His father was two trimesters behind with the tuition.

For various reasons my welcome would be among the warmest. Aristarco rose, came to meet us, and led us to the special sitting room.

Then he took us around the establishment, showing the collection, displayed in cabinets, of the objects used to aid in teaching. I looked upon it all with curiosity, well aware of the glances of the other students, strangers who beheld me, proud and dignified in my new uniform. The building had been whitewashed and painted during the vacation period, like those ships that use time at anchor in a port to improve their appearance. On the walls there were maps, which I was pleased to see as itineraries of extensive travels planned for me. There were colorful prints in black frames on themes from sacred history and rough drawings, or zoological and botanical samples that revealed to me the subjects of intense study in which I planned to excel. Other pictures, behind glass, emphatically laid down moral rules and well-known advice, exhorting viewers to love truth and parents, and fear God, which to me seemed like a redundant code. Among the framed exemplars many—most, in fact—were about the headmaster, and strove to represent him as a disembodied entity, mortared together as a pure essence of love and sacrifice signaled by deep sighs, instilling in me that didactolatry that I vowed to myself I would follow to the letter. We visited the dining hall, adorned with student pencil drawings, the vast tiled kitchen, the large internal courtyard, the dormitories, the chapel. Back in the reception area, adjacent to the side and front entrance to the office, I was introduced to Master Manlio, of the advanced introductory grade, rod-straight, with a full, graying beard, an excellent person who, on principle, distrusted all the boys.

For the entire duration of our visit, Aristarco spoke of nothing but his struggles, the sweat he shed over those youths, none of which was sufficiently appreciated: "It's an insanely arduous job! One must moderate, animate, correct, this mass of different characters where the ferment of inclinations is beginning to boil up; recognize and direct nature when they are prey to those violent impulses; muzzle excessive ardor; restore the will of those who are too quickly discouraged; watch and discern each student's temperament; prevent corruption; forestall evil in its most seductive guises; take advantage of the tumult of the blood to direct those energies toward the nobler teachings;

prevent the depravation of the innocent; watch the dark corners; supervise friendships; distrust hypocrisies; be loving, be violent, be firm; triumph over compassion in order to be righteous; proceed with assurance and then be prey to doubt; punish and then ask pardon . . . A thankless titanic labor that wearies the soul and leaves us exhausted at the end of one day only to start again on the morrow . . . Ah, my friends," he concluded, breathless, "it is not my spirit that falters, it is not about their studies that I worry . . . it's about their character! It is not indolence that is the enemy; it's immorality!" Aristarco had a special intonation for that word, compressed and terrible, unforgettable to anyone who had ever heard it fall from his lips.

And he stepped back, tragical, pressing his hands together. "Ah! But I am formidable when this disgrace brings scandal upon us. No! Let parents rest assured on this point. At the Athenaeum there is no immorality! I watch over the innocence of these children as if they were—I shan't say my sons, but my own daughters! The Athenaeum is a moralized school! I warn everyone well in advance. I have a code . . ." At this point the headmaster leaped up and showed a large picture on the wall. "Here is our code. Read it! All trespasses are thought of, one punishment for each kind: there is no opening there for immorality. There was no parricide in Greek law. Here, there is no immorality. If the unthinkable occurs, justice is the terror I wield, and my discretion is law! And you, respectable parents, may complain afterward! . . ."

I can assure you that mine trembled for me. And I, shrinking, imitated the proverbial shaking leaves. Noting my discomfort, the headmaster rained caresses on me. "But to those who deserve it, I am a very father! I know the bad ones: they are not, as I know you are, the pride and joy of their families; they will not be, as I know you will, one of the glories of the Athenaeum. Do not worry yourself." I took the prophecy seriously and calmed down.

When my father left, tears came to my eyes, but I repressed them in time, to seem strong. I went up to the blue hall, the dormitory for the middle grades, where I had my bed; I changed my clothes, and took the uniform to the cubicle numbered 54, which had been assigned to me. I did not dare confront the recess grounds. From afar I watched my schoolmates, few of them at that time, walking around in groups, conversing in a friendly way, but with little animation, still under the impression of memories from home. I hesitated to meet them, embarrassed by my new long trousers that seemed to me comically exaggerated, and by the sensation of nakedness around my neck scandalously denuded by a recent haircut. João Nunes, guard or beadle, short, pudgy, in dark glasses, moving with the vivacity of a cheerful piglet, came to find me, undecided, on the stairs leading to the courtyard. "Aren't you going down to play?" he asked kindly. "Come on, go down, go meet the others." The friendly piglet took me by the hand, and we went down together.

The guard left me between two young men who treated me with kindness.

At eleven the bell rang for the beginning of classes. My two good friends, from lower grades, showed me the room where the higher reading group met, which would be mine, and took their leave.

Master Manlio, to whom I had been recommended, recommended me in turn to the most serious of his pupils, the honorable Rebelo. Rebelo was the oldest in the class and wore dark glasses like João Numa. The curved lenses of his spectacles hid his eyes completely, concentrating his attention fully on the teacher's desk. As if that were not enough, the zealous student covered his temples with his cupped hands to impede any stray glance escaping from behind his glasses.

This excessive effort was not just the result of wanting to show off an exemplary devotion to his studies. Rebelo suffered from weak eyesight, so much so that only later in his life than was customary had he been able to dedicate himself to his studies. He received me with a grandfather's benevolent smile; he moved over a tad to make room for me, and immediately forgot all about me to sink into the all-consuming dedication that was his hallmark.

There were about twenty students in that class, a variety of types that amused me. There was Gualtério, small, his back rounded, his hair mussed, his movements quick, and his face with a simian mobility—the class clown, as the teacher put it; Nascimento, the beak, built on the general outline of a pelican, with a long, thin nose, curved and wide like a scythe; Álvares, dark-skinned, frowning, his hair thick and unkempt like that of a tavern poet, violent and brutal, whom Manlio tormented, predicting for him a career as a tram ticket collector, the metal identifying tag they wore easier to carry than the responsibility of academic endeavors; and Almeidinha, with his light, almost translucent skin, girlish face, sickly pink cheeks, who would rise to go to the board with the slow movements of a convalescent. Maurílio, nervous, restless, a whiz at the multiplication table: five times three, times two, cast out the nines, times seven? . . . there was Maurílio, shaking, waving his shrewd little finger in the air, eyes bright in his brown face, marked by a spot on his forehead. There was Negrão with his wide nostrils, restless lips, rough features, awkward and angular, incapable of sitting still, always at the teacher's desk and always shooed away, a shameless smile on his lips, flattering the teacher, calling him a dear, seizing any opportunity to give him a hug that Manlio repulsed, leery of unasked familiarity. And Batista Carlos, of Indian blood, robust, an evil mug, scratching himself nonstop as if his clothes bothered him, indifferent to what went on in the classroom, as if he had nothing to do with any of it, just watching the teacher, and as soon as he blinked, shooting at his neighbors' ears with an arrow made of folded paper. Sometimes the Indian's arrow caromed all the way to Manlio's desk. Sensation! All work was suspended and a rigorous inquest was established. In vain; the other children feared him, and he was sly and clever at dissimulation.

Notable also was Cruz, timid, diffident, always on the alert, with the cowardly air of someone who was raised by beatings, clinging to his books, expert on Christian doctrine, going off like an alarm clock spouting lessons learned by heart, while getting an original idea out of him was as hard as pulling out a moist peg stuck in wood. Finally, there was Sanches, big, somewhat younger than the venerable Rebelo, head of the class, very bright, beaten only by Maurílio in the latter's specialty of casting out the nines, careful with his homework, as good as Cruz on doctrine, peerless in analysis, line drawing, and cosmography.

The rest formed an indistinct pack, dozing in the back rows, blending into the lazy shadows at the farther end of the class.

I was also recommended to Sanches. I found him deeply uncongenial—that broad face, sallow, dead eyes of a transparent brown, wet lips with bits of foam at the corners, and the viscous sweetness of a confirmed cad. He was the prize student in the class. He might be first in the choir of the angels, but in my book he was the basest of creatures. I was amusing myself checking out my companions, when the teacher called my name. I paled so visibly that Manlio smiled and asked me, mildly, to go to the blackboard. He needed to examine me.

Standing there, deeply vexed, I felt my eyes blur, as if in a fit of vertigo. I guessed Sanches's viscous eyes fixed on me, Cruz's odious and cowardly ones, Rebelo's blue glasses, Nascimento's nose turning slowly like a rudder; I awaited Carlos's arrow, Maurílio's corrective threatening, tickling the ceiling with his ferocious finger; I breathed in the hostile air of that cursed hour, perfumed by the acrid emanation of resins wafting in from the nearby bushes, a conspiracy against me by the entire class, from Negrão's fawning to Álvares's violent nastiness. I staggered to the blackboard. The teacher interrogated me; I don't know whether I answered. My soul was taken by a strange dread, and I was terrified of being on show, imagining all around me the evil irony of all those strangers' faces. I held on to the blackboard so I would not fall; the floor retreated from me, together with the awareness of the moment: I was blanketed in the darkness of unconsciousness, eternal shame! that drained away my last strength.

I have no idea what happened next. The turmoil chased away my awareness of things. I remember that I found myself with Rebelo in the locker room, and that Rebelo was trying to revive me with sincere and touching kindness.

Rebelo then left, and I, in shirtsleeves, deeply embarrassed, embittered by that disaster, while the attendant looked for locker number 54, considered the difference between my situation and the knightly ideal with which I had dreamed of stunning the Athenaeum.

Since the attendant was taking his time, I picked up a booklet from the table upon which were the records for clothing, laundry lists, and such. Curious booklet, with verses and drawings . . . I closed it convulsively, remorseful about my perverse curiosity. Strange booklet! I opened it again. My face burned with an inexplicable fire of shame, and my throat was constricted with a spasm of nausea. But the seduction of that novelty held me tight. I looked around as if I were guilty of something; I don't know what instinct delivered that jolt of guilt. It was just a piece of paper, blurry and hastily printed. I braced myself against it. Entering, the attendant interrupted me. "Drop that!" he said brutally. "This is not for little boys." And he pulled away the booklet.

The vivid impact of that discovery drove out the memory of my sad performance, growing in my imagination like a vision, taking over my thinking. The terrifying words of Aristarco buzzed in my ears . . . Yes, that must be it: an obscure jumble of unclothed forms, open clothing, a swirl of drunken friars, moving at the whim of every deformity of some monstrous draftsmanship, touching one another, jumping in an endless, diabolic saraband, in the impasted blackness of printer's ink; here and there, the white gleam of a fault, lighting up the spectacle and the print, like the added stigma of chance.

The locker room took up a large part of the basement of that huge building, between the timbers holding up the floor above and the cement floor where I stood. Another part was reserved for the lavatories, hundreds of washbasins along the walls; above them, on a wooden shelf, the glasses and toothbrushes. A third, additional compartment accommodated an arsenal of gymnastics equipment and the servants' dormitory. To reach the central recreation area, one had to cross the room with the basins on the diagonal. Immediately as I came out into the yard, I ran into the benevolent Rebelo, who had been waiting for me. With refined complacency, he insisted on discoursing about my incident, excusing me, explaining me, absolving me. He was unbearable. To change the subject, I asked about our teacher. He said wonderful things, but then such an exemplary student could have done no less. "No master is bad for a good student," proclaimed one of the maxims posted on the wall.

It was the rest period; we ambled around, talking. We spoke of our classmates, and I observed how Rebelo's patriarchal mildness peeled off, revealing an unexpected Thersites, spewing abuse and curses. "A rabble! You can't imagine, my dear Sérgio. Consider it a misfortune to have to live with these people." And he pointed a sarcastic lip at the boys passing by. "There they go, with those sly little faces, oh generous youth . . . Perverts! They have more sins on their consciences than a confessor in his ear; a lie on each tooth, a vice on every inch of their skin. Trust them. They are servile, treacherous, brutal flatterers. They all stick together. You may think they are friends. But they are just partners in villainy! Run from them; run from them. They smell of corruption; from afar they poison the air. Hypocrite rabble! Vicious band! Every day of their lives is ashamed of the use they made of the preceding day. But you are just a child. I won't tell you just what this generous youth is worth. They will teach you themselves what they are . . . That one is Malheiro, great gymnast. He was older when he came to us, bringing with him the good customs of other schools around here. His father is an officer. He grew up in the barracks, amid the mockery of the enlisted men. He is strong as a bull, everyone fears him, many attach themselves to him, the counselors can't control him; the headmaster respects him; everyone turns a blind eye to his abuses . . . The one who just went by, staring at us, is Candido, with his little feminine ways, looking as if he had just got out of bed, his eyes still lazy . . . That one . . . but you must already know him. Yet there are exceptions: here comes Ribas, see him? Ugly, poor thing, like anything, but a pearl. As sweet as they come. Best voice in the choir, a lovely soprano that the headmaster adores. He is studious and protected. Makes a living singing like the seraphim. A pearl!"

"Over there, there is one on his knees . . ."

"On his knees . . . No need to ask; it's Franco. That's how he lives through the weeks, the months, this is how I have known him, in this house, ever since I arrived. On his knees, like a penitent expiating the guilt of an entire race. The headmaster calls him a dog, says he has calluses on his face. If he did have calluses on his knees, there would be no corner in this Athenaeum he had not marked with the blood of one of his penances. His father comes from Mato Grosso; he sent him here with a letter that described him as incorrigible, asking that he be treated with severity. Every so often the agent sends a clerk with the tuition, and best regards. He never goes out . . . Let us move on, there is a company of rascals coming toward us."

A group of boys crossed in front of us, taunting and gibing me.

"Did you see the one at the head of them, who yelled 'frog'? If I told you what they say about him . . . with those moist little eyes like the Mater Dolorosa . . . Look, let me give you a piece of advice: be strong; be a man. The weak are lost here.

"This is a mob. You need strong elbows to get through it. I am not a child, nor am I an idiot; I live by myself and watch from afar, but I don't miss anything. You can't imagine. The geniuses create two sexes here, as if it were a coed school. The timid, innocent, bloodless kids are smoothly pushed into the weak sex: they are dominated, coddled, perverted like unprotected girls. When, behind their parents' backs, they believe that school offers the best of lives, well received as they are by the older students, half-naughty and half-affectionate, they are lost. Be a man, my friend! Begin by not allowing anyone to become your protector."

Rebelo was going on with those extraordinary warnings, when I felt someone pulling on my shirt. I almost fell. I turned and, at a distance, I saw a yellow face, fat and bloated, with squinting lashless eyes, turned toward me, a smiling, cynical grimace. Someone who was obviously stronger than I. Nevertheless I angrily picked up a piece of tile and threw it. The rascal took off, insulting me with a cackle, and disappeared. "Good!" said Rebelo. And at my question, he informed me that the unpleasant student was Barbalho, who someday would be arrested for stealing jewelry, and who was our companion in the elementary class, one of the forgotten boys in the back rows.

Master Manlio was kind enough to postpone my examination, and in order to spare me the consequences of the derision that had come my way after the disastrous incident in that first class period, he bestowed on me the strongest words of encouragement. The boys were generous. Maurílio passed his hand over my hair tenderly, proving that he could use gently the implacable finger of the hardest arguments. Only the yellow tint of his squinting eyes gave any indication of underhanded mockery.

After dinner I did not see Rebelo again. Since he took some extra, more advanced classes, he disappeared at times in the direction of the upper part of the house.

Master Manlio's room was at ground level, by the main building courtyard, as were two other grammar school rooms and the supplementary recreation room, useful when it rained. At a right angle from that building, an extensive construction of brick and painted wood housed the general study room on the ground floor and the dormitory above that, forming one half of the courtyard square, the other half of which was the large building in two wings, like the arms that kept us all closed in. At the back of this huge walled box there was a light, sterile extension of sand, insipid as obligatory cheerfulness, around which a few cambucá trees showed their stiff foliage, the dead green of Palm Sunday leaves in church, yellowed here and there with the precocious senility of suffering vegetation as if it were not allowed to survive in that boarding school; in one corner a slender cypress climbed up to the gutters, trying to escape over the roof.

Without Rebelo I felt lost among the other boys. Those I knew from classes disappeared in the tumult released from the classrooms.

There was not a single one I could approach. Hugging the wall, not to call attention to myself, I crept to where Silvino, the supervisor, tall, thin, with his large nose and moth-eaten sideburns, his eyes swift and alive like sparks glowing in deep eye sockets, watched over the playground, calibrating the excitement with the help of a fearsome notebook. He sat at the gate to the lavatories. Slightly to the side of Silvino's chair, I was safe, and from that protected place I watched the movements of my classmates in the expanse, cooled by the broad afternoon shadow. Here and there arose small disturbances, condensing the scattered students into irregular patterns. Those were the poor new boys, whom the older ones beat up in secret, in a brotherly sort of way.

Near me I saw Franco. Penitent, as always, he stood with his face against the wall. Since Silvino had his back to him, he amused himself by catching flies, tearing off their heads, and watching the little beings die in the palm of his hand. I asked him why he was being punished. "Who knows?" he answered, rudely, without looking at me. "Because they said so." And went on catching his flies. Franco was fourteen, thin and weak-looking, his eyes dead and his lids heavy. With that vague expression in his eyes and the pained slant of his eyebrows, there was a cloud of affliction and patience on his face, like those one sees on images in the *Flos Sanctorum.* The lower part of his face, however, rebelled against the upper half: one side of his lips curled in a permanent contraction of hate-filled disdain. Franco never laughed. He smiled, for instance, watching a serious fight, interested in the outcome as if he were a gambler betting on it, furious when the contestants separated. A fall delighted him, especially when dangerous. He lived in isolation in the circle of the excommunicated into which the headmaster invariably, every morning, dispatched him, as he read, before the students gathered in the refectory, the notes taken the day before.

The teachers knew the drill. Franco's grade, always low, would need to be followed by some disparaging comment, which the popular opinion expected and heard with pleasure, enjoying the occasion to despise him. None of us is as bad as he is! And the Master's zeal renewed the old anathema every day. It was not convenient to expel him. One had to take advantage of a jewel like that as an intuitive teaching tool, exploring it like the misery of the helot, for the sake of the lovely lesson in how, and against what, to feel disgust. Even the victim's repugnant indifference then becomes useful.

For three years the unhappy boy, silent against the torture of small, cruel humiliations, crouching, beaten, crushed under the weight of everyone else's virtues more than under that of his own guilt, stood there, forced into the position of a caryatid holding up the edifice of the Athenaeum's morality, a perfect example of depravation offered to the holy horror of the pure.

Several times that afternoon I was assaulted by Barbalho's impertinent mockery. That small, one-eyed devil pulled at my clothes, bumped into me, and fled with a huge forced laugh, or stopped suddenly right in front of me and, with an expression as serious as could sit on his saffron-colored face, asked, "Will you be changing your pants?" It was hell. Finally, at the end of my endurance, I exploded.

It was in the evening, before supper. We were in a dimly lit corner of the courtyard, almost by ourselves. The scoundrel recognized me and contorted his face into an inexpressible exclamation of mockery. I did not hesitate. I punched his face. Half a second later we were rolling in the dust, at each other like animals. A swift fight. They told us Silvino was on his way. Barbalho fled. I noted that the front of my shirt was covered with blood that was running from my nose.

One hour later, on the iron bed of the blue room, aware of the hospital sadness of dormitories, their depth untouched by the faint light of the gas lamps, I bit into the white cover and reviewed the day I had just lived.

That's what school was like. What should I do with that baggage of plans I had brought along?

Where should I stick the engine of my ideals in the brutal world that intimidated me with its obscure details and the formless vistas that escaped the inquiries of my inexperience?

What would be my fate, in that society that Rebelo had described with horror, his half-words of mystery raising undefined fears, his exhortations to energy making friendship sound like hostility? How could I reconcile any generous and serious behavior with Barbalho's stubborn obsessions? In vain had I tried to find, in the expressions of those young men, the noble seriousness implied by the prizes, which had made me think of legions of workers, like soldiers engaged in a common endeavor, their hearts linked in their collective effort. Broken apart into individuals when they scattered during the free period, as I remembered Rebelo's observations and criticism, they inspired me with very different sentiments. The reaction brought about by the contrast raised in me a feeling of repugnance that would likely abate with habit, but on that evening, it brought me to tears. At the same time, I was oppressed by a foretaste of moral loneliness, an intuition that small worries and inadmissible surprises would not go far in procuring for me the relief that might come from advice or comfort.

No protectors, Rebelo had declared. It opened up a wasteland. And in that solitude, a conspiracy of all kinds of adversities, the treachery of affections, hounding by malevolence, spying by vigilance, and above all, like a stormy sky hanging over the general depression, the thundering fury of the headmaster, the awe-inspiring Aristarco in moments of serious crisis.

Memories of my family changed the course of my reflections. The dear hand that had rocked me into my first sleep was no longer, nor was the prayer, so distant right now, that had protected me at night like a canopy of love. There was only the void that surrounded homeless children taken in by a cold shelter for their misery. Consciousness of my sad plight slowly and quietly annihilated me, prostrated me, and I slept.

All through the night, in my nightmares, various images of that day's trials pursued me: Sanches's slimy tenderness; Barbalho's yellow face; Franco's tortured expression; the laundry attendant's moldering friars. I even dreamed outright. I was Franco. My class, the entire school, thousands of schools, caught in a windstorm, flew for miles over an endless plain. All screamed, yelling out the multiplication tables with the vigor of a hurricane. Dust rose in clouds from the soil; the confused mass waved their arms like the spikes on a hedgehog, in gestures like leafless branches tossed in a winter storm. Gesticulating above the forest of arms was a higher sign still, that of the victor, Maurílio's bony hand, now swollen, enormous, dark, twisting and untwisting its eager fingers hysterically convulsed, correcting some unhappy boy's mistake . . . And I fell, vanquished, alone! And the troop turned and all galloped toward me, stomping me, heavy under their loads of prizes, basketsful of prizes.

The bell ringing in the morning freed me of my anguish. Five o'clock.

Chapter 3

If, when I was a small child, in a flash of luminous prudence, while others were playing shuttlecock, I had sat down to the gentle task of creating autobiographical documents, with the view of making up one more *famous childhood,* I would certainly not have registered, among the events showing me as predestined for fame, the banal case involving "the swim," which, however, had dire consequences for me and caused the greatest bitterness I would know.

The "swim" was what they called the pool, built on land belonging to the Athenaeum. It was a vast, shallow expanse of water, thirty meters by five, that drained into the Rio Comprido—the "long river"—and was fed by large open faucets. The bottom, tiled but invisible, tilted gradually from one side to the other. The difference in depth was marked by two steps, conveniently arranged so that the smaller children, as well as the grown boys, would have a footing. At one point the water was deep enough to cover a grown man.

In the great heat of February and March, and at the end of the year, there were two swimming periods every day. And every dip was a celebration, in that thick water, brackish from the sweat of the preceding classes, the volume of the pool precluding the swift renewal of the liquid. In it, half-nude bodies clashed, squeezed into colorful knit swimsuits, the boys enlaced like lampreys, some ducking down, some reappearing, their eyes reddened, their hair dripping over their faces, their skin streaked with the accidental scratches of their companions, screaming with glee, screaming with fright, screaming in terror, the smaller ones bunched together in the shallow parts, holding hands, terrified at the approach of one of the stronger big boys.

Some of the older boys really inspired fear, cutting through the water with strong strokes, shouldering away the resistance of the water; others shot in head first, fishtailing the air, or belly-flopped without looking where they would land. And bubbling among the swimmers, waves like those at the seashore rose and broke out of the pool, swamping everything.

Alongside the pond there was a dividing wall, beyond which lay the headmaster's private little farm. In the distance one could see the windows of one part of the house where they sometimes kept sick students, their green shutters always closed. Up on the wall, half-hidden by a clump of bamboo, sat Angela, the Canarian, to watch the afternoon bathing. She threw pebbles at the boys, and the boys blew her kisses and dove in search of the stones. Angela, twisting her wrists, leaning back, laughed a big laugh, opening like a flower through her white teeth.

The first time I witnessed that bath, I was frightened by the disorderly commotion.

I sought out the smaller boys' corner. Discipline demanded that the boys should be divided into three groups, according to their ages. But sloppy oversight allowed for the groups to intermingle, and the acting supervisor, holding the stick with which he would prod the latecomers, watched from afar, so that the weaker boys were subject to the abuse of the older ones, hard to see through the splashing water. As soon as I entered, I felt two hands, from below, grasp my ankle and my knee. A jerk, and I fell back; the water muffled my cries, blinded me. I was being dragged along. Asphyxiated and desperate, I was sure I would die. I did not know how to swim and saw myself abandoned in a dangerous spot, and I thrashed around, underwater and about to faint, when someone caught me. One of the big boys put me on his shoulders and deposited me on the rim, where I lay prone, spewing water. It took me a while to figure out what had happened. Finally I rubbed my eyes and realized that Sanches was the one who had saved me. "You were about to drown," he said, holding my head while he brushed my hair from my eyes. Still shaken, I told him, in great agitation, what they had done to me. "Fiends," he said, with compassion, and attributed the brutality to some pest who had fled in the commotion, at the same time trying kindly to calm me down. Later I had reason to believe that the fiend and pest had been he, himself, setting it up so he could render me a service.

The immediate consequence, however, was that I repressed the repugnance Sanches inspired in me, and was all gratitude and warm friendship toward him. And this adventure of mine in trust and attachment proved curious and turbulent.

At the Athenaeum we went everywhere in twos—to the gym, to chapel, to the dining hall, to classes, to the ceremony of greeting the guardian angel, at noon, and to the handing out of stale bread after the singing. For the sake of order and a near-military discipline, the three hundred students were sub-divided into groups of thirty, under the direct command of a decurion or supervisor. The supervisors were selected as an aristocracy of merit, as Aristarco assured us.

Malheiro, the hero of the trapeze, was a supervisor, and so was Ribas, the best voice in the choir, and Mata, wizened and hunchbacked, his spine broken, nicknamed "the peddler," mellifluous and never punished though nobody knew why not, reputed to be excellent because nobody had ever thought of checking him out, yet who was, as Rebelo pointed out, the head of the headmaster's secret police. Saulo, who had three awards in public education, was also a supervisor, as was Ro-mulo, known as "Master Cook," a beast, large, last in gym with his soft corpulence, last in his studies, excused from choir for his old woman's rasp, but who exercised at the school, by virtue of the broad flatness of his ineptitude, the complex and del-icate function of the band's percussion section. I don't know whether it was because of his peculiar talent for drumming, that musical form of advertising, or because of a rumored large inheritance that awaited him from his fortunate parents, but the fact is that, among all the others, Romulo was the one selected by Aristarco to be his future son-in-law.

Several others of the leaders were, like those already named, elected in accordance with criteria that accepted someone who was brave on the high bar even if his performance in classes was disappointing; yet others, like Ribas, an exemplary student, thin and exhausted, could hardly perform the simple straight swing on the trapeze.

Sanches, too, was a supervisor.

These lower officers in the house militia acted like little tyrants by delegation from the higher echelons of the dictatorship. Armed with wooden sabers in leather sheaths, they took their investiture seriously and generally displayed an adorable ferocity. The sabers were used for summary punishment of any infractions of discipline: two words at the back of the line, wobbly legs, a step out of the straight line. A regime, as can be seen, like that in a Siberian prison, the result of which was that the supervisors were held in high esteem.

In the particular case of the fortuitous closeness that had been established between us, the important place Sanches held in the school could not have failed to play a role. But other circumstances conspired to determine the new way I would be seen in that environment, as became even clearer after the incident at the bath.

I could already claim to have been initiated into the inner circles at the school. Called upon by Manlio, I had managed to please, which conferred on me an aura that for a while put me in a favored position. I ran into Barbalho. His face was marked by my nails; he avoided me. At break time I committed the injustice of avoiding Rebelo. It did not help him that, though he made a pleasant companion, he had bad breath that tainted the purity of his advice; in addition, he had the habit of holding one's attention by pinching one hard and of shooting off his aphorisms point-blank. In his turn, my venerable fellow student responded to my avoidance by showing annoyance and sulking. In classes where we sat side by side, he concentrated desperately on his work, and it was as if he were miles away. However, if it became absolutely necessary to talk to me, he would address me with his habitual affability, like a young curate.

I was getting acclimated, but it was acclimating by hopelessness, like a prisoner to his cell.

After I got rid of my baggage of naive ideals, I felt empty; I had never been so aware of the imponderable spirituality of one's soul: an emptiness inhabited me. I was oppressed by the force of things; I felt a coward. Rebelo's injunction to virility—avoid protectors—was lost. I wanted a protector, someone who would help me in that hostile and alien environment, who would offer direct support stronger than words.

If I had not forgotten practical aspects, like Rebelo's personal assistance, I might have noticed that little by little I was being invaded, as he had predicted, by the morbid effeminacy of such schools. But theory is fragile and goes to sleep like larvae when the cold season forces them to. A moral lethargy weighed on me as I slipped down. And as if the souls of children, just like their bodies, had to wait for the time when their individual sexual conformation was finally established, so I was filled with a certain lazy need for support, a voluptuous weakness that was, in principle, unsuited to the masculine character. I realized that the battle of studies and moral energy was not exactly a daily campaign, inspired by the clarion call of rhetoric, as at those celebrations, and by the emphatic lyrics of the anthems, and raw reality saddened me. I was disillusioned as I became aware of what I saw behind the scenes of the glorious parade, as I saw its reverse. Not every day in the military is graced with the spirit of the charge and the glory of triumphant returns; the stagnant routine of peaceful days in the barracks, the boredom of KP duty, had a demoralizing effect on me.

This emotional crisis coincided with the fear that the Athenaeum's microcosm roused in me. Everything is a threat to the defenseless. The tumultuous lack of inhibition of my fellows at recreation times, the ease with which they did their work, looked to me like signs of crushing superiority; I was astounded by the vivacity of the younger ones, some of them so small! For the second time, then, Sanches's arm came to rescue me from submersion, turning up at just the right moment.

I was not studying; my accounts, however, were in order, by a conjunction of unplanned circumstances: recent enrollment entitled me to benevolence; I had been especially recommended to Master Manlio; I could stitch together bits of knowledge acquired earlier. My grade average was satisfactory, but I ran a constant risk of going down from there. The methods used were the worst obstacle—without the help of someone more knowledgeable, I was lost. Sanches would certainly assist me, given his standing as a wonderful student, and especially given the insinuating good will that he kept displaying so disinterestedly. To say nothing of the profit I derived from his affection, as he raised on my behalf his terrifying, leather-sheathed supervisor's saber.

It was not long before he gave me his helping hand, like Fénelon's benevolent Minerva.

I took to geography as if it were my home. The rough edges of the continents dissolved on my maps to speed my work; the rivers did without the complicated details of their meanders and flowed in my memory independent of the natural boundaries of their banks; mountain chains, like large troops of tame elephants, organized themselves into the easiest possible orographic systems; the number of large cities in the world shrank, as they sank into the earth so that I would not need to learn all those names by heart; populations were rounded up and lost irritating fractions, regardless of national censuses and gravamen to national wombs; felicitous mnemonics taught me the lists of states and provinces. Thanks to Sanches's dexterity, no incident ever studied about the surface of the globe failed to attach itself to my brain as if my heart were, on the inside, equal to what the terrestrial globe was on the outside.

In its turn, grammar opened itself to me as if it were a box of Easter candy. Sky-blue satin and sugar. I chose adjectives to my pleasure, like almonds sweetened by adverbial circumstances of the most pleasing variety, and amiable nouns fluttered around me, proper or appellative, like creatures of winged marzipan; etymology, syntax, prosody, spelling were four degrees of the same sweetness. At worst, exceptions and irregular verbs disgusted me at the start, but turned out like those unsightly chocolate curls that, once tasted, proved delicious.

National history delighted me for as long as it could. First, the missionaries of the early conversion and colonization efforts, who came toward me, with Father Anchieta, in visions of goodness, reciting chosen verses of the jungle gospels, sending ahead of them, crowned with flowers, on the wide, white sandy road, the cheerful Indian boys, apprentices of the faith and of civilization, followed by the savage mob of natives the color of tree bark, feathered, painted in a thousand colors, respectfully contrite in their tamed fetishism, bulging out from the bosom, from the depths of the dark forest like a fantastic army of tree trunks. Then on to the era of independence: with a child's patriotic yearnings a complicated evocation of commemorative plaques of sunrises on Rocio Square in Rio with its prince cast in bronze, astride a date, showing the peoples the official mark of the Ipiranga creek, site of the Shout for Independence, on his kerchief; somewhat lower, punctuated by salvos from Santo Antonio, the acclamations of a mixed population that allowed Tiradentes, the earlier martyr to Independence, to die but also erupted into cheers at the coffee plant cutting smuggled into an admirer's bouquet for Domitila.

Every page was enchanting, when prefaced by the complacent explanation of my fellow student. Thanks to the charm of his presentation, I shook hands with the most truculent personages of the past, the most powerful. Antonio Salema, the cruel, smiled at me; Vidigal was gentle; João VI left some snuff on my fingers. I learned to recognize Mem de Sá, Maurice of Nassau, by sight; I watched the hero from Minas march by, calmly, his hands tied together like Christ's, his beard full like that of an apostle to the people, his smooth, wide brow touched by the sun, furrowed by fate better to bear the martyr's crown.

History of religion revealed to me that epic hero—who would have thought it?—the canon Roquette! I felt the musical intoxication of those chapters like the deep chant of cathedrals. I heard the sighs of Belief, the idyll of Eden, the first love of Genesis, envied by angels, under the magnanimous gaze of lions. I heard the soft plaints of the first couple banished toward pain and work; Adam ashamed, clad in the fig leaves of the first prudishness, Eve clothing her young, lily-like nudity in the golden tunic of her locks, covering her body with her hands, the obscenity of mothers, stigmatized by God's curse.

And the song swelled up into the vault, and the organ spoke the entire tradition of human suffering redeemed by the Deity. The psalms rose in a sweet warbling harmony, the sensuous ecstasy of the Song of Songs came from the lips of Shulamith, and the seduction of Booz caught in the honest stratagem of tenderness, and the tragic melancholy of Judith, and the serene glory of Esther, the beloved princess.

Suddenly the sound picture burst open to the choir of Lamentations. The last notes of David's harp died like sparks in the air; Solomon's antistrophe lost itself in ever fainter echoes; at the end of the field the image of Ruth, holding the golden sheaf of wheat, dissipated slowly; the somber Hebrew woman entered the tent of Holofernes, carrying on her lips her murderous kiss; Esther's luminous form was effaced in the slumber of Mordechai's night. It was the dolorous tone of terrors. There were imprecations when the Flood covered the lands, the despair of Gomorrah, and in the skies, the flaming sword of Senacherib's angel; in a lurid dialogue there ascended the supplications of Egypt, the moans of Babylon, the condemned stones of Jerusalem. There rose the deep-voiced concert of the prophets preaching. In vain did the brilliance of the transfigurations, like livid rifle fire, shoot shafts of light over night terrors; did Ezekiel have a vision of the Eternal; did Elijah visit the Mystery in a flight of flames. Nothing. The solemn music was a Miserere. Neither did the flash of dawn in Bethlehem, in Judaea, chase away the shadows, nor did the living mirage at Tabor. The epic was in its death throes as the century rolled on, flowing away in a cavern where there was a tomb; it shouted out in triumph for a moment about the Resurrection of the Just One; it died, in the end, slowly, slowly, like the prayer of the martyrs in the amphitheater, the faraway underground prayer of the refugees in the Catacombs.

Christian doctrine, annotated by the proficiency of my explicator, was the occasion for a double dose of teaching that interested me greatly. It was an open, sky-blue canopy, surrounded by altars dedicated to the consecrated creations of the faith. I was curious about contemplating the greatness of the Lord on high, but there were also windows turned toward Purgatory, and Sanches leaned out of them with me, and that view I found even more seductive. And my preceptor's voice and manner had a seasoning of unction, a seriousness like that of a spiritual advisor who speaks of sin without staining his lips with it. He spoke with a manner close to compunction, his eyes fixed on the ceiling, cracking his knuckles, in a transport of religious abstraction; thus he explained, dwelling on particulars, the hairiest manifestations of Satan in the world. He did not even gild the horns so as not to scare me; on the contrary, with a certain refinement he created the most surprising fantasies of Evil and of Temptation. In Sanches's representation, the devil's tail was about three feet longer than in reality; at one point, however, he suggested to me that the devil was not as ugly as they painted him.

The catechism began to instill in me the kind of fear induced by obscure oracles. I did not believe completely. Considering, I thought that at least half of it was Sanches's wicked invention. And when he started to tell stories about chastity, paying no attention to the paucity of matter on it, theological precept, neighbor's wife, Virgin Birth, the Third Sin of Lust, clamor to heaven about unnatural sensuality, moral advantages of matrimony, and why the flesh, the innocent flesh that as far as I knew was simply the meat forbidden during Lent and by the codfish cartel, the meat of the poor cow was an enemy of the soul—when he corrected my mistake, explaining that flesh was one thing and stew was another and the flesh would be barbecued in a very special manner, I bit back a small portion of indignation at those slanders against the holy catechism reader of my devotions. But the thing was interesting, and I collected the information to judge it for myself when I had a chance.

I could do without my older friend at multiplication tables and line drawing: at drawing because it amused me to follow the capricious lines, and I was diverted by their minute geometry as by a game; at the multiplication tables and the metric system, because I had lost hope that I would ever be better than mediocre as an athlete at arithmetic and had decided to leave the leadership in that domain to Maurílio or whoever else had ambitions in that direction.

Within two months we had gone through, lightly, the materials of the entire course, and thus prepared, I was looking at a magnificent future before me, when fatality struck to derail me.

I have mentioned that Sanches aroused in me a repugnance as if to slime. After the incident in the pool, gratitude predominated over revulsion, and I allowed the assiduity with which my fellow student chose to favor me. After a time, however, the instinctive disgust that told me to distance myself from the boy reasserted itself.

Distrusting the fraternal fellowship of the school, of which Barbalho had given me an account, I was afraid of the tumult in the schoolyard. I found it prudent to remain in the classroom, and I used these intervals of required relaxation to catch up with my coursework. Well, during those moments of exceptional diligence when we were alone, the older boy and I, the foundation of the initially intuited antipathy defined itself. We would sit on the same bench. Sanches would creep closer. Then he leaned hard against me. He closed his own book and read mine, blowing a tired breath in my face. To explain things, he would move away a little and then he would take my fingers and press them till my hand hurt, as if they were clay, darting at me looks of unjustified anger. Then he would repeat some expressions of affection, and the reading would proceed, his arm around my neck as if in a furious friendship.

I allowed it all, acting as if I did not notice anything, beginning to plan a breakup but held back by a lack of courage. There was no harm in those friendly gestures, but I thought them excessive and importunate, especially since they did not correspond in the least to any tiniest gesture of mine.

I noticed that he changed his demeanor when one of the supervisors showed his face at the entrance to the room or when he intended to inform me of some transcendent matter. Then that strange master turned formal and wrapped himself in a severe and distant gravity. This kind of changeableness alarmed me at first and then amused me. I would often lose the thread of what I was reading in order to attend to the wiles of that newest of comedies.

On one very hot day, he had just finished enunciating, like a priest on a page of religious studies, the various acts of Contrition, of Attrition, of Faith, of Hope, of Charity, when he proposed that I repeat them seated on his lap. I thought the comfort unnecessary and repeated the lesson while walking around the room. The devil! That chap really did intend to treat me like a baby! Soon, in his excessive solicitude, he would be trying to put me back into swaddling clothes. Ah, if only I still had in me the audacious bravery I had brought from home, I would for certain have dispatched Sanches with that catechism around his ears. But I was no longer what I had been, and my desire to do so was tender and supple, like a new shoot, after the shock of the first conflict. I kept postponing the confrontation.

Sometimes my passive resistance disappointed my master. He looked at me with a fearful expression, as if to warn me: "You will be losing the protection of a supervisor!" Or else he ignored my impertinence with a forced smile and an abstracted expression on his face that hinted at an obsession.

Physical education took place in the afternoon, one hour after dinner—an excellent time that allowed digestion to stay in the stomach rather than sliding out students' throats as they hung from the bars.

I recognized the handsome parade field when I went there for the first time after joining the school, and I missed the banners flying over the green grass. But even after the cheerful stands erected for the festivities had been knocked down, it was a lovely place. Open to the vast skies, it seemed to have more air, and when I was there, I compensated my lungs for the closed compression of the indoor regimen.

At the conclusion of the exercises, Professor Bataillard would leave, and under the guard of two supervisors—Silvino and João

Numa or João Numa and the old Margal, venerable invalid Spaniard beloved by all, or Margal and the "Counselor"—we students would have free time till nightfall.

One evening, as it got dark, I was walking in silence, as was Sanches, watching the day flee behind the mountains, and I noticed that my companion was mumbling a question. He spoke distractedly, admiring the sunset with a frown, in the slightly absent way that was usual in him. We were at one of the bends in the avenue that surrounded the field, opposite the gate where the supervisors were chatting. The other students were playing catch in the field or leapfrog farther away. As I had not heard the question, Sanches repeated it. I laughed almost involuntarily: he was offering me the strangest kind of proposition! I was laughing frankly but was also completely taken aback. That Sanches was definitely a unique character. These days he is an engineer, at a railroad in the southern part of the country, a very grave engineer.

As it became clear that we could not understand each other, he put the splendor of the afternoon between us, and we resolved the embarrassing moment by agreeing unanimously on how we felt about it.

In the following days, Sanches was cool toward me. I was afraid of losing him. He taught me the necessary lessons without a single one of his unbearable tender gestures. He spoke in short sentences, partly angry, partly sad. I suspected a change in his character and thought I had found a position that suited me, as a moderate friend, and that freed me from the indignities visited on the younger boys. But that was not the case. Sanches had understood that my innocence had neutralized the zeal of his teachings. And he was positioning himself to return to the charge. Meanwhile, he was careful to insist on some edifying preparations.

He invented an analysis of *The Lusiads*, a book that would be on the exam, and the difficulty of which he ceaselessly emphasized.

He led me to the ninth canto, as to a disreputable street. I was guiltily enjoying the thrill of the unexpected. My mentor took me along the stanzas, ripping open the noble face of the poem to show views of bordellos reeking of lavender. Barbarian! As if its words were a modest cover hiding the truth, he would tear those tunics from top to bottom, roughly. Out of each graceful sway of a verse he made some offensive brutishness. I followed him without remorse; I thought vaguely of myself as a victim and gave myself up to his cruelties, submissive, relaxed in the position of passivity. The analysis whipped up the rhymes; the rhymes went by, leaving the image of an impudent sway of the hips. And Sanches's air of severity was unperturbed.

He took up every phrase, every sentence loftily, with the somber demeanor of an anatomist: subject, verb, complements, subordinate clause. Then, the meaning, zap!—a cut with his scalpel, and the sentence fell dead, repugnant, gutted in its filthy decay.

Using the same method, he started a picturesque course about the dictionary. The dictionary is the universe. It drools enlightenment, but at first it makes you giddy as in the tumult of great foreign cities. Lined up on those countless pages, nouns follow each other strangely with their numerous offspring of cognates, or they appear alone, foppish little masters, in the French style, or conceited dandies from Albion. They vex us with their disdain when we don't know them. Meanings go on forever, crossing each other in a confusing topographical network. The inexperienced visitor will not get ahead a single step in that huge capital of words. Sanches knew his way around. He went with me to the most humble shelters of the metropolis, to the core of the sewer system of dirty words. He flayed into a caricature the magisterial circumspection of the lexicon, just as he had polluted the Parnassian elevation of the poem.

I felt myself shrivel under the weight of his revelations. The knowledge of things never dreamed of terrified me. That honorable spiritual director of mine realized that he had now an ascendancy over me, a dominion under which I bowed. He began to look me straight in the face and to laugh open and daringly malicious laughs. After days of acting reserved, he now approached me again with the assurance of one who exercised a powerful hold over me. I, on the other hand, felt drained of energy. From time to time Rebelo embarrassed me, looking at me through his blue glasses, with an air of disdain or, more humiliating, of pity. My father came to see me every week; I showed him my prizes for scholarship, talked about home, was silent about the rest. I still distrusted and feared everyone, and Sanches was almost my only companion. We were always together, he and I. They knew at the Athenaeum that he was my tutor, and some even thought he was being paid. They did not think our relationship strange.

Meanwhile, like all those of evil intent, Sanches avoided busy places. He liked to wander with me, in the evening, before supper, crisscrossing the darkened yard a hundred times, hugging me nervously, tightly, to the point of lifting me from the ground. I put up with it, imagining, in resigned silence, the artificially weakened sex Rebelo had defined for me.

Encouraged by my compliance, which he took for tacit assent, Sanches pushed toward a resolution. One rainy afternoon we were wandering around the room with the washbasins, dark, humid, smelling of moldy towels and toothpaste, in favorable solitude, increased by the obstacles to sight offered by the large, square pillars that held up the building, when, with no preparation, my companion put his mouth near my face and whispered.

Just that voice, the simple, cowardly sound of that voice, creeping, sticky, as if every syllable were a slug, revolted me, like touching a filthy instrument of torture. I pretended not to have heard, but inside I felt an explosion of all my disgust for that individual, and very calmly, just turning my eyes away, I found the excuse that I needed a handkerchief because the cold had gotten to me, and . . . I went to procure one.

Beyond the magnetic zone where my good friend imprisoned me, my repressed instinct of rebellion recovered, and Sanches became a stranger. With one blow, I sacrificed the friend, tutor, and supervisor: it was heroic. At our first meeting after the breakup, the older boy saw it was all over. He started to hover over me, his eyes glinting like knives.

The thing was, it had not been the best time for that conflict. The demands of the course load had made it necessary to divide Master Manlio's class in two, and I had been included in the group entrusted to Sanches as a competent teacher's assistant. The result turned out just as it had to. Mistreated and condemned by the assistant, doing badly on the exam to which the teacher subjected me, demoralized by a solemn reprimand that pleased Sanches mightily, I swore revenge. I would shock the world with unprecedented idleness. I had gone over the entire content of the course, so I'd quickly get my bearings. That was not, of course, enough. But it would have to do. I made that my motto. And down I went. I sank lower than Barbalho, lower than any decent ranking—lower than Álvares. I managed the lowest grade in the class, a reasonable result for the purpose of using a discreet surge of energy that began to bubble up.

At the same time, like troubled philosophers everywhere, I sought the sweet solace of the stars: Aristarco had started a night course in astronomy.

Stars were his specialty. Ah, the noble task of teaching! No other teacher, under pain of expulsion, would touch the nocturnal robe of the astronomer. And one just had to see him, at his window, indicating the constellations, pushing them through the night with his pointy finger. We, his disciples, saw nothing, but were lost in admiration. All he had to do was eruditely delineate a group of stars for each one of us to feel more in touch with it. And off he flew, leaving a trail of luminous dust.

As for me, what mostly filled me with wonder was the way Aristarco hooked the stars with his fingers, when everyone knew that pointing at stars caused warts.

One night, full of enthusiasm, our Master showed us the Southern Cross. Soon after, whispering to each other what we knew about the points of the compass, we figured out that the window looked toward the north and raised that question. Aristarco recognized the mistake but did not want to admit it. And, unwilling, the Southern Cross remained where he had planted it, in the same hemisphere as the North Star.

I developed a love for everything related to space, and studied all I could of celestial mechanics in Abreu's compendium.

On cloudy nights, Aristarco brought out his machines. He had an infinite number of apparatuses for the study of astronomy: models of the solar system, demonstrations of the theory of eclipses, the gravitation of satellites, concentric spheres, terrestrial and celestial, the inner ones in polished cardboard, the outer ones in glass. On the table there was an incredible confusion of stars, twisted wires, tin gears, weak naphtha lights representing the sun. Aristarco turned a handle, and everything moved. With his thick tortoiseshell pince-nez perched on the tip of his nose, he controlled the throng of worlds.

"Do you see," he would ask, explaining nature, "do you see my hand here?" And he showed his right hand, turning the hurdy-gurdy, a great big hairy hand that Esau would have envied.

"This is the hand of Providence!"

Chapter 4

Serene period in my moral life; chapter to be written on an altar bench, or with the blue alphabet that the smoke of incense draws in the air; the quietest, most unforgettable period of truce and inner peace of my entire youth—that was what my bitter descent into the deepest scholarly abyss turned out to have been.

Astronomy, like the skies in the psalm, brought me to contemplation. Earthly evil, described by Sanches with the skill of an expert practitioner, grew in my mind as I meditated. My initial disbelief came to an end in my soul, as I recognized the disaster that was this vale of tears where we live. The time I should have spent redeeming myself through my studies, I took instead to study—as Ignatius of Loyola had, perhaps at the same age I was—the redemption of the world.

I incarnated sin into the figure of Sanches and blackened him further. Perhaps, deep down, I had the ambition to reform mankind with the pontifical example of my virtues on the pontifical throne of Rome, but the truth is that I dedicated myself conscientiously to the holy task of deserving this exaltation, preparing myself in time. Having abandoned the theatrical ideal of work and fraternity that I had wished school to embody, I had to release into another direction the doves of my imagination. A reasonable goal was heaven. I was left as the sales representative for eternal bliss, immeasurable.

The oppressive sadness I felt over being a bad student predisposed me to this kind of rapture. And since nobody paid attention to my weak attempts at rising from that trough, I remained insensible, resigned, as if unconscious under a landslide. My conscience, the spectacle we offer to God, was at peace. My faith served as a soft mattress of comforting roguery.

In passing, let it be noted that despite my yearning for heavenly bliss, I was doing as badly in catechism as in everything else.

The most terrible of the Athenaeum's institutions was not its famously arbitrary justice, not even the *dungeon*, refuge of darkness and sobs, punishment for enormous misdeeds. It was the Notebook.

Every morning, without fail, and in front of the entire school, gathered for breakfast at eight, the headmaster turned up at one of the doors, with the slow solemnity of apparitions, and opened the record of deeds.

It was a long and thick memo pad—a book, really—leather bound, a red label on its cover, the cover edged in the same red. On the previous evening each teacher, in the order of their schedules, had recorded in it his observations about the diligence of his disciples. It was our journalism. From the open book, as from the shadows of the magic boxes in fairy tales, there was born, there appeared, there grew, there imposed itself, the opinion of the Athenaeum. Capricious and unreliable queen, this opinion tyrannized us beyond any appeal, final as a judgment from the highest court. The fearful newscast, compiled at the whim of the unreliable justice of the teachers, often violent, ignorant, hateful, immoral, reared itself up as an irredeemable attack on reputations. A judge could be driven from the bench by conclusive evidence of his defects; the written defamation was irrevocable.

The worst part of it was that conviction was contagious, and everyone who heard the judgment was surprised that he had not noticed how very ordinary that disciple really was, or that fellow student—thus reinforcing it passively till the work of vilification was completed and, at last, the victim, without even a suggestion of rebellion, accepted it all as fair and just, and bowed his head before it. Public opinion is a devilish opponent that can count on the ultimate complicity of the victim himself.

With the exception of the privileged, the supervisors, the intimate friends, who slept in the shade of a reputation cleverly arranged by means of a fair collusion between hard work and captivating sweetness, there was for the rest an expectation of terror before the reading of the notes. The book was a mystery.

As the broadsheet was reeled off, the tension eased. Those who had been victimized slunk away, bowed with shame, oppressed by the incalculable punishment of three hundred little faces looking at them with ironic superiority or offensive compassion. They had to pass by Aristarco on their way to the penal task of writing. The headmaster, gathering into one of those Olympian rages he knew so well how to create on the spur of the moment, slapped the book on the back of the condemned, adding injury and mockery to the sentence of defamation. The unfortunate student staggered down the hallway.

When the thing was not serious enough for a rage, Aristarco simply underlined with some comment what the teacher had set down: at times it was an expression of surprise, at other times a threat; sometimes a stinging and swift insult, sometimes advice shrouded in funereal pity.

Sometimes he caught the boy by the neck with two long fingers and turned him, shaking and submissive, toward the attentive audience, offering him to the slaps of public opinion: "Just look at this face! . . ."

And the child, livid, closed his eyes.

In compensation, there were no literal corporal punishments.

For a long time, Master Manlio, mindful of the recommendation, spared me the formidable public punishment. But in the end he lost patience and fulminated at me.

The next day, at breakfast, I could not put enough sugar in my coffee to take away the bitter taste in my mouth as I waited (because Manlio had warned me) until the moment when I heard Aristarco, pausing dramatically with emotion, as he read, clearly, severely, "Mr. Sérgio has been degenerating . . ."

I had already appeared in the Athenaeum's news sheet as the object of praise; the bad grade would be a sensation. The headmaster eyed me darkly.

In the depths of the silence, usual in the cafeteria, an even deeper silence dug in, like a well at the bottom of an abyss. I felt that gaping silence devour me. The student body, a congregation bent on severe justice, turned toward me, against me. Those sitting next to me at the table moved away, on both sides, better to expose me to everyone's view. From the pantry, in the distance, came the horrible, silvery sound of spoons being washed; in the park, the tamarind trees swayed in the wind.

Aristarco was clement. It was the first time; he forgave.

The worst case in this system of justice by pillory was when the student became hardened by habit, his sense of shame murdered, as in the case of Franco.

A few days after the terrible grade, I was back on show for another bad grade, less philosophically written up, but made more serious by recidivism.

Aristarco did not forgive. There was a third, a fourth, and more. Each one of them hurt tremendously, but they did not anger me. I wanted that suffering, in the devout humility of my current disposition. I cried at night, in secret, in the dormitory, but gathered my tears in a goblet, like the martyrs in the holy pictures, and offered them to heaven, for remission of my poor sins, the bad grades floating on them.

At recess I walked around alone and silent like a monk. After my experience with Sanches, I did not go near any other student except to exchange necessary words. Rebelo tried to attract me; I avoided him. An angry Sanches followed me, like a demon. He said filthy things. "Just you wait," he'd swear in a hiss, "I'll get you!" In his quality as a supervisor, he beat me brutally with his sword. My legs were purple from his blows; my shins were swollen. While Barbalho remembered to revenge himself for the slap, I went by the gospel injunction.

During that entire period of contemplative depression, only one thing pained me: I did not have Ribas's angelic air, and I did not sing as well as he did. If I died, what would I do among the angels, if I could not sing?

Ribas, at fifteen, was unattractive, skinny, lymphatic. A lipless mouth, like that of an old keening woman, drawn in anguish—a mouth-shaped plea, a perennial prayer drawn over his teeth. His chin slipped away from his face, forever, like a drop of wax running down a candle . . .

But when, kneeling in the chapel, with his hands folded before his chest, he turned his eyes toward the blue medallion on the ceiling, what feeling! What dolorous charm! What piety! A penetrating, adoring look of rapture that rose and pierced the sky like the extreme needle of a gothic temple.

And then he sang the prayers, with the feminine sweetness of a virgin at Mary's feet, high, tremulous, airy, like the heavenly prodigy of sound of the nun Virginia in one of the novels by Counselor Bastos.

Oh, if only I were angelic, like Ribas! I clearly remember seeing him at his bath: his shoulder blades stuck out from his skinny back like wings!

And I was happy then, when envying Ribas.

There were a few reservations in my religious fever, which looked like the germ of a future *libertine*, as the priests in Minas called them: I did not hold with confession, did not think about communion, found the excesses of public worship strange, felt an antipathy for the men in cassocks. But I was a devotee of St. Rosalie.

Why St. Rosalie? There was no real reason. She was in a small picture on cardboard, a delicately colored etching given to me by a cousin, now dead, which I kept in loving memory.

The little cousin had been a good person. Three years older than I, she was affectionate and motherly toward me. She did not play much, but took care of her brothers, of the household, like a lady. Her eyes were large, very large, and seemed to widen still when fixed on something, black and animated by a movement like clouds in a soft sky; her face was light, white, pure, pure like marble, transparent to the blood that colored her cheeks. She spoke only rarely; she did not know what it was to be agitated; she did not know impatience. Maybe she knew she was going to die. Seeing her pass, noiseless, like the female specters of the American dreamer—light upon the earth like the swish of an angel's gown—one would feel, with a tightness around one's heart, that this child did not belong to our world: errant in this life, she sought only the repose that would come in a silent spot, under the gravestone, in the sun, where roses would weep in the morning—and the ethereal freedom of sentiment.

One day, perhaps due to the tears in my eyes, I saw a sign of animation in the face of the small picture. I was thinking of my cousin: I found in the image a moving resemblance to the deceased. And I then kept the picture of St. Rosalie as if it were a portrait.

As my mysticism grew, it was natural that the consecration of the print would be completed, and she was triumphantly canonized in the ecumenical council of my most intimate vows.

The general studies room, to the side of the central courtyard, was a huge hall, longer than it was wide. It would be difficult for a person standing at one end to recognize another at the other end, unless he were endowed with extraordinary powers of vision. To one side were lined up four rows of varnished wooden desks, with their benches. Against the wall, on the other side, large cupboards stood at attention, with numbered doors corresponding to deep compartments for books. But books were the least of what was kept in many of those compartments. The owner would put a lock on the little door and arrange the inside according to his preferences. Some, the future sportsmen, raised mice, carefully pulling out their teeth with a pair of scissors, then hitching them to small cardboard wagons; others, the future politicians, raised chameleons and lizards, showing a precocious affinity for crawling about and shedding their skins. The entomologists filled the shelves with dormant cocoons and kept watch over the efflorescence of butterflies; the collectors, who someday would turn into so many Ladislau Nettos, established make-believe mineralogical museums, botanical museums, where the delicate dry lace of fleshless leaves abounded; others dedicated themselves to zoology and had bird skeletons, hollowed eggs, snakes in bottles filled with cheap spirits. One of the latter suffered a great disappointment. He was carefully keeping the precious cranium of I don't know what phenomenal quadruped he had found while digging in the kitchen garden, which was eventually identified as a chicken carcass.

I had the idea of turning my numbered compartment into a chapel. There would be subcompartments adorned with colored prints and drawings: mine would be a bed of flowers, and I would find a tiny lamp to keep lit there. In the background, gold-matted paper would house Rosalie, the patron saint.

The project foundered on the difficulty of arranging the flowers. If I paid a servant, I would barely manage to get one sprig of jasmine or some other bud a day. In the end I had to accommodate the picture in the drawer of the dresser we had in the dorm, close to the beds, among brushes and combs.

And every day, on the paper, as proof of assiduous veneration, I deposited one flower, keeping in the drawer the tepid climate of my fervor, symbolized by a tribute of perfume.

When, on the first day, the mystic roses of May smiled at me, I greeted them, deeply moved, from the windows, high in the blue hall, as messengers of the Virgin Mary's love.

The morning chants were about to begin in the Athenaeum's chapel. Blessed moments of contrition and tenderness, in which one's body, happy after a bath, could live, for a moment, the fullness of Christian poetry, in the magnificent parlor, preserving, at the same time, like the morning mists on mountain slopes, the last shades of night among the stucco ornaments.

The sun came to chapel as well and, from the outside, pressed his face against the windows, still soft from waking, fresh from the dew of dawn, blushing with shame at not being able to pray, poor atheist star. Through the open windows fragrant bows of jasmine peeked in, like an invasion from the forest, and the tired jasmines of the day before scattered small nacreous shells on the floor, the free soul of perfume expiring in the air.

On our knees, under the moral influence of our surroundings, we prayed sincerely. There was not much evil to harvest in all those young hearts, at that moment, resting in the truce of prayer from the little miseries of the time of convocation.

I never looked at the altar. There she was, lavishly adorned, on her illuminated throne, resting on three ranks of palm fronds, the image of Our Lady of the Immaculate Conception, carrying above her brow the silver crown where the reflected light set a glory of gems. My contrition, my song, belonged to St. Rosalie, to the beloved and simple cardboard image that I carried inside my denim shirt, that I pressed against my heart with my hand, heightening the ecstasy of faith by the thrill of the holy touch.

May brought the height of the anagogical period of belief. By coincidence it was also at that time that my father's ailments made him take to his bed, keeping him from his habitual visits to the Athenaeum. I thought of his suffering, and that became one more theme on which to play the variations of my mysticism.

The fog of melancholy that fell over the school from the mountains, a repercussion of the green sadness of the forest, weighed on me like a seminarian's cassock, like a friar's vows.

I walked within the enclosed space of the schoolyard as if in a cloister, looking at the walls, white like whitewashed tombs, limiting the preoccupations of my spirit to my humiliation before God, without looking up, in the bowed modesty of brute beasts—effacing myself in the anguish of religious thought, as if caught in the black, pointed, cloth hood of penitents in a procession.

The sky, which my imagination had sought before, just as canticles seek church domes, sat now on my head like a bronze helmet.

Sad and happy.

Nobody knew my dreams, and all thought my love of solitude and silence was simply a form of eccentricity.

When it was time to sing the anthem to the guardian angel, in the protected yard, at noon, the students, hot and sweaty from their games, their coats wet above their leather belts, their hair mussed, did not take the rite seriously, and only the severity of the supervisors forced them to respect those ten minutes of religion. Only Ribas and I . . . and if worldly afflictions and our troubles did not lessen, it was not for lack of entreaties to the angel . . .

We sang the first stanza (Ribas set the tone) and those following, up to the very last, and all ended in a long note, rising like a rocket; we sang with an effort of adoration that would easily, if balance were needed, make up for all the irreverent levity of the other students.

Ribas's tone was a delightful note, treated with throat lozenges, protected by a woolen scarf on cold days, probably stolen from some thrush's treasury of warbles. Aristarco loved it. Sometimes, in the middle of a music class, he would call Ribas and ask him for that tone, the one from the hymn . . .

Candidly, to please the headmaster, Ribas let out that note, like an amber-colored gumdrop at the tip of his tongue. Noon was the time. Ribas rolled his eyes up and let out, before all others, the precious sound. The students together then intoned in his wake, and all our voices took off after that first one. Wasted effort: Ribas's voice joined the heavenly choirs, greeted with the fraternal cordiality of celestial harmonizers, while ours returned from their assault, disillusioned, falling like Icarus, gangling, dismembered, through space, like a band of disoriented egrets. From a distance, the noise could have passed for a canticle.

The most annoying prayer time took place in the evening, before we retired.

The day's business sat heavy on our shoulders and caused a reaction of irresistible exhaustion. Sleep weighed down our eyelids like a casting net. The harmonium in the chapel, played by Sampaio—who is now an obstetrician and dedicates himself to extract newborn wails as he then extracted the chords— slowly produced snores like those of a tiger at his nap, snorts like those of a sleepy abbot digesting his dinner. Some of the boys were nodding off as they sang, their voices trailing away in gaping yawns. In the first rows, many of the younger ones had their eyes closed, far from caring about the prayers. I myself was enjoying the pleasures of self-mortification, my fervor sustaining me during those evening devotions.

For that purpose, I carried in my pocket a handful of pebbles, which I scattered on the ground to create a *prie-dieu*—a kneeler of sorts—to keep me awake, while I stared wide-eyed, as if alert, and gritty-eyed with sleep at the shivering tongues of the burning candles . . .

I have mentioned several times how Aristarco habitually took on the external trappings of divinity.

It was a transparent cloak, like the floating breezes woven in Gautier's later poetry, a supernatural cloak that Aristarco threw over his shoulders, revealing no more about itself than that it denoted majesty, far above the mundane industry of weavers and the material weft of shuttlecocks. Nobody had ever been able to touch the mysterious purple. One felt, however, the aura of impalpable royalty. Thus it was that a simple glance from the headmaster immobilized the school, as if his glare carried the threat of despotism in its fullest cruelty.

The headmaster manipulated this talent for imperiousness with the skill of a jockey on a responsive thoroughbred.

The general study room had countless doors. Aristarco would appear suddenly, at any one of those doors, when one would least expect him.

Thus he materialized in the classrooms, surprising teachers and students. By this method of sudden vigilance, he kept up throughout the establishment, everywhere, the perpetual risk of being caught red-handed and an atmosphere of alarm. He accomplished more in this manner than with the spying of all his beadles. His refinement went so far as to designate some doors and windows as having to be kept shut permanently, the only purpose of which was to make it possible for him to open them of a sudden so as to catch any clandestine form of truancy. He would smile to himself at the awful effect of his traps and stroke his copious white military moustache, slowly, as the jaguar licks his chops in anticipation of a blood-soaked meal.

It was in his moments of anger and eloquent exaltation that he knew how to make himself truly divine. It was more than a fearsome revelation from Mount Olympus; it was as if Jupiter had sent Mercury to gather on earth the thunderbolts he had already fired and had added them to the incalculable stockpile of Aetna's arsenals, ready to be released, all at once, at this one irate moment, in one single bolt, annihilating all nature with that single, all-powerful assault.

But it was not only the Olympic furors he parodied. That supple artist's soul knew how to descend to blandishments, even to the purposeful tear.

Jupiter kept in reserve the softest feather-like caress, the swan's insinuating gesture. There were times when a burst of fatherly love engulfed the Athenaeum, so generous, so cunningly sincere, that we could only answer in the same tone, with a madrigal of filial tenderness.

And we admired him.

Aristarco used the solemn hour of noon to distribute a luncheon's worth of advice, after the singing, and before the actual one, composed of sliced foods and received with incomparably greater pleasure. Often it was not just advice, but also mass reprimands for collective sins, confiscation of cigarettes, or small summary judgments that brought to light important offenses like filling a room with shredded paper, spitting on the walls, wetting the toilet, or even more serious ones, as in an episode involving Franco that in my recollection is connected to this pious period of mine.

The headmaster was attending with his usual concentration to the sung prayers and turning over, with his fingers, a medallion attached to the chain of his watch fob, showing between the lapels of his cutaway. At the end, after a preparatory pause, like an appetizer of the emotions, he started to speak, in a solemn tone reserved for revelations, and appealed, with all the grandeur it seemed to demand, to the vengeful indignation of the Athenaeum.

On the Sunday before, taking advantage of a relaxation of vigilance induced by the free day, Franco had gone to idle away time in the garden. And in order to have a drink of water from a well there, whose pump did not always work, he decided—horrors!—to prime said pump with a liquid that Moses would have been able to gather in the desert without divine intervention and without reference to Mount Horeb. Now keep in mind that this well provided the water with which the dishes were washed.

A horrified murmur rose from the rows of students.

"Step forward, Franco," ordered Aristarco.

With the stony insensibility he used as his armor against humiliation, Franco left his seat and, head bent, went to the center of the room. There he stood for a few seconds, exposed, in the middle of the enormous square of students. Their glances hit him like the bullets at an execution.

What made everyone angriest was thinking how they had all eaten from the dishes washed after that irremediable profanation of the waters. After achieving that effect, on which he counted, to impose the moral punishment, the headmaster completed the assault. We should not worry; our lips were clean and pure. Franco had been seen by one of the mess boys, who had apprehended him, and immediately the pump had been declared out of bounds.

Many doubted the interdiction had been imposed in time. They were scraping their tongues hard on their handkerchiefs and rubbing their lips till the skin came off.

"The pig!" roared Aristarco. "The filthy pig!" he repeated like a god beyond himself with ire. Around him, all supported the energy of the reprimand. It was nevertheless resolved to allow the criminal to live.

Aristarco only assigned him ten pages of punishment to be written at night, and ordered him to spend recess on his knees, starting immediately.

The verdict having been pronounced, Franco fell with his knees on the ground, with a thud, as if a spring had suddenly been released in his legs.

"Not here, scoundrel!" shouted the headmaster, indicating the door. As you know, the midday prayers were recited indoors in the great hall, three large doors of which opened to the central yard. Aristarco stood near the middle one.

On his knees at that point, Franco was pilloried: before him the taunts of the nastier boys and everyone's free delight. As that door was on the boys' way to the trays where the seductive piles of their snacks were heaped, the culprit was subjected to petty additions to his punishment. As they passed by him, the more irate ones pushed him, pinched his arms, insulted him. Franco responded under his breath with a curse word repeated in rapid succession and spat on them, dirtying them all with the only resources left him in his position.

Finally one of the bigger, reckless boys pushed him hard against the door frame, injuring his head. To him, Franco did not react; instead, he started crying.

The overseers were busy checking the distribution of the food, making sure nobody misbehaved. They never saw the attacks.

The poor boy's misadventures and my own had made me come closer to Franco. I had become an almost-friend. Franco was quiet, as if fearing everyone, sad, with a melancholy that could look like stupidity; he had bouts of controlled fury, complaints that he did not know how to formulate. Books, the primary causes of his troubles, were a horror to him. The need to write as a punishment had developed in him the ability of galley slaves: he had acquired an astonishing facility for scrawling pages and pages of words. This endless writing had created calluses under his nails: "my fingers have lost their mettle," he would say, with the bitter wit he used to improvise sarcasm at his own expense.

At first he would run from me, muttering indecipherable things. Then he accepted me. But he never confided in me beyond the very strict boundaries of a few growls implying a dislike for this person or that, stories of off-color scrapes he had heard about, naive observations about childish matters, and references to his hatred of those in power.

Once he received a letter from the provinces, one of the few that reached him in a year. After he read it, I noticed he had tears in his eyes. Crying unfolded like a spectacle on his face, whose usual expression was a masklike apathy. I was interested in that suffering, and he handed me the letter to read. Franco's father was a pitiable judge exiled to the depths of Mato Grosso, with his eight children. A painful letter. It had been delivered to him directly by a clerk of the sender's, thus escaping the curiosity of the headmaster, who liked to snoop into his students' correspondence. It spoke of coming to the Court, in Rio, by the end of the year, with all the sacrifices that entailed, and of finding his son to be a good boy, well educated, and a good student. And then it told, with many expressions of consternation, how one of his daughters, the eldest, had disappeared from her school in the company of a piano teacher, a married man, and had been found three or four days later, abandoned. In vain had they questioned the unhappy girl with the purpose of punishing the culprit; the girl had wrapped herself in a desolate silence, as if she had lost her voice, refusing food, never lifting her delirious eyes from the ground, enslaved to the demented contemplation of her shame.

"How Sérgio has fallen," the supervisors would say to each other, sorrowfully, in their daily reports to the headmaster. "He is now close friends with Franco."

Even though that was not precisely true, I was not surprised to have the shunned one invite me on an extraordinary adventure one night. "Revenge against the rabble!" he murmured, with a sour half laugh, deep in his throat. That was in the afternoon, after gym class, on the same day as the trial about the pump.

At dusk he had managed to escape from the room where he had been shut up to write all those pages. And together, he and I—because I had accepted his invitation with an ease I still don't understand—climbed up one corner of the wall enclosing the yard and jumped down into the wooded garden.

Under the trees, gloom had already settled in. We walked around in the dark along the curving alley. Franco walked ahead, in silence, light and quick like a shadow in the air. I followed unresisting, as if in a dream of curiosity and wonder. What was Franco going to do? Where was he going? We arrived at an area of tall grasses, at the edge of which was the swimming hole. Right at the gate of that area there was a garbage dump, where the gardeners gathered the sweepings from the kitchen garden, to let time turn them into compost, and there they lay, black and putrefying.

Franco stopped beside the steaming heap. Always silent and active, as if not wanting to lose that precious stimulation of his will that pushed him forward, he tested the garbage with his foot.

At one corner, among bamboo stumps, there was a clink of bottles. Franco bent down and as if mechanically, without turning, picked up one bottle, and another, and another, and handed them to me, then gathered several more, and we went on, Franco ahead of me, light and swift always, like a shade, as if suspended and diffused in the shimmering mist of the open field.

We crossed the grassy area almost invisible among the high rows of buffalo grass, the dark expanse of which was punctuated by glowworms and vibrated from the intense chirping of crickets and the clamor of frogs. Arriving at the pool, Franco stopped and made me stop. "My revenge!" he said between gritted teeth and showed me the unbroken surface of the pool. The liquid mass, motionless in the stillness of the night, looked like a shining surface of pitch; a few stars were reflected on the black surface, perfectly sharp.

In the same busy way in which he had conducted the entire strange enterprise, Franco approached me, took back the bottles he had handed to me, and disappeared from my sight.

I heard him breaking the bottles one by one. Shortly, he reappeared, having made the bottom of his shirt into a carrier. And with the greatest tranquility, he started to throw into the pool, in all directions, as if sowing them, the shards into which he had broken the bottles. There was a short bubbling noise as the pieces touched the water and sank, and the reflected stars moved over the concentric circles they left. Many times, against the lighter shade of the wall before us, I saw, going to and fro, the shadow of the sinister sower.

"My revenge!" he repeated. "Blood for blood," he added with a dry laugh. "Tomorrow I will laugh at that rabble! . . . I brought you here so that someone would know that I am taking my revenge!"

And as he spoke, he showed me the handkerchief with which he had wiped the blood from his forehead.

The full terror of that adventure, in that forbidden place, at that time, only hit me when, as I jumped over the yard wall, I fell into the hands of Silvino. In my plight, I hardly saw Franco, held by the neck, like a thief caught in the act.

In the presence of the headmaster, in the inquisitorial office, I improvised a lie. We had gone to pick sapodillas, I asserted, as I justified, under intense interrogation, the purpose of the strange excursion. The headmaster assigned a punishment of eight pages. Franco, who owed at least twenty, had to add that many to his unredeemable debt. In order to shame us for the attempted larceny and in accordance with the system of moral punishments, another observance was added: we, the delinquents, were to spend the next day's lunch and dinner hours standing in the refectory, holding in each hand as many sapodillas as we could carry.

Those refinements in our punishment did not worry me; on the contrary, it was part of the conditions of my private program of martyrdom *ad majorem gloriam*. Something else weighed on my mind, a burning remorse—I had the glass shards on my conscience. Franco's sanguinary trap obsessed me as if it were my own crime.

After the evening study hours, when the pupils were leaving for the dorms, I stayed behind, working, with Franco. After four pages I had to stop. Remorse devoured me like a fever: I was terrified of the time when we would all go bathing the following morning, the boys jumping into his perfidious revenge, the water turning red. It was impossible to write another line. I left him and fled to the older boys' room.

The excitement increased; I tossed on the bed feeling as if I were lying on sharp glass shards. What to do? Denounce Franco in the morning? Run out in the dark and let the water out of the pool? Warn the other boys and ask them to scatter? The controversy grew in my head like a swelling of meningitis. Could it happen that Franco, driven by remorse, would, first thing in the morning, denounce himself to the supervisors? I even tried to fool my conscience by considering that perhaps they would not all jump into the pool at the same time so that the first one who was wounded would save the others. But the fever won out, with visions of blood. Ten, twenty, thirty boys, at the edge of the pool, moaning, extracting from their flesh, with difficulty, the shards embedded in it! And I, the accomplice who had allowed it, was the greater culprit; simple reason made it very clear, in sum, that any retribution would be only fair.

I rose from my bed and, barefoot on the cold floor, hoping that my unease would diminish, wandered through the sleeping halls.

The other students, quiet in the rank of beds, buried their faces in their pillows, relaxed in their dreamless sleep. Some affected the touching outline of a smile; some had the hopeless expression of the dead, their mouths half-open, their lids half-closed, showing the blurred tenderness of death. Here and there, the sheets rose with a stronger intake of breath, exhaled then in one of those long adolescent sighs, generated in their sleep by the unconscious vigil of the heart. The younger ones, children still, held one of their hands on their chests, while the other hung down, preserving in the abandon of their sleep the ideal gesture of flight. The older ones, contorted in the spasm of precocious aspiration, bent their heads and enlaced their pillows in a caress. The outside air entered through the open windows, fresh, smelling of the nocturnal exhalation of the trees; one could hear the rhythmic croak of a frog, hammering the seconds, the hours, with a cooper's hammering; others and others answered, farther away. The gaslight shone weakly in milky sconces, flickering in the cut-glass sleeves, bathing all the beds equally with the dispersed sweetness of a mother's glance.

What happy safety in the museum of sleep! And tomorrow, O my poor fellow students! The swim, the return, bleeding feet marking the way with crimson smudges!

I returned to my own hall. I took the image of St. Rosalie out of the drawer and kissed it, in tears, asking for advice as if I were her son. The restlessness persisted. I crossed the dormitories again, slowly, so that Margal, ensconced behind a screen in one of the corners of the blue hall, would not hear me. A cracking of the bones in my ankle almost betrayed me. Behind the screen, someone coughed. I stopped for a moment; the cough stopped; I went on.

I went down to the ground floor of the building. I entered the chapel.

The chapel was the deep black of a sable merino shawl. The darkness gave it a subterranean amplitude, mysteriously felt as in space. I was not afraid. I went up to the altar. I stumbled on the dais. I knelt on the floor and rested my head in my arms at one of the angles of the platform to the oratory. I prayed.

In my status as a bad student, I did not know any prayer to the end. I devised my own entreaties, improvising vehement, anguished supplications that should force St. Peter's gates. I implored God directly, without the intermediary endeavor of my patron saint. Until, and I cannot tell how, I fell asleep.

A slap woke me. It was day. I rose, embarrassed, in my night-shirt, standing before Margal and a lot of students who looked at me. "He sleepwalks, he sleepwalks," they explained.

For me that was a way out: I did not need to explain what had taken me there, and I took up that explanation. "What time is it?" I asked. "Six," they answered, "we have just come back from bathing." Their hair was pasted over their eyes. "What about the shards?!" I cried, terrified. I checked their feet. I saw no blood in the slippers they always wore to the morning bath! They explained: an order had come down that they should shower in the appropriate room, on the lower floor of the school, because the water in the swimming basin had been used six times. Thank the Lord! This solution of the dirty water had come from heaven itself, in answer to my prayers. My soul expanded in happy relief.

My exclamation about shards, however, convinced the other boys that I was still under the influence of some dream. But not the supervisor, who called on me to explain. Another lie became necessary: while on the sapodilla-gathering excursion, I had thrown a bottle awkwardly against the wall, and it had broken into many pieces, right above the basin. Measures were taken. The servant in charge of sweeping the basin called attention, with the zeal of the perfect domestic, to the number of fragments, but the hypothesis that there might have been some perverse intention was so extraordinary that it did not arise.

On that same day, I met up with Franco during break, as he finished his punishment. Feeling compromised, he concentrated on the numbness of the carapace that defended him, expecting anything: my snitching, a storm of abuse, the dungeon, an addition to the permanent deficit of his punishment. What annoyed him most, however, was that he might be punished for a failed attempt.

As for the refined torture of being exposed in the lunch hall, my hands full of sapodillas, there was no way Aristarco could force me to do it. I would stand there, no mean concession. Franco, of course, submitted, and there he was, his arms extended, making like a fruit bowl in the interest of the system of moral punishment. So much the better for the system.

Given my reluctance, they effected a conversion of two handfuls of sapodillas into copied pages; it was a difficult calculation, which the school's system of justice reached mathematically, decreeing a result that would keep me busy till after midnight.

This burst of vigor went against my religious regimen of submission and suffering. It was the sudden harbinger of the next reorganization of my spiritual geography. And since the movements of the will know how to extract from any fact a deterministic hermeneutic, right away something occurred that weighed heavily in the transformation.

In the evening, again beside Franco, tiring myself out at the task of copying those pages, I had to stay late in one of the second-floor rooms. At about half past ten, the headmaster, before leaving for his own home, came to see us. "Are these . . . rascals still writing?" he asked from his great height, by way of wishing us goodnight, before disappearing and leaving us in the charge of João Numa, the piggish overseer of the upper rooms. In his capacity as designated fatso, João was not diligent. As soon as he saw Aristarco leave, he locked the last door of the Athenaeum and went to sleep.

Depressed by the events of the preceding evening, I was so sleepy that I could hardly hold my head up. At one point, having given in to exhaustion, I was woken by a caress on my hand. I had fallen asleep with my right arm against the desk, with my face on the inkwell, and my left arm hanging on the seat. One instant later, I was out of the room, in one bound, as if I had realized, in my dream, that Franco was a monster.

The next day I rose from my bed as if from a metamorphosis. I imagined, in a faulty generalization, that contemplation was an evil, that mysticism was degrading me treacherously: the ease with which I had befriended Franco was proof of that. At the time, the Athenaeum honored me with a reputation that I was not able to evaluate until later. I did not see how much support I had received, but saw myself on a straight road to a fatal moral plunge. If my soul had hair, I would have registered at that moment a phenomenon of moral horripilation.

I was perplexed.

At the school, triumph might look like Sanches, while Franco represented defeated humility. Between those repugnant extremes, three typical examples of the right life revealed themselves to me: Rebelo, the ancient; Ribas, the angelic; hunchback Mata, the secret police. I had clearly proven my lack of talent and of thin shoulders for the angelic role; I could not be an ancient, as I lacked age, blue spectacles, and bad breath; to be like Mata, I lacked the love of justice and the crooked back . . . Where then did duty lie? In the primer? In Aristarco's opinion? In the senile misanthropy of the blue spectacles?

And that was when I saw, contrarily, my blinding light on the road to Damascus: independence.

Chapter 5

Thus, I owe my religious epiphany the greatest debt of gratitude. Divine complacency smoothed for me that period of profound truancy and hypnotic enervation at the Athenaeum. Any pursuit of punishment, without prejudice to my moral delicacy, slipped away over the hair shirt of penance; I had become stronger through the ordeal. How comforting, in my apathy, to have God as my bondsman!

On Sundays we went to Mass. All opened their booklets, so the headmaster would see they were attentive. I did not open mine. I simply let my spirit escape upward and attach itself to the dome like the sacred decorations, and adjust itself closely to the temple's architectural details, like the gilders' subtle gold, staying up there, still yearning to rise, to reach the heavens like the smoke of the censers.

There were infectious fits of coughing running along the pews. I did not cough. There were convulsions of laughter—suppressed with difficulty by means of handkerchiefs pressed against faces, and by a look from Aristarco, who knelt before the school, his hands folded over the knob of his unicorn—as when a mischievous and unprincipled dog entered the chapel at the precise time of the elevation of the Host and ran out again after a slap with a student's cap. I resisted the general merriment.

We sang in choir on feast days. Orpheus would have a better vocal organization than mine, but if hearts had been singing, instead of lips, no hymn would rise to heaven more expansively, more beautifully than mine. They brought us sugar water in a glass jar to wet our vocal cords. I rejected that worldly sweetness.

The Athenaeum contributed to the brilliance of processions. I enveloped myself amply in the ceremonial cape, red as something offered in sacrifice, that would wrap around me three times; I grasped a torch, which martyred my fingers with drops of hot wax. And there I went, wishing I had a back as strong as those of itinerant salesmen so I could carry, by myself, one of the heavy litters that served to take saints' images. I envied the aplomb of the president of the private philharmonic orchestra, called the Long River Pleasure, that marched behind the parade bearing a standard with the group's initials, and the tightrope walker's athletic wrist that held up the flag.

How sad then, when, as the procession entered the field, the headmaster told us to go on back to the school; how sad to have to watch from afar, through the door, the flaming interior of the temple! That was where the feast of the Lord was held . . . and meanwhile, we were on the inexorable march toward the grim Athenaeum! I shook my head in despair; I could not suffer being deprived of that joy, of delighting my soul with the fire on the altars, of scaling in thought the step—the steps—to the glittering throne, hurling myself upward in a climb toward glory.

After those bursts of enthusiasm, religion began to darken for me.

My neighbor in the general study hall was Barreto, a double personality who, during breaks, was enjoyment personified but who also had moments of inky melancholy with flashes of terror when he spoke of death, and of another life. He prayed much and carried pagan wooden amulets (in the shape of closed fists, thumbs peeking from between the index and second fingers) and blessed medals representing saints, small medals on ribbons, which jumped out of his shirt when he played.

Sanches initiated me into Evil. Barreto instructed me in Punishment. He opened his mouth and showed a cauldron of hell: his words were flames; in the heat of his practices, faults burned like sardines frying at a cheap eatery.

Barreto had been to a rigorous seminary that subjected the boys to a regimen of saltpeter in order to tame the ardors of their age. He was thin, with a Romantic poet's forehead like Alexandre Herculano's, thin lips, black, shining, protruding eyes, his whole head skull-like, his skin dry like a mummy's. From his chin sprouted two single hairs, curling, each to one side.

Maybe only he really knew of my pious preoccupations. In possession of my weak point, he began to inform me about the horrors of the faith, with the self-satisfied importance of a tourist guide. I remember one subject: sacrilegious communion! Barreto gave me a book to read about it, a cruel book that described things worthy of Moloch: children suffering the direct weight of divine wrath, one of whom, having deceived the priest and taken communion without first going to confession, was caught by his clothes between the two steel drums of a machine, and reduced to pulp, dying impenitent, cursed, with no time for a last call to mercy . . . It was incredible to me that, starting from a simple wafer, a thaumaturgy of superstition could derive such terrors.

Barreto embellished his accounts. He stoked fears with a preacher's sacred ire, demonstrating how far from the tortures of eternity were the punishments of Providence on earth. He described hell as if he had seen it. A fiery, ruby-red cave, green-and-black dragons, the color of slime, red-hot iron serpents twined around the condemned, fulvous demons stirring vessels of molten tar, while other tailed sprites, on their spits, carried swarms of inconsolable reprobates to the cauldrons.

I went and read the *New Forest*, by Father Bernardes. That most reverend author reinforced Barreto's words with his terrifying narratives and illustrative commentary.

I began to think religion a source of unbearable melancholy. Death certain, date uncertain, hell forever, pitiless justice: nothing could be darker!

It was too early to consider philosophically what was being revealed to me, but I did develop an insurmountable resistance to the ceremonial rituals. In my best days, I had been unable, literally, to formulate a single one of the prayers in the catechism, and now I could not get through the fastidious imposition of precepts. Going to Mass, well and good, but the rest, and the obligatory dependence on the masters of the cult, that was another matter. In two words: the sacristy and hell, probably inevitable scandals and horrors, filled me with disgust for all the rest. Also, I had several times tried to fulfill my obligations, by studying a little and praying a lot, even throwing in a bit of fasting, and the following day—a bad grade! It did not speak well for the favor of the divine. What would it cost the highest Omnipotence to transform tolerable ignorance into a properly learned lesson, just as it had changed into incalculable abundance those miserly five loaves of bread?

That had been the course of my religious fervor when I got involved with the episode of the glass shards. The tribulations of remorse revived for a moment the dying flame: the result of my entreaty in that harsh ordeal had been more than acceptable. Still, the decomposition of my ecstasies had been too far advanced. I forgot the circumstances with the easy ingratitude of the successful petitioner. And I came to an audacious conclusion.

Too weak to suddenly stop the torrent of centuries of Christianity, I managed, at least, to stay on its banks. Knowing nothing about atheism, I simply turned my face away from the phantoms of eternity. I walked upstairs to the dormitory, took St. Rosalie out of the drawer, put away the last flower offering—dried up, because the punctuality of my cult had already suffered—and kissed it goodbye. Then, without further profanation, I took the image back down to the study hall, where I assigned to it the modest task of marking the pages of one of the books. My patron saint had been discharged!

Shortly afterward, someone who prized those little pictures kidnapped her, and all I felt was regret for the loss of that memento of my little cousin.

May had come and gone, and so had the roses; the prayers to the Virgin ended. Without the morning anthems, without the pink smile of St. Rosalie, all that was left to me was the God of the newest students, the sacrilegious communions, Barreto's savage God. I definitely refused to have anything to do with that executioner, and jettisoned metaphysics as if it had been just a nightmare. And once again I found myself alone at the Athenaeum, more alone than ever. All I had were the stars in my compendium, a comforting nightscape.

Just as well, then, that I could return to belief by way of the Milky Way, which had also led me to belief in the first place. It was an honorable retreat from disillusion.

Every two weeks we were allowed out. We would leave on Sunday, after Mass, and return on Monday, before nine in the morning. On religious holidays we could go on the eve. The cellarer and manager of the commissary argued with the headmaster that he should relax the holiday system. These boys need to be *out*, he cried, with the freedom of a confident butler. Aristarco replied with the soothing invention of lower-quality foodstuffs, strengthening budget flexibility.

There were, however, extra releases, as reward or favor.

For every assignment deemed well executed, the teacher would issue a scrap of yellow paper, a *good point*, and hand it to the student who had thus distinguished himself. Ten of these prizes were worth a printed card, a *good grade*, just as ten times twenty copper pennies were equivalent to a two-hundred *réis* coin. The decimal system was applied to achieving an honor fund, equivalent to a deck of ten "good grade" cards. With that distinction, the student could apply for the winner's medal, silver or gold, depending on whether, on the scale of superlatives grading his achievements in the class, he was more or less excellent. Thus, personal value was reduced to paper in the director's "*clearinghouse,*" or rather, Fox's theory was adapted to the reward mechanism, with all the risks of an uncertain exchange system, subject to bankruptcy panics, without a criterion of justice that would guarantee, undergirding the flashiness of paper money, the reality of a currency of solid value.

In any case, what was certain was that, with the "good grade" tickets, one could buy an outing, and that's what was important, as in nations with bad finances: if the economy is based on paper, what constitutes value?

No need to say that I never achieved outings as a prize. That made the other kind even more important.

In the first fortnight of school, the idea of a holiday and return to the family intoxicated me with the anxiety of a fabulous ideal. When I saw them all again, it was as if they had undergone a miraculous resurrection. I entered the house in tears, dominated by the exuberance of a deadly joy. I was surprised by the incredible happiness of seeing myself reflected in all those dear eyes after the cruel eternity of those two weeks. No! The magnitude of the feared cataclysm privileged the home roof. God, in the prodigal largesse of his kindness, had permitted that I revisit our home, still standing on its foundations, the remembered roof still topping it, and the peaceful fireplace still smoking from the endless melancholy of all unmoved and elevated things.

In time I got used to the happy probability that I would find the dear domestic gods in their usual place and dared, in moments of schoolyard meditation, base my plans for enjoyment on the hope that, even if it used my absence simply to torment my heart, still, the earth would not open to devour, precisely and exclusively, what was dearest to me.

But it was not childish fears or plans for amusement that I took home on the first day of my first release after the dismissal of St. Rosalie.

A servant had come to pick me up. And with that emissary, in my gilt-buttoned uniform, I left the Athenaeum, serious and mute like a diplomat on his way to an international conference. I was in fact ruminating the most serious of intentions: to brave a frank interview with my father, to describe to him, courageously, my situation at the school, and to ask for help in responding to it.

My father had just gotten out of bed. He knew nothing of my latest failures. He showed surprise and consternation. Thus the complete success of my interview.

Days later, at school, I had become a small potentate. I toppled Sanches; I managed to repeal the discipline by sword; I regained Manlio's benevolence; I held my head high!

Free from the arbitrary power of a pretentious supervisor, I found pleasure in my work. One piece of advice I brought back from home was that if there was the noble opinion of Aristarco, and the even nobler one of the primer, there was also a third one—mine own, which, if not as noble or authoritative as the others, had the great advantage of originality. With one word, an anarchist was born.

From there on, a conflict between independence and authority was inevitable. Aristarco would chafe. In compensation, goodbye to any hope of ever rising to the position of supervisor! And above all, goodbye to the happy indolence of my devout period.

For the opposition campaign, I stockpiled an inexhaustible amount of vanity and decided to disdain as well as I could the prizes and applause with which the model students graduated. As I became used to life at the boarding school, I was certain that I would be able to achieve by myself all I had not been able to do with the support of a friend or with help from God.

With the firm intention of not turning into an exemplary student nor applying myself to the expert groveling that the role of model student made necessary, my new plan of action was to establish myself in a position of reasonable mediocrity with no obligations.

I earned few of the yellow paper prizes; in compensation I eased the few that came to me into the bohemian freedom of the trash bin. Some of those, with my name on them, ended up in the headmaster's office. That show of contempt was an insult that would never be forgiven.

In the upper echelons there grew an antipathy toward me that flattered me like a kind of consideration. And thus I arrived, on a path very different from the one I had dreamed of, at the desired moral status of a real man.

Envious of my haughtiness, my enemies found each other. Sanches was the chief, behind the curtain; Barbalho was the leader, openly. I smiled, proud of myself, pushing the hostilities ahead of me, like foam before the prow of a speeding boat.

And that was the character I settled on, after all those oscillations. For it seems that it is only tentatively that we arrive at the outlines of character, like a sculptor molding the flesh of his own face in accordance with some ideal; or perhaps it is because, before moral individuality can manifest itself, it will try on different costumes, available in the psychological wardrobe of possible manifestations.

Two pernicious influences reigned at the Athenaeum, readily undermining the doctrinal wisdom oozing from the walls, decoratively framed, and even the policy of ubiquitous and sudden appearances of the headmaster. It is difficult to pin it down, something like the dissemination in a society of a principle of evil, that primary element of theogonic dualism. The middle, let us say, is a reversed hedgehog: instead of the centrifugal explosion of darts, we have a convergence of spines toward the center. Caught in the stinging mass of spines, it is necessary either to find a duct toward the exit or accept the unequal contest between the skin and the quills. Generally, one chooses the duct.

The maxims, the headmaster, the inspections by the beadles, for instance, were three such quills; the influences mentioned were two further ones. Youth transgressed them as best it could, under the circumstances.

Those corrosive influences manifested themselves under two incarnations, fused into a hybrid built on absurdity: its female form was personified in Angela, the Canarian, or rather, Dona Ema's chambermaid; the other was a corner made up of humble boards hastily joined, under the pressure of the uncivil banality of an episode of bodily economy.

Thus they spoke to the imagination, those impressions gathered with a glance: a lascivious look; a storm of clothing in the disorder of flight, calculated to irritate; a careless strap loosened from a corselet; purposeful puddles on rainy days that forced skirts to be held up and shins to show (once at a run past an open door, once across the leafy park, or at the office with messages from Dona Ema so frequent they filled the headmaster with despair, or over the wall surrounding the swimming basin, or in corners with the mess boys in an idyllic duet one espied); or a coarse jest flung toward the overseers, who drooled at it.

The big boys joked; the younger ones looked on, solemn, as if learning a lesson.

Then, the conspiracy of the slats, the opening to vice in the shade of tarry pines, the penury of smoke, the neediness of puffs granted in exchange for dedication, the "bird's eye" butt going from lip to lip like the maté gourd in Rio Grande, bitten, spit-wet, savored with all its acrid taste of something hidden and forbidden. The solitary, devastating memory of the images of distant evil, unattained, a dance of deranged flowers in the wind; cowardly correspondence sheltered in a crack of the rafters as in an asylum of measly miseries; obscene readings, and the thrill of perpetual fear, caustic compost of evil pleasures; the pride of concealment, the secret mockery, the termite's appetite for the invisible demolition of what is firmly constituted, the intense, extenuating weft of a delicate tissue of minimal and complicated hypocrisies—vermicular life of vile stimulus breathed in with the corrupt air of the retreat, born low, oozing from a hole, obscure spread of mire.

And on the faces a cream-colored pallor spread; one saw the sunken, glassy eyes of regions where malaria was endemic.

Barreto's sermons preaching asceticism still sounded in my ears. For him, evil was female. Sanches thought it was male. He tied a tail to his coccyx and fashioned an outlaw Satan, immoral and cheerful. The tail of Barreto's devil was made of lace. On the fashionable Rua do Ouvidor, Satan would be—a bauble. A horrible thing, with two eyes, designed for the perdition of men. The only skirt worthy of notice was that of a priest, which, however, is a cassock, not a skirt. The rest was no more than a Parisian fashion pretext to hide the cloven feet. Beware of the smiling Satan! A smile with two legs, an embrace with two breasts, a hellish pantomime, foppish and treacherous, graceful and combustible, where through chance or carelessness humanity burns off, like the pyrotechnic little snakes of the Pharaoh. At the smallest slip-up, eternal disgrace!

Barreto told me that the doorman at the seminary where he studied had been ordered, if he did not want to be fired, to reject his own sister. God, when He wanted to enter the world, had severely constructed the extraordinary miracle of an immaculate virginity. And but for the prophecies, which could not be compromised, the vehicle for the Conception, for love of asexual purity, would have been the carpenter Joseph, or even old Zacharias, more respectable still, for his baldness.

Barreto's theology had made a deep impression on me, and piously I had resolved to banish any image of a smile that might alight in my mind. I had turned the page on his fervors, but the theory of the female Satan remained. With the purity natural to my age, I mocked Angela and the trappings associated with her. My bosom closed, like his temple, on the days of Janus's peace, and outwardly, vanity upheld me.

To warn me even more emphatically, an event occurred that served to prove conclusively that Barreto was right about feminine power. It was an event that bloodied the annals of the establishment, saddening the headmaster, though in the end he found it agreeable because of how much talk it provoked about the Athenaeum.

We had just finished dinner, and it was the usual recreation time preceding gym. From the pantry, usually very quiet, we suddenly heard a tumult, then the noise of a fight, the crash of a table falling over. Then calls for help, more screams, and Aristarco's voice, high-pitched, giving orders as if in combat. We were dumbfounded.

All at once, we saw, at the door that dominated the yard from the top of the stonework stairs, a blood-covered man. A cry of horror escaped us all. In two leaps, the man flew down the stairs and into the yard. He held something made of iron, dripping red, in his hand, a thin-bladed knife or a dagger.

"He killed! He killed!" came from the pantry. "Catch the murderer!"

Various people were running down in the wake of the fugitive. João Numa, fat, livid, and trembling as he came down the stairs, rolled over, breaking his glasses on the stonework.

From a window, Aristarco, assured of his personal inviolability, pounded the sill with endless energy, demanding that the man with the knife be caught. The yard supervisors had vanished. The boys yelled like madmen.

Unexpectedly, Silvino returned, very pale, his sideburns even blacker in contrast with the sign of his fear.

"Wait! Wait!" he cried, convulsed, as if he were carrying the saving device in his pocket. "Wait!"

In the precise center of the yard, he opened his long skinny legs, posing like the Colossus at Rhodes, and put a whistle to his lips.

Unfortunately, he blew so hard that the whistle choked after two failed cheeps.

Surrounded by the servants, who ran after him with bars and bludgeons, the man with the knife, whose intention was to flee to the garden, pressed himself against a wall. "Let me through or I will kill someone else!" he growled, his face glowing. "Open the way for me!" he repeated, waving the weapon with shivers like a rattlesnake's.

Some of the young men, fearless, had approached him and closed the imprudent siege.

"Open!" roared the cornered criminal. And with one feral leap he threw himself against the besiegers, brandishing the knife.

With the miraculous dexterity of the preservation instinct, every one of them escaped as fast as he could; the prey went through the open ranks like a shot. Cries of "He fled!" came from all sides.

And then we saw him fall on his face.

Someone had flung himself unexpectedly at him and, stopping him with his knee and grabbing him by the throat, with one blow had brought him down.

It was Bento Alves! . . . With one hand, our valiant schoolmate was pressing the creature's face against the ground, grinding it into the sand, while with the other, in a marvel of vigor, he held down the arm that held the knife. His left arm free, the criminal tried to rise, but was crushed by the pressure of a monolith.

By the time they got around to helping him, Bento Alves had already disarmed his adversary, who had relaxed his grip, giving in to the vise around his neck.

From all sides they acclaimed the hero. At his window, from afar, an enthusiastic Aristarco forgot his divine aplomb and waved his arms like a windmill, unable to give voice to his emotion.

Bento Alves withdrew, holding the knife as a trophy, leaving the criminal half-suffocated under a pile of last-minute braves.

When the poor devil was able to stand, manacled, tied up in a thousand ways with leather belts and looking like a mummy in its linen-strip wrap, Silvino approached him and hit him, coward that he was, with a sermon on morals.

He was a criminal, they said. Of what crime? Within moments the entire school found out.

The man with the knife was one of the Athenaeum's gardeners. During dinner he had confronted one of Aristarco's house servants and killed him. For a time they had been vying for primacy in the heart of Angela, a terrible dispute. Aristarco's servant thought he had legitimate possession of the shrine of his affections, as he lived in the same house as the beauty he desired, consorting maritally in the intimacy of the washbowls where their hands touched among the dishes or in the affectionate relationship established as they cleaned the headmaster's and his lady's rooms, exchanging sweet words, or during the flagellation of the carpets.

The gardener, who came from the same part of the world as the chambermaid, based his claim on the fact that they were fellow countrymen and had arrived in the Americas in the same group of immigrants, as well as on a complete set of bona fide vows from the seductress.

When thus tightened, it is not possible to loosen the knots of passion: they must be cut. The gardener cut them. Adding to the bitterness of the situation, it was said that Angela incited the adversaries, declaring to each in turn that she desired him exclusively.

Once the murderer had been entrusted to the police, the victim became the object of general attention.

He was a big man of thirty, brown-skinned and pleasant. The murderer was darker than he, something of an Andalusian bullfighter type, short, solid, sturdy like a butcher's table.

As soon as the criminal had been taken away, the entire school stormed the stairs, eager to see the murder victim. However, at the door of the lunch hall, Aristarco declared: "None of your business!" At the same time the irritating bell called to class. Professor Bataillard, all in white, except for his red sash, turned up beside the headmaster. The boys ground their teeth with rage. Never in the history of the world had there been two more hated authorities.

But the tissue of discipline was not that tight. Some of the boys found a way to creep to the pantry, and I was one of them.

For a long time, I had had the wish to see a dead body, the real thing, fists clenched, lips turned up. The iconographic charts on the walls had left me cold, with their theoretical pictures of naked brains, eyes popping out of their sockets, bellies cut open with the skin folded back, showing the entrails, human figures standing straight or with their weight on one hip, spines curved with an air of passive complacency, skinned so we could see their veins, living models of science in poses of torture, Brahmin constancy as if waiting for us to learn by heart the circulation of the blood so they could dress up again in skin and muscles. It was not enough for me.

In the large cabinets there was better fare: anatomical pieces made of plaster, bleeding red varnish, a very hemorrhage; huge hearts, pulsating, moist to the sight but with lids that came off as on soup tureens; Cyclopes' plucked-out eyes, which still seemed to live, strangely, the solitary and useless life of vision; but also eyes that opened like those of figures on Carnival parade floats. But I wanted reality: death, alive.

I remembered having seen the body of a small child, surrounded by candles in the coffin trimmed with gold braids, the simple, yellowish little face shadowed with scattered blue stains, hands clutching a ribbon, flowers covering the immobility of the last sleep. I had also seen, on the elevated bier, an opulent old woman who had died heirless. Around her, torches were crying their waxen, honey-colored tears, inconsolable, stretching out long flames that seemed to reach the ceiling with their thread of smoke. One could clearly see the two feet turned to each other, in cloth boots, and the long nose under the lace kerchief.

That did not count as viewing a dead body. I wanted an openly exhibited corpse, not covered by the artifices of display and religiosity that make of the dead a mere pretext for ceremonial apparatus. What I wanted was the broken bough, fallen any which way, cut from the tree of existence, just so.

The servant's corpse fulfilled those conditions, with the advantage of the dramatic trappings of blood and crime, just as in the theater.

I was therefore on my way to the kitchen, and my heart beat fast, somehow unsettled by a pleasant dread. The Athenaeum's kitchen, beyond the living quarters and the pantry, was as spacious as any parlor. On the walls gleamed ranks of polished copper pots, lined up like a gallery of shields or bucklers. At the center, a long table was the servants' refectory.

On that occasion there were many people around the table. I saw the backs of persons who did not belong to the establishment. I was told that the authorities were present and engaged in removing the dead man. All those people with their backs to me must be the police authorities, an aspect of public power that I had not yet become familiar with, but respected. I saw the corpse lying on the floor, on a sheet of blood.

He still showed the awkward contortion of his agony: there was a pink lacelike foam around his mouth. He wore a tightly buttoned vest and thick woolen trousers. One could not see his wounds. His eyes were completely open and turned up in a way that made me shiver.

A few minutes after my arrival, two men came in with a hammock. The mess boys helped them lift up the body. The two men took it away.

I will always remember the limp languor of his arms and legs when they lifted the corpse, the head hanging down, turning on the neck with the characteristic movement of those who are suffering from an intolerable anguish, and the sudden backward fall that froze my blood, lifting the chin and the Adam's apple, the mouth opening wide, abruptly, as if the wounded man were vomiting a last tenacious trace of life.

After the hammock, all left down the kitchen stairs. I stayed. I was looking, one more time, at the floor, puddled with blood, when someone, walking past me, touched my hair. It was Angela.

"Morió," she said, indicating the blood and lifting her eyebrows, and she disappeared, swaying her hips.

For the first time, I noticed that the Canarian was beautiful. Indeed! And toward the demon responsible for such a horrible incident I was so benevolent in my judgment that remorse arose in me.

Angela was about twenty years old; in her body, however, she looked older. Large, fleshy, voluptuous, and fiery, she was one of those excessively sexual exemplars that seem shaped expressly to be spouses to the multitude—those revolutionaries against the monopoly of matrimony.

Bold in her manners like a dithyramb of ephemeral love, empty like a hollow statue, unfeeling, material, and stupid, she still had the satanic power to widen her large sepia-and-gold eyes, animate her face with expressions that looked as if in it there lived a powerful surface soul, capable of high martyrdoms of tenderness, and able to interpret the most tragic poems of devotion.

She liked to pull up her sleeves and show her arms—luxuriously white, perfect princess arms that brought sweet thoughts to the humble duster in the morning. When exposed to the sun, the white skin on her face turned a warm tawny color, the fugitive tone of wilting magnolias, invulnerable to the rigors of the open air—just what, in other times, might have been called the skin of Ceres. Let her complexion be battered by the corrosive darts of the sun, and her face was covered by an even more lovely blush; the sun could take no more from the youth of her flesh than from the earth itself, under the calcination of other ardors; all it could do was bring forth a springtime of roses.

Conscious of her beauty, Angela indulged in it.

And it was hard to escape it. She started by playing virtuous. With a serious air, she dried her moist lips; she lowered her eyelids, with their long lashes, over her eyes, over her face, like modesty's impenetrable visor. She invited adoration by wrapping the mantle of innocence around her shoulders, taking refuge in the hieratic indifference of a vestal. Then, there was a small, ingenuous smile, her eyes still closed, in a gradation of innocence that replaced the vestal with an elusive and timid child, laughing, turning her face away. Finally, her eyes ventured a glance, simply the temerity of, perhaps, a bride, nothing more, retreating then, pensive. Next, a bolder, more trusting look—the whole plot, line by line, of the novel of virginity. Then, suddenly, my most chaste Barreto! that virtue, that tenderness, that elusive candor, that melancholy nobility, that honest expression, sorry perhaps about being so friendly, opened in two leaves like a magic door and wheeled around in the explosion of a sabbath of lewdness.

Her eyes smiled, distilling a tear of desire; her nostrils flared, trembling, at intervals, with the spasmodic animation of birds making love; her lips, animated by titanic convulsions, murmured challenges, promising the submission of a bitch and the sweetness of Oriental dreams. At that point, her dominion rested on an abusive, sudden proffer; she bowed down in the lowest abjection, in order to attract from below, like vertigo. There she was, crawling, the prostitution of the vestal, the virgin's hymen, the perversion of the innocent, three forms of servility asking to be lorded over, to be owned; appetite, appetite for this rare guestless orgy.

She was not choosy about bestowing her love. It belonged to all, like the elements, and, like the elements, with no remorse for the destruction and disorder in their wake. She was open to all rivals. There was room for all in the shade of her chestnut hair that could serve as a dress for her opulent form, thick, perpetually dry, that she shook as she ran like the dust of hay.

That look, from Angela passing, threw light on the terrifying shadows that, in my imagination, curled around the excitement of the afternoon's event and the horrible sight of the corpse.

After his feat, Bento Alves, the hero, disappeared. Everybody was talking too much about his bravery. He did not even come to the field exercises.

Bento Alves was a mystery. Mysteries, at schools like ours, were those who did not clutter the available space with their antics. He attended the upper classes; though he was not a student of blinding merit, he had garnered the respect of the teachers and fellow students. Serious, like certain boys of lesser intelligence, afraid of ridicule, it was not only by his seriousness that he imposed respect. His reputation rested mostly on his being known as herculean. The strong really formed a kind of aristocracy of privilege at the boarding school. In the tumult of common living quarters, class distinctions melt in a kind of collegial democracy; distinctions of fortune are erased in the required fashion statements of dun-colored shirts. Superiority is affirmed in more primitive ways, in accordance with the semibarbarous criteria of early years; a strong fist can trump even the advantages of favoritism.

Alves did not parade his strength; he avoided quarrels, he did not wrestle, and he preferred to practice his gymnastics without spectators. Sometimes, as a joke, he would circle another boy's arm with his thumb and middle finger, and create, under his sleeve, a painful purple bracelet. Those who had been subjected to the formidable tattoo by compression would thenceforward approach Bento Alves with the greatest show of prudence.

Nevertheless, he was sluggish, with the monumental laziness of a large, powerful animal. He was fast, but detested racing; he was cheerful but avoided play. He liked peace and quiet, made a wide loop around the inconveniences of the more exuberant conviviality of the school favorites. One did not speak of him at the Athenaeum; one just feared him in silence.

After the feat of valor that chance had led him to, he was forced into the role of hero. He hated it. If anyone was foolish enough to say anything to him about the gardener's crime, Bento Alves would tear up the conversation with an impatient monosyllable, bristling up like a boar. Despite all that, the poor modest Alves was hammered, and laminated on the anvil of fame.

Luckily, the enrollment in the Athenaeum of a famous young man freed him from that odious repute.

Nearco da Fonseca had just matriculated in the school, a young man from an illustrious Pernambuco family.

He presented himself with his father, a political figure at the peak of his importance. He was seventeen, with a hollow face, abundant hair, uncommon talent; his eye was lively, heavy with his own importance, his nose aquiline, protruding, dry, almost translucent, as if made of glass. Puny as from a deprived childhood, thin like an osteology lecture, he surprised us, among other things, with a recommendation from the headmaster himself, to his father's face: Nearco da Fonseca was a great gymnast!

We would grant that he was talented, for his mane if for nothing else . . . But that the hunger specter before us should be a gymnast!

Youth, however, is forever hopeful; we waited for proof from a show of that talent.

The tribe of athletes and acrobats was shaken; anyone with any mettle—Luis at their head—who considered that a creature's highest powers resided in the knotty bulge of a bicep, prepared, in a spirit of the most intense admiration, a large enough chamber in which to house the new member of their tribe.

It was when three hundred of us stood in formation, in the afternoon, before the apparatus, that we heard Bataillard, in the gentlemanly way that characterized him, invite the great Nearco to show what he could do.

The headmaster was present; the most respectable parent of that Blondin was present. The Athenaeum was watching.

Nearco left the formation, stepping out with his left foot, according to the rule, hands on hips, as serious as a bishop, and walked toward the trapeze with the measured pace of an emu, imperturbable as one who has a profound knowledge of the rules governing the act of marching. Before the apparatus, still with his hands on his hips—right turn!—he turned toward the school, rigid, and folded himself into a stiff bow, keeping for a few seconds the angular shape of figurines representing farmworkers drawn on ancient Egyptian stonework.

Anxious, we stared.

After the greeting, Nearco grabbed the bar of the trapeze, thumb down, in accordance with the requirement of the position. And executed a flexion. Ah! little do you know, profane as you are, the worth of a flexion of the upper limbs. In the ideal world of mechanics, it is Archimedes's lever; its practical and painful application is the Britannic boxing jab. This is what it consists of: pulling in the wrists.

Nearco did it once, twice, five times! He followed up with a flip and, squatting on the trapeze, was able to flabbergast the audience with a backward flip. But that was not all! Nearco found a few more fantastic somersaults that could change radically all the established principles of the art of tumbling and favored us, sweating, with a triumphant smile.

Still to come, the last lot. Nearco stretched as much as he could his lamentable lack of musculature and gave us . . . a *siren!* The siren is the most elementary, the most contemptible, the most stupidly ostentatious of all the apparatuses. The athlete holds on to the ropes, lifts his feet from the bar, exchanges feet for hands and, upside-down, pushes away with his abs. Poor Nearco, belly-less, had no abs with which to push.

He pushed nothing; at most, some little bones that protruded around his navel like knife handles. He jumped to the ground.

The acrobat had been displayed. We looked at each other, stupefied, in the dispirited posture of those who had been conned. Aristarco noticed and rebuked us with his eyebrows. We understood, tactfully: the respectable father of a schoolmate was there, looking on.

A round of applause, clear, noisy, endless, ran through the ranks with the communicating electricity of an acclamation. Haughty, Nearco thanked us with his nose.

Chapter 6

For Nearco the future had set aside a sheaf of the very best victory palms, and another of the most legitimate laurel branches, to season his triumphs.

The Love-of-Learning Literary Guild, recently founded, would be the true theater of his superb achievements.

Twice a month, its members, the friends of knowledge, gathered in one of the upper-story lounges, the same where Aristarco's astronomy lessons took place. To illuminate those sessions, there were still leftover bits of cosmic matter in the corners of the room, tattered by the Master's analyses. This does not mean that the meritorious association deserved the eternal luminaries of irony.

I took part in the meetings, timidly, for no other reason than to take advantage, if possible undue, by reason of excessive consumption, of one of the students' statutory rights: all were allowed, at the Athenaeum, to glean in humble silence whatever had been left behind by the reapers in the wheat fields of literature.

Assiduous participant, I would leave the room filled with spindly rhetoric, which I would then press between the pages of the dictionary, as preserves of the spirit, invaluable relics of the Beautiful.

The difficulty in joining the association, encountered by any student who applied, made me venerate it even more deeply.

Nearco had not been in the least embarrassed. He had joined the establishment as an advanced student. He was immediately nominated, accepted, and inducted. At the first session, after his triumph at the trapeze, I had an occasion to appreciate his proficiency at verbal gymnastics.

The following problem was being debated, one of the inexhaustible array of such questions raised in such associations: who had been greater, Alexander or Caesar? A historical question that could obviously never have been resolved without resort to a measuring tape.

Nearco gave the thing an estimate, and excelled with the expected grace. He spoke for an hour and a half with a fluency that forever guaranteed him his reputation for eloquence. He compared, with the delicacy of a fine fabric salesman: Caesar spread out over Alexander. Caesar objected to the way it was done, belly-up, not at all artistic; in addition, Alexander's armor was poking into him. Pompey would have laughed, in his legendary closet, and the senate would have gossiped, compromising the secular seriousness of the man who came, saw, and conquered. Nearco kept him down, inexorably, for the entire course of the critical comparison. Caesar could not count on the legionnaires of his better times, and lay there, grimacing helplessly, the *anima vilis* of which the documents spoke. Alexander, who, not counting his helmet, was a little taller than the other, was more patient, allowing himself to be measured up to the peroration, with the good will that characterizes the departed. He won, in effect. Nearco proclaimed him the most magnificent of the magnificent, several inches greater than the daredevil from the Rubicon.

Enlightened, the Guild cheered. The argument was closed; no one else would speak. And anyway, for the last five sessions they had measured poor warriors against one another.

From that memorable day on, Nearco's position as a notable was assured. All forgot that he had been matriculated under the almost-condition that he would never take a step that was not a somersault, that he would not rest except on chairs balanced on bottles, that he would know no recreation unless it was on a tightrope, just so as not to belie his reputation. His acrobatic debut was forgotten. The Love-of-Learning Guild took him on, with pride and exclusive ownership.

There was no lack, meanwhile, of poets, journalists, polemicists, novelists, critics, broadside writers. The society had its own organ, *The Guild,* printed at Lombaerts, of which all paid-up members could be the pipes, and in addition, for the sake of richer harmonies, so could the honorary members.

Among the honorary ones was Aristarco, president, reliably contributing to the periodical with piecemeal transcriptions of the maxims hanging on the walls, and placing, on the fourth page of every issue, an ad in huge print praising the Athenaeum, which he paid for so as to help the enterprise. In that interesting publication there appeared as well Ribas's mystic verses and lubricious sonnets by Sanches. Barreto published meditations, a kind of *Believer's Harp* in exploded prose.

The serial novel was an imitation of *O Guarani,* decorated with indigenous words and signed *Aimbiré.*

Nearco threw himself into the subspecialty of comparisons, starting right away with two: Cilla and Marius, Titus and Nero. A preview promised a third, most curious comparison: Plutarch and the Boeotians.

This preference for parallel lines—a talent visible also, by the way, in urban tram lines and the mules working them—was one more reason for the extraordinary youth's prestige.

Eloquence was represented at the Guild in a number of categories: Ciceronian tragedy (cavernous voice, with gestures as of one stabbing with a poniard, that seems to cry out from a tomb, that raises the audience's hair on their heads, and furrows their brows, and that, were rhetoric prone to signing its name, would add, at the end of each speech, heavily, "the late great orator's hand"); Ciceronian modesty (formulating excellent thoughts awkwardly, in the embarrassment of a perpetual debut, with many apologies in the introduction and still more in all supporting arguments, teary voice, constrained style, choice expressions, and halting presentation); Ciceronian circumspection (short sentences built as if setting up bricks to build a wall by a man of order and integrity, stressing "which" and "whom," long-winded, time-consuming, careful to show itself shallower than it really is, a friend of sentences square and empty like coffins, attenuating in each opinion the attenuation it had suffered in the preceding expression of that opinion, conservative, in fact, ultraconservative, because what has been established absolves one from thinking, entrenched apologist of Quintilian, slowing down, by means of pauses, his impossible speech, to prove how well he parses his elocution, with all the requisites of oratory—purity, clarity, correctness, precision—except for one thing: content, ideas); Ciceronian storm (verborrheic, rushing over boulders and tree trunks, fluency precipitating him down the stairs, accumulating avalanches like a boreal tempest, annulling the astounding effect of one discomposure with the shock of the next discomposure, a sweaty, breathless, disheveled, deafening eloquence punctuated by jabs as in a boxing bout); Ciceronian candor (positive, indispensable for the closure of the arguments, saying it all in two words, generally coarse and ill-spoken, with a ready offer to meet his adversary at a venue of his choosing, a dangerous species in a debating society); Ciceronian priesthood (solemn, orating in tremolo, lifting his forehead like a miter, requesting a cathedral for each statement, on his feet two rostrums instead of shoes, a venerated and respected species).

Nearco introduced another type, not then represented: Ciceronian penetration—incisive, twangy, and annoying, gesticulating with his little hand in front of his face, the crooked index marking precisely in the air, on the floor, on the palm of the other hand, the place of everything he said—even when it was not apprehended—surprised at not being understood, impatient to the point of desiring to poke out the eyes of his audience with the points of his argument, or melting with compassion for our disgrace when we did not understand him, pearls and swine.

His incisive gestures and flowing eloquence, as well as his talent for historical parallels, established his primacy in the Guild.

The effective president of the society was Dr. Claudio, home-room teacher, a knowledgeable man, tolerant of the young people's nonsense; he would be depressed for a week if any-one imagined that he might miss any of the sessions because he did not take it seriously. This constancy of its leader was one of the main elements in the prosperity of Love-of-Learning. Dr. Claudio conducted the meetings with the skill of an expert coachman, disentangled entanglements, forged expressions of praise that he would hand out to each participant in turn and to every guild member, proposed some topics and found others amusing. On the more solemn occasions, he was the speaker.

For me, the greatest benefit of the Guild was the library. It had a collection of five or six hundred volumes on the most di-verse subjects, under the zealous guard of Bento Alves, a very Cerberus of a librarian, unanimously elected.

Alves belonged to the Guild, like almost all the students in the upper grades. He was friends with the pleasant group of the more silent ones, grateful that chatter was not obligatory. In addition to keeping the library, his duties to the Guild were limited to a firm and conscientious "Hear! Hear!" always at the service of the better idea in discussions of more elevated questions, and of the most sensible suggestion in questions of order.

Some boys who were not members of the Guild, and who, in their writing, had not shown a grammatically noteworthy penchant for the surreptitious conjugation of the verb "to ac-quire," could obtain from the president the right to enter the book room. As a friend of the beautiful printed page, I presented my candidacy. And since I was not sufficiently attracted to playing on the bars in the sun, or shooting tops on the ground, the library became my habitual retreat.

My assiduity there earned me two friends dear to my memory: Bento Alves and Jules Verne.

To the famous storyteller of *Around the World in Eighty Days* I owe a multitude of amiable phantasms from my first flights of imagination: eccentrics like Fogg, Paganel, Thomas Black; cheerful ones like Joe, Passepartout, and the Black Nab; noble souls like Genarvan, Letourneur, Paulina Barnett; attractive ones like Aouda, and Mary Grant. Above all, big as a demigod, with his shining beard, luminous like the mist of dreams, the legendary Nemo of the Mysterious Island, morose with thoughts of the kind of justice brought by revenge, waiting for the cataclysm that would dig his grave in the bosom of the ocean, his subject, his accomplice, his domain, somber home of his homelessness.

I had there a complete literature of boys' treasures: I read tales by Schmidt; on my little donkey I visited, one by one, the wisdom fairs of Simon of Nantua; by following the adventures of Gulliver, I made a deep study of the ups and downs of life, where, as soon as we are done scoffing at extreme smallness, we are beset by derision from extreme tallness, a kind of infant Pascal between Lilliput and Brobdingnag; I even arrived at the perfection of doubting the veracity of Münchausen's enterprises. All of this, not to mention Sanches's version of the *Lusiads*, the reverend Bernardes, the refined humor of Bertoldo, and in *The Rooster's Will*, a rather philosophical symbol of the odious nature of succession, in which an heir authorizes the disemboweling of the fowl, an instance of torture worthy of the Shakespearean treatment of King Lear.

Jules Verne was celebrated as a migration to new worlds. Wherever the *Forward*, or the *Duncan*, or the *Nautilus*, or the balloon *Victory* took me, whether a Floridian columbary or

Saknussen's cryptogram, on I went, hungry for plot resolution, jolly, avid like Columbus three days before America, breathing, in the smells of the bindings, the different climates of my readings, from the African sands to the crystal fields of the Arctic, from the great sidereal cold to the adventure at the volcano Stromboli.

Bento Alves's friendship for me, and mine for him, makes me think that, even without the dejection that caused Rebelo such moral indignation, there can be a certain effeminacy as a phase in the development of one's character. I esteemed him in a feminine way, because he was big, strong, brave; because he could protect me; because he respected me, almost shyly, as if he did not dare be my friend. If he wanted to look at me, he waited till I turned my eyes away from him. The first time he gave me a gift, a gracious, educational book, he stepped away blushing, as if in flight. That timidity did not alarm me; rather, it moved me, though I should by rights be on the alert against new disappointments. Interesting, the vague element of materiality in this childish affection, just like what one can observe in love—the pleasure of a chance touch, of the pressure of a hand, the scent of the clothing, as if we were absorbing something from the object of our affection.

In the library, Bento Alves would choose the works for me; he considered what might interest me, and suggested those books be bought, or bought them himself and donated them to the Guild, so he would not have to give them to me directly. During breaks between classes we did not stay together, but I saw my friend from afar, attentive, following me with his gaze like a watchdog.

Later I learned that he had threatened to break the neck of anyone who even considered offending me; he declared I was his adoptive brother.

And I, who had quite a while ago adopted, toward my fellows, a great air of fearless haughtiness, changed when I was with my friend; I felt comfortable in my voluntary submission, as if my bravery had been artificial, like proverbial feminine petulance.

But Barbalho's and his group's malignity did not sleep. Fearing Alves's reprisal, they whispered evil worthy of their nastiness, in the corners they had been chased into.

Sometimes, in the library, while I read, Alves watched me from the other side of the table, covered in green cloth, that occupied the middle of the room, with his hand on his forehead and his fingers sunk in his hair. He looked at me, and I felt him without looking up, understanding, in the depth of my slumber-heavy vanity, that this contemplation expressed the horror of ridicule that was customary in Bento Alves, and that rigidly suppressed any effusive demonstration. Were disapproval not a creature of its time, I could have found comical this situation of our two characters playing out this platonic scene. But since no outside disapproval was present to falsify the psychology of this development, I simply engaged to be sincere, just like my poor friend. Sometimes a tear came from nowhere to his eyelid.

In the general course of boarding-school life, he was attentive and diligent; he knew how to be inexpressibly fraternal, paternal, I would almost say loving, so particular was he in his care. There was no treat, small but costly in the perpetual famine of this school prison of ours, that Alves would not forgo for my sake, despairing pitifully if I tried to refuse. In conversation, he would tell me of his family, in Rio Grande do Sul. He had two sisters; he spoke of them and of how long it had been since he had seen them. Both were very light-skinned, with beautiful eyes; one was fifteen, one twelve years old; he was eighteen. He suggested what I should do to stay healthy—I should switch beds in the blue room; mine was too close to the window, that must be harmful . . . There were other trifles, his voice mild and full of feeling as if he were trying to shrink away from the solid proportions of his build to the stammering smallness of a grandfatherly carcass, shrunken with age, barely animated by the fever of a last breath, and the need to carry, for a few last days, the weight of a heart, an affection.

According to the statutes of the Guild, two solemn dates were to be kept: the yearly feasts at the opening and the ending of its activities. In addition, there would be any commemorative occasions its members resolved upon.

For the literary celebrations a big podium was erected in the recess pavilion covered by a rich wine-colored cloth with striations in black dye resembling ominous ink spills, and a rostrum affectionately known as the "rattletrap."

This rattletrap, huge and heavy, that seemed to object, at each jolt, against the character of furniture they were trying to force on it, turned up in all the rooms of the Athenaeum, in response to current rhetorical exigencies. Once the venue for the speech, the lecture, the solemn affair was set, the poor thing went bumping along on its way, an ambulatory showcase for eloquence. In those circumstances it was not a simple rostrum, but a veritable prognostication. If the rostrum was on the move, speechifying was imminent. It did once have a reasonably proud day: it was used at the Athenaeum by Professor Hartt, for a talk on anthropology.

When we saw it on its way one day and learned that it meant the installation of Love-of-Learning, the Athenaeum congregated, united in the same movement of enthusiasm, and for the first time the rostrum marched on without the ceremonial bumps. We dismissed the servants, and took it on our own shoulders, carrying it in triumph.

The inaugural feast was spirited. More than expected, unfortunately.

The vast hall filled up with benches and Austrian chairs. At the center, to the front, the directors' table; on the left, the guests; to the right, the other students—the rest, as one calls voiceless majorities.

On the winy and ink-decorated cloth lay open the secretary's briefcase; on the rostrum a crystalline water glass sparkled, ready for an emergency.

There were few speakers. Aristarco, honorary president, opened the session with the key of his peregrine word, recommending the new association as an honorable effort that could bear much fruit for hardworking young men who would, there, have an opportunity to cultivate oratory and belles lettres.

Then the actual president of the Guild stepped up to the rostrum.

With his easy elocution, Dr. Claudio presented a critique of Brazilian literature over the years: the satire of Gregório de Matos, the unction of Sousa Caldas and S. Carlos; influenced by Magalhães, the first attempts at a national novel, the glory of Gonçalves Dias and José de Alencar.

And from there he shifted to the present.

The listeners, who had been interested, but quiet, began to show agitation.

The speaker described the nation as a morass of twenty provinces, stagnating in the boggy lethargy of the most disgraceful indifference. Any small germ of life would be lost in the deep muck; on the surface, putrefying clots would at intervals release bubbles of noxious miasmic breath, fermenting in the sun, rising in clouds that darkened the sky like vapors of death. The birds, silenced, fled; the few remaining trees, close in the still air, collapsed into themselves in vegetative despondency and seemed to grow downward with the melancholy prosperity of weeping willows. The horizon, clean, remote, threw shafts of an oblique light, reptilian, that slithered in mirrored parallel bands, motionless on the sleeping mud.

Among the scarce reeds there emerged the eyes of frogs, meditating on the advantages of that somber peace, that inky indolence amid which the desire to twitch four spurts through the oily waves toward a female counts as vigor. Art is either the joy of movement, or the cry of supreme pain of societies that suffer. Among us, joy is a cadaver. If at least we suffered . . . The general condition of souls is the comatose prostration of a morbid inertia. If only we had the lethal energy of a convulsion. We ground at life as if it were a bone; we gnawed down our days, patient, prone, on our bellies, like dogs in the grass. Let us go eat Rogério's cranium, then at least we would have a tragedy . . . But no! The prevailing condition is the uninterrupted repose of annihilation on the infinite plane of monotony. And it is not the burning ceiling of tropical summers that oppresses us. Ah! how deep is the sky of our actual climate! What radiation for thought to take flight on descends to us from our stars! The marsh of our souls is the immense factory of a grand entrepreneur, an organization of artifice so long in the making that one would think it the protozoan accumulation of many centuries, yet dissolving rather than building itself up. It is the moralizing work of a long reign; it is the decanting of a single character that floods, as far as the eye can see, the moral surface of an empire—the putrid, expansive decomposition of a flaccid tallow tyrant! . . .

Keep in mind now that among the guests was Dr. Zé Lobo, father of one of the students, devout defender of the established institutions, brother member of I don't know how many sodalities, cousin to all the convents, lawyer to all religious causes, a conservative, in sum, angry and militant. The flaccid tallow of tyranny fell on his resentments like a drop of wax from a blessed candle.

"I protest!" he roared, red-faced and hoarse, pulling on his beard and raising his fist. He would not stand for anyone besmirching the institutions in his presence! To compound the offense, there was in the audience also Senator Rubim, the grandfather of another of the students, an irascible member of the Upper House, not a father, but a stepfather of the country, who had neither respect nor scruples:

"Anyone protesting against the tallow of tyranny is an idiot!" he replied to the one making the comment, with the frightening calm of the old and insolent.

"Not an idiot!" the first one exclaimed, paling under the lash of the insult, nervous and upset by the attention of the entire hall gazing at him. "Not an idiot! Such talk is unworthy of Your Excellency, a senator and an old man."

"Idiot indeed!" the other reiterated slowly, with a disdainful grin that underscored the insult. "Idiot indeed."

Aristarco presided still, with the wooden passivity of an affronted idol. The huge hall, students and guest, surged in a tumult, breaking into opposing parties, some for the senator and anarchy, others for the lawyer and public order. Many stood, waving their arms; students were shouting from atop the benches. Insults flew like buckshot; protests clanged like shields under heavy blows; hands were raised, asking for swords.

Taking advantage of the racket, the lawyer had dared hurl a few insults toward the senator. The latter, not having really heard what was said, replied with the impertinence of his refrain: "Idiot indeed," until, impatient, he closed the polemic with the five letters expressing the energy of the people, letters that Waterloo made heroic, Victor Hugo made epic, and Émile Zola made classic.

Crushed by the weight of this conclusion, Zé Lobo gave in.

Aristarco decided it was time to activate the presidency, and rang the bell of order over the tumult.

The orator at the rostrum, straight-backed and calm, a promontory above the storm, had been waiting for the commotion to end. As soon as he noted that the furor of insults was abating, he went on: "Let us draw a veil over this desolate landscape; may the hope for a rebirth come to succor us all." And from that start he skillfully drove his oration to a picture of the future, rising like the sun over the rostrum, a portal of light dazzling his listeners with the enchantment of happy prophecies, and chasing away the mists of dejection that had covered the expanse of the room, with the sweet breath of a morning breeze.

After that, two students spoke, grinding out a profusion of commonplaces about literature and letters. The son of the headmaster, the little republican we knew, had ten sheaves in his pocket, ten fire ships of incendiary eloquence that he had decided to smother after the colossal scandal of the used-book store.

The second solemn session of the Guild, though more peaceful, was no less important.

It took place at the beginning of October, around vacation time. Attendance was greater; ladies were present in large numbers, which had not happened at the installation. There was greater care in the decoration of the rooms; the rostrum was covered in the national colors of green and yellow, and on the program were the champions of oratory who had signed up at the Love-of-Learning. The school turned up in uniform, and the administration in dress coats.

Dr. Claudio's talk was subversive, but differently from his first one. It did not address literature in Brazil, but art in general. To wit:

Art, aesthetics, aesthesia, is the education of the sex instinct.

The preservation of individual existence rests on the life instinct of the species. The present moment of the generations is nothing more than the prolific connection between the past and posterity. And what is the reason why the species exist? The question has no meaning.

For the individual to persist, a generative moment of specific existence in time, it is necessary to adapt to the demands of the universal environment. The flowing river does not neglect the most insignificant backwater, and neither can it reason away the obstacle of the smallest rock in its bed. The unconscious criterion of instinct is what guides adaptation.

The work of human life, from the first wail in the cradle to the movement of the sick man on his deathbed who seeks a more comfortable position to die in, is the selection of pleasure. The senses function as the saving antennae of the tottering insect, going forth to find impressions, opportune and careful warning systems.

To each world of notable sensations there corresponds a sense. The senses, theoretically limited, number five, the transformation into several of just one: touch, precisely that rudimentary sense of the antennae.

Feeling one's way, instinctively, one searches for pleasure: visual pleasure, gustatory pleasure, tangible pleasure, in sum. The pleasant is essentially vital; if it is at times fatal, that is because instinct can be betrayed by illusion.

The evolutionary perfectibility of functioning organisms, in its prodigiously complex manifestations in the human type, corresponds to the revelation, in the animal orders, of the mysterious phenomenon of personality, able to view instinct critically, just as instinct can criticize sensation.

The reported information coming from each sense does not therefore awaken, in man, the cerebral activity of the impulses of preference, of repugnance, simply as in other animals, but amplifies, by means of the entire psychology of spiritual phenomena, the infinite variety of comparisons, in thousands of permutations within the unity of the spirit, like the pieces of a wondrous jigsaw puzzle spread out on the same cloth.

There are two elementary representations of realized pleasure: nutrition and love.

Inferior animals, not favored with a reasonable coefficient of progress, have for centuries produced the condition of their inferiority: they look, they touch, they smell, they listen, but they do not taste with great scruples and they feed coarsely and then love, as they have done forever.

Man, however, by his desire for nutrition and love, produced the historical evolution of humanity.

Nutrition demanded easy hunting—weapons were thus invented; love demanded shelter, and huts were built. Unperturbed digestion and procreation without anxiety demanded protection against the elements, against monsters, against malefactors—and men joined together tacitly for mutual safekeeping by the increased strength of the union: thus were born society, language, the first instances of peace and contemplation. And shepherds noted, for the first time, that there rose in the sky the evening star, large and pallid like a sigh.

But it was necessary that the beds for loving be covered with the gold and tawny pelts of lions, and that there be ivory, shiny petals, sparkling stones on the milky whiteness of the beloved's skin, for it was not enough to cover it with kisses; it was necessary to delight gustation with the refinements of exotic tastes. And men went to conquer the kings of the forest, the womb of the earth; they garnered the rarest inhabitants of the air, feathered with light like trilling creations of the sun, and went to gather in the waves of the ocean the most elusive travelers of the abyss, sailing swift, fantastic, in the blue shade, a vague reflex of their tail fins—to bite off their lives.

But hunger did not abate, love did not abate, and war came, violence, invasion. Captives bowed under the whip of the victor, and slave girls lay down under the talons of bloodthirsty lasciviousness that hungered for scattered limbs, soulless eyes, wordless lips, powerless shapes, miserable pretexts for the spasms of lust. Race hatred, class oppression, vengeful and destructive corruption came into being.

But thought evolved as well, that early pastoral, poetic thought that sought out the stars in the sky to adorn idyllic contemplation. The quiet and dark depths of souls, where the billows that heave the surface do not reach, lit up with phosphorescence; there came the halos of the gods, Olympic glories found their medals, religions were born.

But it was necessary for the spectrum of divinity to be palpable; thus were rocks chiseled into statues, metals became flesh, and there were cults, there were laws, prophets came and ambitious pontiffs. And this evolution of thought, which had been loving, made of it an instrument of tyranny, and was replaced by the practices of terror, by the apostles of slaughter.

But one lyre remained from the first generation of thinkers, and the strings still sounded, and the sounds spoke into the air the epics of the Orient and of Greece. The monopoly of the gods was wrenched away from the tyrant priests and yoked to the harness of meter; let them carry through the centuries the triumphal carriage of the stanza, a sound wave with immortal vibrations.

And the sculptors of idols bequeathed the secrets of their labor, revealing that those arrogant bronzes came from clay molds, that gods were made in the same way as amphoras. And modern artists started over, calling religion back to their workshops, like a model paid by the hour, and in paint, they daubed on walls the mystic visions of belief.

The artistic sharpness of forms led men to believe that indeed a sacred spirit resided in the porosity of marble and that there really existed an infinite canvas of Olympuses and paradises, where the colors of artistic anthropomorphism were sovereign, watching the world beneath, spilling out the providential urn of sufferings and joys.

When sentimental fantasies decayed, the face of the world changed. The gods were banished, inconvenient aftereffects of a dream. Following upon the order imposed from Above, a positivistic order was proclaimed in the name of the Belly. The fatal necessity of nutrition was made into a principle: it was called industry; it was called political economy; it was called militarism. Death to the Franks! Reaching for the black flag of Spartan Darwinism, civilization marched toward the future, fearless, undaunted, crushing underfoot the artistic prejudices of religion and morality.

What still survives, however, is the supreme and comforting poem, the eternal lyre.

First, marble and form were sovereign, then colors and shapes, now sounds: music and words. The ideal has been humanized. The anthem of the poets of marble and of colors, which looked up to heaven, speaks now to me, a strong advocate for feeling.

Dreams, artistic feeling, our contemplation, is the attentive pleasure of harmony, symmetry, rhythm, the sweet accord of impressions with the vibration of nervous sensibility. It is sensation transformed.

The history of human development is nothing more than a long story of the disciplining of sensations. The work of art is the manifestation of sensation.

As sensation is divided among five kinds of senses, sensations must correspond to five kinds, and so must works of art.

From acoustic sensation comes acoustic aesthesia: the sensations of sounds, of words—eloquence and music; from visual sensation, visual aesthesia: sensations of sight—form, line, color, namely, sculpture, architecture, painting; from the gustatory and olfactory sensations there arise the sensations of taste and perfume, arts that receive less consideration, given the relative inferiority of their effects. The sensation of touch, aided by all the others, gives rise to the complex sentiment of love, the art of arts, the mother of the arts, the reason for the existence of all the other kinds of aesthesia.

A lover's first moment of contemplation was the beginning of aesthetics, in the visual pleasure taken from the lines of beauty, in the auditory delight of an inarticulate expression uttered in the emotion of contact, in the inebriating inhalation of the indefinable aroma of the flesh. The work of art that comes from love is the offspring; the instrument is desire.

After the primitive and fundamental art of touch, there came the art of sound. The work of art is the felt utterance, skilled at calling forth emotion; the instrument is language.

This art then branched out into eloquence proper and folk poetry, thanks to the hybrid approximation of the third art, that of music.

With human progress, the artistic feeling of symmetry and harmony differentiated itself analytically from the art of love. And after that primordial art, direct descendant of the erotic instinct, from which it had detached itself under the savage form of primitive yelps, the art of eloquence; and then, under the form of homometric expressions, popular poetry, and the first instances of music, there arose the imitative, intentional arts of sculpture, architecture, drawing. In the wake of popular poetry, lyric or epic, came the rhapsody.

Furthermore, following a most natural filiation, the sense of symmetry, translated to the sphere of social relations, became the blueprint for religions, daughters of terror and morality, invention of a majority of the weak. With the insensate dominance of religions, love ceased to be a phenomenon and became something either ridiculous or obscene.

Reasoning retrospectively, if we consider that morality is the symmetrical organization of common weakness; that religion is the symmetrical organization of terror; that symmetry—that is, harmony and proportion—is the artistic norm of plastic imitations created by the simple-minded admiration of primitive creatures; that this pleasurable admiration—witness attempts at a drawing or a sculpture, a popular song or a vehement exclamation—that all of this is no more than a marked form of an effort at attention; and that the first attempted attention of early men—as we see in the legend of Adam—must have been directed by an individual of one sex toward an individual of the other sex, then we will have demonstrated the paradoxical aphorism that subjectively, art, or artistic sentiment in its highest, most ethereal manifestations is simply . . . the centuries-long evolution of the instinct of the propagation of the species.

This is its greatness, and this is why, across the ages, it laughs at the tempestuous vicissitudes of the fight for nutrition, even at the homicidal exasperations of love.

Art is at first spontaneous, and then intentional.

At first it manifests itself coarsely, by eruptions of sentiment, and makes love concrete with exclamation, elementary eloquence, primitive poetry, primitive chant. Later it manifests itself, progressively, through the effects of calculation and meditation, and originates the epic, high eloquence, highly developed music, drawing, sculpture, architecture, painting, religious systems, moral systems, ambitions of synthesis, metaphysics, and even modern literary forms, the novel being the present face of poetry in the world.

The spontaneous manifestations appear in all societies, coeval with the others. For instance, popular poetry does not disappear; neither does eloquence, and least of all, love. The intentional manifestations, extensions, and improvements of the primitive mode of sentimental expression are affected by the movements and vacillations of all that is progressing.

The heart is the universal pendulum of rhythms. The coordinated movement of its muscles is like the natural gauge of the harmonic, nervous, luminous, sonorous vibrations. Feelings and impressions of the world are measured on the same scale. There are states of the soul that correspond to blue, or to the bass notes in music; there are brilliant sounds like red lights, which harmonize with feelings of the most vivid liveliness.

The representation of sentiments is effected in accordance with these repercussions.

The study of language demonstrates this.

A vowel, the graphic symbol of the primitive exclamation, born spontaneously and instinctively from sentiment, is subject to the chromatic variety of timbre, like the sounds of musical instruments. Vowels are graded in a rising scale: *u, o, a, e, i,* with an infinite variety of intermediary sounds, which the sentiment of eloquence suggests to the lips, that are not acknowledged, but that live a real life in words and bring expression alive, their energy felt, free from pedagogical precepts, improvised, almost invented in the moment.

There is also in language the rhythm of every expression. When feelings speak, language does not splinter into words, as in dictionaries. It is the utterance of a prolonged sound, crackling with consonants, rising or falling according to the timbres of the vowels.

What moves the hearer is the impression made by the whole. The sentiment of a sentence invades us, even if spoken in an unknown tongue.

The timbre of the vowel, the rhythm of the sentence, those are what gives elocution its soul. The timbre is the coloring, the rhythm is the line and the outline. The law of eloquence governs music, coloring, and line, the sequence of notes and the tempi; it governs sculpture, architecture, painting—it is all still a matter of line and coloring.

As it is the primary representation of sentiment, after one has accounted for the fact of love, eloquence is the highest of the arts. Thus the supremacy of the literary arts: written eloquence.

In the beginning, eloquence was free, faithful to the rhythm of sentiment; influenced by the monotonous music of the most ancient times, it organized itself into regular cadences, monotonous like music. Used as a mnemonic device, it then freed itself from music, keeping, however, the same form of a meter and a quantity equivalent to what would later become a syllabic meter, and then resulted in the monstrosity of rhyme, the pun turned into the miracle of perfection.

Music evolved apart from that.

In the present, the art of eloquence offers a powerful reaction against the classic meters; critics expect that in a few years conventional and artificial meter will have disappeared from the workshops of literature. Sentiment will incarnate itself in eloquence, which will be free, like the nakedness of gladiators, and powerful. Style will topple versification. Stanzas will be measured in accordance with the breath of the spirit, not the thumb of grammar.

Today, when there are neither gods nor statues, when there are neither temples nor architecture, when there are neither *dies irae* nor Michelangelo, when mnemonics is useless, style triumphs, and it does so through primitive form, through vehement sincerity, as in the good times when the heart for loving and speaking well did not need to crucify tenderness on the four difficulties of a sonnet.

What is the mission of art? Originating in an erotic propensity detached from love, art is useless—as useless as the colorful splendor of petals to the fruitfulness of an ovary. What is the mission of colorful petals? What use is it to us that spring is green? Birds sing. What profits us the song of birds? Art is a consequence and not a form of training. It is born of the joy of life, the vigor of sentiment, and bears witness to it. It always pleases because joy is as contagious as a fire. The soul of the poet invades us. Poetry is the interpretation of our sentiments. It is not its purpose to please.

And then, to demand usefulness of the graceful digressions of the soul's energy, what is the purpose, after all, of the first manifestation of the very perpetuation of the species?

In addition to being useless, art is immoral. Morality is the artistic system of harmony transplanted to the relations of the collectivity. It is a *sui generis* art. The future will show whether it is possible to organize efficiently the social regimen of the symmetries of justice and fraternity. In any case, it is a different art, and the arts do not join together except as false products of convention.

An intentionally moral poem is like a polychrome statue or a relief painting. Only one of these forms of expression is possible, no more—though there are also those who fashion flowers with the wings and legs of cockroaches.

True art, *natural art*, knows no morality. It exists for the individual and does not care about the existence of other individuals. It may be obscene in the opinion of morality: Leda; it may be cruel: "*Rome in flames, what a spectacle!*"

All it has to be is artistic.

Cruel, obscene, egoistic, immoral, indomitable, eternally savage, art is human superiority—above clashing precepts, above transient religion, above self-correcting science; it intoxicates like an orgy or like an ecstasy.

And it disdains ephemeral centuries.

Considering the calm reigning in the audience, it is hardly necessary to state that the two heroes of the first solemn session were not present. Dr. Zé Lobo had not come, so he would not meet up with the senator; Senator Rubim had not come so he would not meet up with Dr. Zé Lobo: equal forces in opposite directions, annulling each other.

Many in the audience did not quite keep their attention on the flights of eloquence with which the orator hovered over them.

One of those was Bento Alves; another, Malheiro, olive-skinned, nervous, sullen, top gymnast; a third, Barbalho.

Bento Alves's thoughts were on an injury. Between him and Malheiro there was an old antagonism, a rivalry. Malheiro never forgave him his bravery. The very prodigies of strength and agility applauded and proclaimed by the Athenaeum wounded his vanity. What was the point of being strong, if it was not possible to apply his efforts to the loosening of the least fiber in Bento's muscles? Ah! That it was not possible, by the force of suggestion, to unravel one by one those bundles of steel, reduce to weak boyishness that odious muscularity! Why couldn't the wishes born of envy, like vampires, drink, drop by drop, the blood that gave him strength and life, reducing that iron vigor?

Bento Alves gave no sign of noticing the rivalry. Malheiro avoided him. It was not possible for him to spend even one minute near that classmate of his without feeling an impulse to assault him.

His rival's exploit in apprehending the criminal definitely took away from him the glory of being the only valorous man on campus. Malheiro locked himself into melancholy. The olive-colored face became darker; not the least glint of animation came into the window of his eye; no smile opened a door on his lips. One would think a house in mourning.

He meditated the plan of an encounter.

My good friend, always afraid to show himself at his best, or to importune me with a more lively manifestation, invented a new surprise or pleasure every day. He began to go overboard with the flowers. At first, dry magnolia petals with a date and a signature began to turn up between textbook leaves. Then petals were fresher and more frequent; then there were full flowers. One day, as I opened the numbered bookcase in the study room, I found an imprudent posy. St. Rosalie had never received one like it from me. What should a girlfriend do? I caressed the flowers, very thankful, and hid them before anyone saw them.

But Barbalho was prying, having lately made himself the hidden inspector of my movements.

Circumstances had brought him close to Malheiro, and the saffron-colored one-eye intended to manage the rivalry of the two older boys: a conflict between Malheiro and Bento could redound in embarrassment for me.

Malheiro, with his deep bass voice, started to torment me with epigrams. He wanted to annoy Alves by mortifying me, counting on my complaining. I swallowed the affronts of the older boy, unable to think of an appropriate way to retaliate. Barbalho then thought of defending me. After inciting Malheiro against me, he incited Bento against Malheiro. He sought him out and in great secret informed him: "Malheiro can't cross paths with Sérgio without asking him when the wedding will take place . . . it is imperative to wed . . . Even today he asked for an invitation to the ceremony. Sérgio is desperate."

Alves's rage was indescribable, the powerful furor of the quiet. An apoplectic redness rose into his face. With one simple movement of indignation, he clenched his fists, as if strangling someone. He sought out Malheiro, and—his voice altered, perhaps, but without emotion—he issued his warning: "Tomorrow is the closing ceremony; in the middle of the celebration, we will both leave; I need to speak to you about the wedding."

Malheiro understood: it was the meeting he had dreamed of.

As soon as the Guild's acting president left the rostrum, the adversaries left their seats. Barbalho left shortly after. I noticed their movements and more or less guessed what was going on.

When we left the pavilion, after the ceremony, a servant handed me an envelope, a letter from Alves, in pencil. "I am a prisoner; before anyone tells you I did something unworthy, I am letting you know: I taught Malheiro a lesson."

Minutes later, a very happy Franco was telling everyone: "They fought in the garden, Malheiro and Alves. What a fight between the two brutes!" Alves had been wounded by a blow to his arm, they thought a knife; Malheiro was in the dorm. Warned by Alves, the servants had gone to fetch him, unconscious, in a small copse at the end of the garden. "Unconscious!" Franco assured all. "What fun! What blows! There was Malheiro mauled!"

It came out that Barbalho had watched the combat from behind some bushes. Before it ended, he ran, busily, and fixing his cross-eye with a schemer's attention, prepared things so that, returning from the garden, Bento Alves was met with a detention order from the headmaster.

Never to snitch is a sacred loyalty precept at the school. The combatants refused to tell what had gone on. Bento Alves refused to have his arm checked and treated. Malheiro, wrapped in salt and sheets, feigning prostration, offered the most impenetrable silence to Aristarco's inquiries and promised to break the nose of anyone daring to stick it into what was none of their business.

"Oh, well, that's the mauled one! . . ." muttered the boys; nevertheless, they concentrated on forgetting the whole business.

For my part, I threw myself heart and soul into the despondency of the damsels in romances, standing guard and sighing under the barred window of a prison where the gentle knight allowed himself to be kept, for the sole purpose of furnishing subject matter to medieval lays and troubadours.

Chapter 7

Boredom is the great disease at schools, that corrosive boredom that can be generated by the monotony of work as well as by that of leisure.

Our lives were surrounded by the tended, garden-like forest of the park and by the rugged emerald mountains of the Tijuca, that ostentatiously chesty and plush colossus: the spectacular vistas only for moments broke the white dryness of our days, packaged within the boundaries of the central yard, hot, unbearably bright at the end of the high walls of the Athenaeum, whitewashed and tedious, white, ever whiter.

As vacation approached, the boredom increased.

The boys, most of them endowed with practical minds, thought up a thousand ways of fighting the tedium and breaking the monotony. Games had their season like fashion, changing rapidly like a series of essays.

The shuttlecock was no longer fun, slapped loudly, rising like a rocket, falling in a spiral on its feathered cockade? One went on to rubber balls. Tired of rubber? There were marbles. Had enough of those little glass spheres? There appeared hopscotch lines drawn with chalk on the floor or with a nail in the sand, in all their variants, first house, second house, third house, rest, hell, heaven—one kicked the little flat pebble along with the tip of one's foot in a risky progress of skips. Then there came the running games, notably the nostalgic and tough game of tag. Certain forms of recreation varied, so that the central area was alive with the flight of feathers and the elastic pop of the balls that passed like howitzer shots hitting their targets with practiced marksmanship, the multicolored crawl of the glass spheres on the ground, and the shouting of all those voices of pleasure and excitement.

Then there were the betting games where feathers, postage stamps, cigarettes, and even money circulated as coin. Speculation moved like the well-known brokerage snake. There were capitalists and usurers, the sharp ones and their marks; idiots who took it upon themselves to take to market, with the ease they found outside the school, large and very valuable supplies of Mallets and Guillots that the clever ones cleaned with the care of stock exchange big shots, and stamps of incalculable value that the practical collectors talked down so as to buy them cheap. Smokers, drunk on tobacco that belonged to others, acquired easily as the market moved, reclined Turkish-style on the cushions of their cut-rate bounty.

The transactions were forbidden by the Athenaeum's code of conduct. That made them all the more interesting. The letter of the law, incubated under the pressure of a veto, spawned other games, more expressly characteristic: dice that burst like popcorn; cards of the same suit fanning out, proud of their handsome trumps, the belly of a king showing here, there the gallant smile of a jack, the symbolic ear of the queen, the smiling landscape of the ace; small roulettes; little lead horses; a flood of cardboard tokens swarming like dice and pink like the mailman's standards.

The main currency was the stamp.

One would give anything for the postal token. There were no lesson prizes as valuable as the most vulgar of those used coupons. On that currency one could exchange rights to bread, to butter at lunch, to dessert, to the secret delights of nicotine, even to personal decorum itself.

The rage of the collectors, vying to display the richest and most complete album, communicated itself to others, simple agents in speculation, and from those to others still seduced by the fever. In the entire school, only Rebelo, maybe, and Ribas—the former anchored at the haven of senile misanthropy that kept him apart from the tempestuous rest of the world, and the latter acting perpetually like the ugly angel at the feet of Our Lady—escaped the general mania of the stamps, or rather, the general need to equip themselves with valuables to weather an emergency.

The stamp market was boiling with the agitation of commerce, with contracts showcasing greed, usury, cunning, fraud. Stocks accumulated, circulated, bore fruit; syndicates conspired; bears and bulls roared at ups and downs. Rookies were ruined, and there were clever bankers, fat with prosperity.

One spoke, with the halting circumspection of flunkeys to millionaires, of imponderable fortunes . . . There was the lucky one who owned those huge exemplars of the first English post, both of them extremely rare! The blue one and the white one, of 1840, with the distinct cancellation of Mulready: Great Britain with its arms open above the colonies, above the world; on the right, America, the civilizing propaganda, the conquest of the grasslands; on the left, the dominion of the Indies, coolies carrying bales, the backs of subjugated elephants; in the background, toward the horizon, ships, the Canadian sleigh rushing away pulled by reindeer; above, like the winged voices of fame, the messengers of the metropolis.

Jewels of that price had to stay put in the collections, inalienable by nature, like certain diamonds. But that did not lessen the acquisitiveness in the feverish mass of small deals; the infinite quantity of other stamps: rectangular, octagonal, round, elliptical, elongated, broad, smooth, perforated; ancient and recent; English, Swedish, Norwegian, Danish; with sword and scepter, sumptuous Hanoverians, like tapestry swaths, the double eagle of Lübeck, the Prussian white eagle, the relief eagle of modern Germany. Or Austrian; Swiss with the white cross; French, imperial and republican; from all of Europe, from all continents; with the picture of a dove, of ships, or an armored arm; Greek ones with the effigy of Mercury, the only god left over from Homer, Olympic survivor after Pan; stamps from

China with a dragon sprouting talons; from the Cape, triangular; from the republic of Orange with an orange tree and three horns; from Egypt with the sphinx and the pyramids: from the Persia of Naser al-Din with a crest; from Japan, embroidered, lacy like the tissue of folding screens and fans; from Australia with a swan; from the kingdom of Hawai'i, showing King Kamehameha III; from Newfoundland with a large seal on a field of snow; from the United States, with all the presidents; from the republic of San Salvador with a halo of stars floating over a volcano; from Brazil, starting with the huge and ill-made stamps of 1843; from Peru with a couple of llamas; in all colors; every seal with which states tax sentimental or mercantile correspondence, in indiscriminate exploitation, posting a minimal tariff on gigantic speculation as certainly as a blood toll on the refugees from hunger longing for their homes.

The study room, long, with its four rows of desks and the opposing wall of bookshelves and the inspector's podium, was a microcosm of subterranean activity. Studying was pretext and show; book covers covered craft rather than the readings they should have hidden.

At certain times the entire school gathered there, from first-graders to students at the highest grades. They grouped themselves according to their abilities, those just learning their ABCs by the entrance, on the right; on the far left, the philosophers studying their Barbe, the Latin scholars, the admirable students of German and Greek. All the ages mingled there—an older boy might be stuck on the right with the illiterates or a baby-prodigy might be weaning himself on philosophy on the left. Chance could place me between Barbalho and Sanches or separate me from Alves's affection by a mile. It all depended on the station.

Compensating for these disadvantages, there were the telegrams and hand-to-hand correspondence. The telegraph wires were of the best Alexander 80 brand, very fine and strong, installed under the wood of the desks and kept there by hooks made of pins. For vacations they were taken down. Two friends interested in communicating would establish the apparatus; at each extremity there was an alphabet on a strip of paper and a plectrum of sorts, tied to a wire, a true Capanema. There were so many lines that, seen from below, the desks offered the pleasant configuration of stringed zithers, so many that at times the service was tangled up and the message zither turned into an Italian peddler's harp.

There was a genius of inventiveness at the Athenaeum, and there were hopes of wealth through some miraculous discovery that chance would offer, as had been the case with Newton's apple. One clever scheme comes to mind: a concession to explore the gold left in the teeth of the dead, a veritable mine! Of such caliber was the ill-fated invention of the hammer-telegraph. Each letter, a certain number of little blows; some more, some fewer, formed other letters. The inventors thought the system of written signs had the disadvantage of not being useful at night. The basic element of their reform was a total trust in the deafness of the inspectors, ill-placed, as it turned out.

The first touches went unnoticed; only the students closest to them smiled knowingly. But the little hammer went on working and gained courage. In the silence of the hall, the short blows dripped, sounding like a chick pecking on the floor.

Up on the podium, Silvino scratched his ear and paid attention; it was beginning to irritate him. Silence . . . silence and from time to time the low knocking.

Then all hell broke loose. Unexpectedly Silvino precipitated himself from his high seat like a vulture, and with the expertise gained in his office, landed precisely on the best part of a dispatch. Devastation followed. Checking out the desk, he found the extended network of the other telegraphs. It was all leveled. Brutal like the Furies, implacable as war—O, Havas—Silvino did not leave one wire, not a single ball of correspondence twine. From desk to desk, cursing, he tore off, tore up, destroyed everything, the vandal, as if our telegraph, our modest imitation, crisscrossing heavens with the wide staff of the hymns to progress, were not our homage to the century.

The violence only served to increase the volume of little notes, suspending the telegraph for a while.

From hand to hand, like the Epistles, went the manuscript periodicals and the forbidden novels. The periodicals carried along the desks the mordant mockery of fellow students, teachers, beadles, even the odd, blasphemous joke about Aristarco, a pure temerity. The novels, thickly plotted with feverish tribulations, enticing descriptions, shocking resolutions, some spiced with gross sensuality, awakened in our imagination idealized pictures of life on the outside where there were no schoolbooks to guide one: the fights for money and love, the access to salons, the diplomatic victories among duchesses, the celebrated bravery at duels, the dignity conferred by a sword at the waist; or also the drama of rough passions, torments of an ill-fated and sublime bosom against the dirty scenery of a tavern, between vomit from bad wine and the verbal abuse of a low-class whore.

With the approach of the long vacation, everything disappeared. Boredom reigned.

Impatience at the expectation of freedom made the confinement of the last few days unbearable.

The great exhibition of works completed in the drawing lessons was being organized; the lower grades were about to start their exams, the half-year assessments where the headmaster checked progress. These preoccupations were not enough to lessen the expectant inertia that took over the students' spirits.

In the study hall few opened their books. The boys spread their elbows on their desks, stuck their chins on the backs of their hands, and lost themselves in thought, their eyes motionless, in an idiocy of waiting, as if they were trying to trace the course of hours in the space before them. Behind the house, in the headmaster's yard, one could hear Angela singing Spanish songs, soft and sinuous; farther away, much farther, in an indistinct buzz, like a horizon of sound, the cicadas chirred, stirring the hot air like the vibrations of boiling water.

During the very long hours of study breaks, the boys walked around quietly, destroying the usual communion of games, as if they were afraid to waste their pleasure in that prison, sure of a better use for it soon. On the walls in coal, on the blackboards in white lines, scratched on the plaster, written in pencil or ink, everywhere one read the proclamation: "Long live the vacations!" documenting the general eagerness, urging time not to be so slow, not to oppose, so cruelly, the impalpable resistance of the minutes, the seconds, to the desired arrival of the auspicious date.

After assuring me that it had been only for my sake that he had subjected himself to the humiliation he had suffered, Bento Alves kept away, on purpose.

As for me, solitary, I came and went like the others, crisscrossing the yard, punctuating with yawns the alternating periods of impatience and resignation, watching a kite, flown by street boys who lived near the Athenaeum. I envied them, and their cheerfully bobbing kite, weaving and diving in the wind, whimsical bird, commanding, all red, the vast blue rectangle that the walls cut out of the sky, solitary, solitary like me, tethered like me, but high up, and outside.

The class schedule became looser; teachers were absent; inspections were less invasive. Students went everywhere at their whim. They set up bull sessions in the dormitories, grinding away peevishly at the hardest topics, ground-up gossip, pulverized scabrousness, crushed malice, sometimes naive malice if that is possible, the gatherings characterized by the sour volubility of a rotting end-of-year weariness according to the temperament of each hall.

The dorms were poetically named in accordance with the decorations on their walls: the Pearl Room was the children's, policed by a dried-up, nasty old woman with tiny glittering eyes, her mouth buried between nose and chin, bright red throat, a large population of warts, a fuzz-covered head like a vulture's on a witch's body, who had made pinching into her only disciplinary weapon; Blue Room, Yellow, the Forest Room with the appropriate tree branches, where the innumerable middle-graders resided. The older boys' room, in a separate building, above the general study hall, was known by the gentle appellation of "cottage." The cottage had a separate and mysterious life.

The policing of the dormitories was carried out by various inspectors, conveniently distributed.

At that time of the year, the police's zeal was attenuated. Even the Pearl's vulture flapped her wings at the revelry, an innocent ninety-year revelry.

Chatter circulated fearlessly.

Some lay in groups on one bed, others gathered around the neighboring beds and tackled different subjects.

In the middle-graders' room:

"Dona Ema . . . Dona Ema . . . it's not for nothing that people whisper . . . Check out how Crisóstomo speaks . . . He has good reason, a strapping guy . . . I swear I caught them alone, close together, talking, at the right distance for a kiss . . ."

"The thing is, Crisóstomo won't be fired . . . Hang it, the Greek isn't worth so much, that he should be paid in discounted kisses from the wife . . . I think that this business is going to have a dirty and nasty end—*kakós kai ruparós*, with a bang . . ."

"Really! Headmasters! Operators is what they are! Providers of cheap science and prodigies of shabbiness, with which they cheat the gullible parents. What they want is repeat business . . . They are talking about taking out ads . . . A woman bending over a balcony . . . What a come-on, a pretty face! If I were a headmaster, I'd start a kindergarten for grown-ups: a beautiful principal at the head of four amiable adjuncts. Any grown mother's son would die for intuitive learning. They'd pay a mint to chat up the beauties in my garden! And what service to my country's progress: stimulating feeble minds and belated adolescence in accordance with Froebel's methods . . ."

"Well, as for me, I might go to war against the establishment. If I were headmaster, I'd make sure to also be a minister of the empire. I'd revoke the Public Education Act and approve my people by decree, all at once, and with distinction."

"Bah! If I were headmaster, I'd be just shameless! Nothing in the world as good as being shameless! A beautiful collection of young'uns, what a feast! The boys like us, we like the boys, and the school grows. *Crescite!* Soon there'd be so many applicants, we'd have to get a bigger house."

"What a rabble! What evil tongues . . . Go away! For me, all I'll mention is that guy from the Lycée Marcellus, whose face shows the sewn-up scar of a slash by one of his disciples, in the course of a certain adventure, engaged in with the most peaceful of tools and who, even after that, was caught at the casino having left on a sofa his dance card, carefully illustrated with "pedagogical . . . symbols."

The chat at the Pearl was much more candid, and mostly not all that personal.

It consisted of an improvised course in elementary obstetrics, pure speculation. All wanted to know; twenty little ones were crowded around the problem, like the figures in Rembrandt's *Anatomy Lesson*. What was the origin of the species? They were researchers. Nobody got ahead by even one step. The vulture was absent, and might have been able to explain. Happy is he who can learn the cause of things! What is it like, the gate to life? Doric? Ionic? Composite? Busy imaginations crawled, avid as ants, all over the question: nobody penetrated to the truth. Home-brewed theories flowed, angelico-gynecological.

There was in Paris a big export firm; its agents around the world were midwives, and its representative in Rio was Mme. Durocher. The merchandise appeared in the cradles, boxed, pissed, and weepy. This theory had the philosophical merit of not needing final causes. The metaphysically inclined tended toward the intervention of the supernatural: around Christmas there was, during the night, a general distribution of little heirs around the world, it rained fat little babies, compensating for the killing of the innocents, so destructive at the time of Herod. Needless to say that in those times said innocents entered the world by the same carriers of revelation credentials, no longer in use.

And the little academy of scientists procured documents, some of them smiling at the credulity of the others, and showing in their refutations a different kind of credulity; others, more positive, and referring to their own observations, since boys see things, offered to the scrutiny of their fellows a ponderous note, and slowly the system was built up in the way systems are built, using only elements that receive general support.

Two final opinions contributed opportunely to resolve the embarrassments, and the assembly scattered. One scrawny kid from Ceará, his hair in a crewcut, smart and silent, who liked to respond by rolling his eyes in a special way, and who had a disconcerting smile he knew how to fire off at appropriate moments, speaking low and explicitly, introduced into the debate the detailed description, including all flounces and ruffles, of the bathing outfits of backwoods women on their way to the riverbank, a beautiful, appealing canvas that emphasized the glow of the rising sun. Another contribution was the coarse mockery by the paunchy and quarrelsome son of a wealthy cattle farmer from Paraná, his forehead very much like a young steer's, brutal and knavish, a small muleteer, conversant with all the practical demands of the paternal calling. He had been listening from the beginning, saying not a word, waiting for the conclusion. Supposing that the kid from Ceará was about to explain, he threw himself forward, interrupted him, and concluded in a torrent, wallowing among the boys as a young animal at the ranch would in the mud.

The idleness in the dorms did not just take the form of talking. Depraved by boredom and sloth, the boys came up with extravagant instances of cynicism.

Cerqueira, the rat, a comedian whose face consisted mostly of thick lips that split into a mouth like a ripe pomegranate, with enormous hands like feet in disguise, galloped on all fours through the halls, shirttails flapping, heehawing and kicking, as sincerely happy as a mule. Maurilio, the one who corrected everyone, was not just the champion of the multiplication tables we knew; he had another notable talent and obliged, to general applause, with original experiments involving flammable fluids. This one just escaped dying in one of the latest shipwrecks on our coast; one of his former fellows wrote to him: he who sows the wind harvests the storm.

Provocations were frequent during recess, the result of boredom; all were sensitive as sores; constantly the inspectors had to intervene in conflicts; harassment was on the lookout for sensitivity, and sensitivities searched for harassment. They saw Franco on his knees and pulled his hair. They saw Romulo go by and tossed his nickname at him: Master Cook!

This provocation, however, was unfair. A cook, Romulo! Only because he looked culinary, with his loose flesh bloated with meat pies, or because he was fat with the deceptive corpulence of the bouncers at cheap dives, from a morbid paste of sardines and oil disguising voluminous health? Romulo was simply and completely the pastry cook for Aristarco's sweet hopes.

Sleek in appearance and more ample still in fortune, he was precisely what is understood as a good catch. Aristarco had a daughter; health, fortune, an ideal son-in-law, and, in addition, one who was good-natured and peace-loving.

Melica, the haughty and hip-swaying Amalia, insipid, built like a stick, long and thin, dark-skinned, and full of airs, spent her time making like a princess. Two large black eyes, exaggerated versions of her mother's, took up her whole face, giving her front the precise look of a beautiful capital "I" with two dots. From those eyes and from her shoulders, which she carried high and Mephistophelian, disdain poured over everything and everyone. She had and enjoyed the easy certainty that the entire Athenaeum had fallen for her, and lived as the saint in a procession, carried on the imaginary litter of that idolatry of three hundred boys. Three hundred hearts, three hundred doses of disdain. Her father's eminence over that little despicable world gave her life and vainglory, and she enjoyed visiting the school to exercise her haughtiness, a mixture of sex and hierarchy. As for Romulo, he was the first in line for her disdain. She made a show of paying no attention to him. She referred to him, splendidly, as "the chucklehead." Melica herself was a sweetheart and precious.

Romulo philosophized in the wake of Epicurus. Disdain does not kill. There were advantages to that situation of perennial engagement, a kind of usefulness: the job of supervisor, privileges and benevolence, the occasional dinner with the headmaster—a vacation for the taste buds dreamed of by many mouths, caught in the bland regimen of the house menus, inviolable like the letter of constitutions.

When Melica came to the Athenaeum, Romulo was the first to come up to her, the last to be seen. Sometimes Aristarco called him and took him on a walk with the girl. Melica, all airs and pride, walked ahead and, at most, allowed Romulo to follow her, mute, head down, like a tame hippopotamus. But truth be known, he expected to have the last laugh at father and daughter.

At as famous an establishment as the Athenaeum, one could not fail to include a marching band as one of the offerings in the arts.

Sampaio's pump organ went unnoticed, religious and muttering. Cunha's little fiddle was paid no mind, whiny and expressive in the hands of the slim violinist, the instrument whimpering like a maternity ward, the musician pale, skinny, and tall, leavening the language of the pegs with sounds that imitated Cunha's fearful and childlike aphasia, degenerating into swoons and, from time to time, stretching out into hysterical squeals of idle love, hopping pizzicati that sounded like the patent-leather toe caps worn by Cunha, that friend of the waltz, nimble at the dance like the ribbons, feathers, and the vaporous tulles.

Alberto Souto's piano playing was reasonably well respected, as he sat, with his large maestro cheeks, a portentous pianist who had come to rest at the Athenaeum after wandering around Europe to collect triumphs, round, short, and musical like a hurdy-gurdy drum. He was famous for his vulgar laugh, which sounded like the wrung-out residue of vanity and greed that had stayed with him after his success on the stage and the beatings he had sustained as he practiced, as well as for the dry stupidity he showed in class, as if his intelligence had leaked out through his fingers onto the keyboard, in an irrecoverable desertion.

But Aristarco's preference was for the band, the noise, the vibrant shouts of the brasses, the fusillade of the drumsticks, bringing people to their windows when the Athenaeum passed, marching under admiring glances around corners, roaring with the double-march pace like an echo of combats, an unbridled furor, irresistible like bass drums at the fair.

The band had its own house and a well-paid teacher. The instrumentalists enjoyed particular favors in the form of relaxed discipline; on festive occasions they were regaled with extra sweets; they were decorated with silver insignia that not even the harmonious members of the choir, the Orpheum, managed to secure.

Even within the band there were degrees of Aristarco's favor, according to the importance and sonority of the sounds produced. The deep bombard, the serpent-like bass brass ophicleide, the bugle, the trombone, even the saxophone, destined for the secondary job of accompaniment, retiring like lackeys in the hierarchy of sound, men-at-arms, servile and brave in the brilliant charges, or timid pages, picking up the spread trains that escaped the regal luxury of the high notes of the singers, were in even lower esteem by the headmaster than on the pages of the score.

A favorite was the piccolo, a rapier made of sound, slim, penetrating, stinging like needles; another favorite was the clarinet-like requinta, a kind of cracked flute, aggressive like the vibration of a serpent's hiss; the bassoon, a bigger, louder requinta, the only apparatus that could produce artificially the nasal scolding of mothers-in-law; the clear oboe, metallic larynx of a singer of epics, heroic and beautiful; the cornet, frantic and lively, a flag showing above the fray, harmonious, gathering the other instruments around it like a cavalry regiment. They were favorites because they were louder. But the greatest favorites were the drum and the bass drum, at the forefront in noisemaking, the thunder of the stretched skins, which loosened the storm of scoundrel Carnival ecstasies on their special days, embraced by Romulo, the greasy Romulo, sleek, opulent, the dear son-in-law of dearest hopes.

It was precisely by means of this hierarchy of acoustic preferences that Aristarco had come to discover his favorite. And that, by chance.

During one school feast, the band was showing off. The bass drum lost concentration and let go, out of tempo, a magnificent explosion that went with the piece being performed like a splash of India ink on a watercolor. Half the listeners thought that was a Wagnerian touch, inserted on purpose; the other half could not control their laughter.

Aristarco admired the frame drum in a solo, the solitude of salvoes on the vast ocean, a grand factor in the sonorities that are amplified by the rest of the drum section. But he was bothered by his guests' laughter.

At the end of the festivities, he called the artist, author of the detonation, to his presence. The musician presented himself, and I don't know how they came to an understanding, but instead of being punished, Romulo left the office with the advantageous franchise of honorary son-in-law.

That scandalous favor gave rise to envy.

Romulo was disliked. To squelch excessive demonstrations of that, he inspired fear through brutality. At the slightest joke by one of the little ones, he threw against that poor soul his entire corpulence in all its loose fat rolls, in a shower of punches. He took revenge on the stronger students by muttering intrepidly.

To drive him crazy, the little ones took advantage of darkness. In their midst, Romulo became disoriented, spouting death threats, showing his fists. In general, he tried to recognize at least one of his tormentors, marking him for revenge. Inexorable revenge.

During the tedious period of the last weeks, Romulo was chosen as the main victim of amusing pranks. Fantastic voices, coming from the earth, called to him: "Master Cook!" Voices from space, raucous or shrill: "Master Cook!" He sat, woebegone, trying to remember whether he had ever touched a pot in his life; the unanimity was impressive. More often, he had fits of fury. He threw himself against the groups, snorting, foaming, his eyes closed, fists back. The boys ran, laughing, opening a lane for the cursed elephantine fury to roll away.

I was present at one of the jeering incidents. Romulo noted me. Soon afterward, we met in the hallway that led to the Guild's library. Embarrassing situation. I was coming; he was going. Should I stop? Should I retreat? While I hesitated, I kept on going. In a leap, Romulo grabbed my shirt collar. He shook me to the point of crushing my chest. "So, you cur, tell me now, if you can, who is the *master*."

The pain woke me from the shock. Everything was lost. I chose bravery: "You *Master, Supermaster Cook!*" I cried into his face. I am not sure what happened. When I came to, I was stretched out under a staircase. Three nails from the last step had poked into my head. Considering that the future would offer me time enough for revenge, I got up and shook the humiliating dust of defeat from my clothes.

Finally, exam day arrived.

There were official tests for the transitions within elementary grades: from first to second, second to third, third to secondary school.

Tables and desks were taken to the oratory hall, the altar covered with a curtain, and the solemn commission installed itself, composed of personages from the Department of Public Education, the headmaster, and the teachers.

At that table Aristarco represented the carefully considered vote of the accountant. Balanced accounts: passing with honors, at times slightly adjusted to simple distinction. Behind by a trimester: full passing grade with risk of lowering. Behind by a semester: failing grade.

The Athenaeum also had some nonpaying students, who fell outside that scheme, carefully chosen to represent concrete objects of charity, timid as if crushed under the weight of that largesse; they had all the duties, none of the rights, not even that of not being good at anything. In compensation, the teachers had the duty to make them shine, because a charity that does not shine is pure loss.

In the third-year exams, passes with distinction were so numerous that one came to my hands, with no scandal, by the way, since I had lost my fear long ago and started to feel at ease about the accolades, which I saw as an evil and a contamination originating with the headmaster. Looking very much like a winner, I picked up the delicious certificate, which I carried home to show the family as if it were a rare little pet, stroking its fine pelt, kissing its muzzle. Sanches got honors; Cruz got honors as well, thanks to his proficiency in the catechism of which he was a specialist, astounding the judging commission with the entire litany to Our Lady, and threatening us with the entire saints' calendar, which he knew by heart. Saint by saint, with appended observations, in addition to the movable feasts and the phases of the moon: even Doctor Ayer, the one with the cathartic pills, could not have done better. Gualtério, the clown, failed. Nascimento, the *beak*, sniffed with satisfaction: pass, if simple. Negrão, Almeidinha, Álvares—distinction. Against the distinction award to the latter, Professor Manlio protested under his breath: the idiot Álvares getting distinction! Batista Carlos, the Indian with the arrows, failed! Before the commission he looked very surprised about the questions, as if wondering what they had to do with him. Barbalho failed. Barbalho senior was late with his payments by about a semester and a half, and Barbalho junior made sure to save appearances with a scrupulous presentation of nonsense that justified the rejection. The wonderful, venerable Rebelo did not participate. He had left the school months before, because of his eyes.

While I waited in the green room, walled in polished porphyry, with the other students, for the inspector who would read the results of the scrutiny to turn up at the door, my eyes settled on the high-relief scenes of arts and industries, the smiling boys naked, fraternal, in pure and innocent gypsum. I felt old. What a long journey of disillusionment!

It had been only a few months since, for the first time, I had seen the ideal children coming to life in the stucco by contagion with my naive enthusiasm, in that happy round of activities . . . Now, one by one, as I saw them, the little hypocrites, with their white buttocks, the reverse of candor, one by one as I judged them, all the gypsum of those little chubby faces seemed as if it should blush from a general and bruising round of spankings. The little scoundrels no longer fooled me. They were childish, cheerful, frank, good, immaculate, the ineffable nostalgia for the first years, the first school times that would never return! And they were liars all! Each of those images of childhood masked a deceit, the prospect of a betrayal. Purity clothed corrupting malice, gross ambition, intrigue, flattery, cowardice, envy, the arch sensuality of erotic caricatures, the savage mistrust arising from incompetence, the depressed emulation from spite, the impotence, the whole school, barbaric like incipient humanity, under the fetishism of the Master, a confederacy of instincts on show, passions, weaknesses, shame, which society exaggerates and complicates in proportion to the scale in which it appears, respecting the embryonic type, characterizing the present as disagreeable to us, who only see the past as a blue haze because it is made up of illusion and distance.

For the show of the drawings all the desks were removed from the study hall, and the walls and tall cupboards were covered with dark satin. Against that background they pinned the sheets of drawing paper stained with pencil marks from the shading of the drawn figures, of the landscapes, then pinned a gilt border around the frames of the works deemed worthy of that ennoblement.

I had had my small success in drawing, and the doodles had improved so as to garner praise. At first, there had been a simple attempt, linear, trying my hand; then gradations of tone that I had managed to turn into a cloud; then views of fields, leaves with lacy borders, picturesquely collapsing shacks modeled on the French school, like the ruins of rotting tree trunks, set up for the artists. After many an old mill, many a straw dwelling, many a decaying mansion, exhibiting its misery like a beggar, many a towering village pyramid sketched out in the background, many a vague figure of a peasant woman, her triangle of a shawl falling down her back, round haunches, thick pleated skirts, curved clogs, I went on to the great copies, parts of a human face, complete heads, horse heads; I was brave enough to copy, with all its silken magnificence, all its strong grace of movement, a Tibetan goat.

After the distinction in primary school, that goat was my greatest pride. Retouched by the teacher, who had the good taste of doing to a drawing all that the students had not done, the Tibetan goat, twenty inches high, was very close to a masterpiece. I was proud of my work. But fate did not want me to enjoy it for too long. They denied my goat the golden frame given to the good works; in addition—imagine my despair!—on the very day of the exhibition, in the morning, I found the animal defaced by a cross in ink, wide, from top to bottom, which the gentle hand of a stranger had traced. Unhesitatingly, I tore the wretched piece of paper from the wall, and tore to pieces the effort of so many days of perseverance and love.

When the visitors invaded the room, they noted, in the array of works, two enigmatic edges of torn paper. They wondered, not knowing that what they were seeing was the interesting last chapter of the story of a goat, and a cross, a drama of despair and the miserable spoliation of a masterwork.

The art shows took place every two years, alternating with the prize distribution ceremonies. That way it was possible to gather a fabulous amount of lined paper for the greater wealth of the galleries. The satin was covered from floor to ceiling. There was everything, not just drawings. Some oils, by Altino, and smiling watercolors interrupting the gray monotony of pencil and charcoal. Future engineers applied themselves to architectural drawings or colored diagrams of machines.

Among the heads in black crayon, the horse manes, the wooly fuzz of onagers tilting their funnel ears, hirsute setaceous boars' heads with bared fangs, audacious lace collars, presumptuous felt brims, wind-tossed plumes, savage, frowning sailors' faces buffeted by the wind, unkempt beards, hoods pulled over their foreheads, pipes between their teeth: among all those faces there was a notable collection of portraits of the headmaster.

This delicate subject had been invented by the courtesy of an old teacher. The model was prepared; one student copied it successfully, and after that there was no amiable draftsman who did not conceive of the idea that he should try his hand at that most respectable Veronica. Dear God! with what noses did they endow poor Aristarco! It could almost count as an insult. What blepharitic eyes! What black-lipped mouths! What libelous whiskers! What an inventive collection of stupid expressions for the dignified countenance of that noble educator!

Nevertheless, Aristarco felt flattered by the intention. It was as if he could feel on his face the subtle tickle of the crayon as it traced his features, playing with the soft wrinkle on his eyelid, the crow's-feet, soft around the ear, firm on the outline of the lips, peeking into the white threads of his bangs, defining the severe shaven jaw, rising along the oblique lines to the nose, hovering over the pituitary, extorting a pleasant and cheery sneeze.

That was why the Veronica sketchers were respected.

All the portraits, good or bad, were lodged within the prize frames. After the feast, Aristarco would take the drawings home. He had piles of them. At times, in moments of spleen, the deep spleen of great men, he would take apart the pile; then he covered tables, chairs, floor with the portraits. And an ecstasy of vanity would overcome him. All those generations of disciples that had passed before his face! All those fawning caresses to the effigy of an eminent man! Each one of those sheets of paper was a piece of an ovation, a chunk of apotheosis.

And all those ill-made things became animate and gazed out with shining eyes: "Look, Aristarco," they said in a chorus, "look at us who are here. We are you, and we applaud you!" And Aristarco, like no one else on earth, savored that unparalleled delight, he, the incomparable, the only one able to properly understand and admire himself, applauded by a multitude of alter egos, glorified by a multitude of his own selves. *Primus inter pares.*

All, all he himself, acclaiming himself.

Chapter 8

The following year, the Athenaeum revealed a new aspect of itself. I had thought it interesting, with the attractions of the new, with the obscure projections of perspective, challenging curiosity and fear; I had thought it banal and insipid like a mystery solved, silent out of tedium; I now found it intolerable like a dungeon, walled in with desires and privations.

Having grown by force and become competent in the moral whirlpool of the boarding school, I had taken advantage of the two months' vacation to watch the bustle of outside life. The movement of the great world no longer seemed to me a play of shadows: the parlor, social life, the business of the public square, which during childhood were like fog touching the imagination, from which we awake as from the tumult of a nightmare, which flee, disappear, leaving us asleep again in the oblivion of our age, at the time when, at a gala, we go for the sweet morsels and, of the dresses, we prefer the frills in their glowing colors, ignoring that there might be in life something more sugary than sugar and that a soft touch can at times vanquish garish colors when, among all social positions, we modestly envy the elegance of Phaeton exhibited by coachmen for hire or the crimson bravery of the trousers on a military dress uniform, not knowing that ambition could reach higher and that there are commanders; the activities of the wider world no longer appeared to me as a play of shadows. I had begun to penetrate outside reality, just as I had touched the truth of existence at the school. I despaired, then, at finding myself doubly shackled to the contingency of being still irremediably small and just a schoolboy. A schoolboy practically in leg irons, marked with a number, slave to the limitations of the house and the despotism of the administration.

There was the scant compensation of outings. The school would then don a white uniform, as for the gymnastics celebrations, and braided caps, and march out in twos, four pairs to a group, drums and trumpets before us.

The year before, the outings had been insignificant, happy marches around the neighborhood. Young girls came to the windows, and we, with military pride, were prodigal of our elegance. Outings to the mountains were better. We would climb the Two Brothers, the trail to the Corcovado, and march toward the water tower. There we scattered on a most pleasant plateau.

Those outings took place after dinner. Toward evening we would return, drawing up an account of our experiences: the green glory of the forest; a scrap of fiery sunset; a corner of the city, in the distance, diluted in pearl-colored smoke; or the glance of a lady and another's smile, inoffensive projectiles in flirtations that, given we were marching in formation, had the shortcoming of uncertainty about whether they were directed to ourselves or to a neighbor, reaching us simply by the chance of a ricochet—the eternal question for the last in line, well known at the Praia Vermelha.

Our outings became more substantial.

First, to the Corcovado, challenging the giant, now tamed by the vulgarity of the cable car.

At two in the morning, the drums roared, as in barracks under assault. The boys, who had hardly slept, in the excitement of the expectation, tumbled out of the dorms. Shortly after three, we were at the mountain range.

Aristarco headed the march, valiant as a young knight, encouraging the troops, like Napoleon in the Alps.

Nocturnal outing and nameless joy. The trees bordered the road with walls of shade laced here and there with the clear sky. The road was dark as a tunnel, with agitations like clothes on a line from the slabs of soft moonlight—a long reptile in gray and milk slowly rising. That colossus must have dreamed of being tickled, in that stony drowsiness that still held him in its thrall, under our trudging invasion. We climbed. Through openings in the trees we glimpsed abysses; beyond, the lines of streetlights, like golden rosaries on black velvet.

At a reasonable altitude, we camped for breakfast. Servants who had gone before us with the provisions improvised a counter and served us in the order of class rank. Some were lucky and got a drop of fine port wine, warmer than the coffee, the inner warmth serving as comfort against the dampness of the place and the hour, rousing their courage like a glass of punch, stoking their delight like a fiery draft.

The air seemed lighter under the lace of the branches; the last stars among the leaves faded like jasmine blooms and closed up. Aristarco gave orders to the band. The ascent started again, festive; a triumphal marching song tore the silence over the mountains, frightening away the night. Romulo's bass drum roared, to the intense astonishment of the birds that watched him, their beaks peeking over the rim of their nests, perhaps desiring him as a son-in-law, as he announced the sunrise with that brutal burst of sound.

As we rose, so did the day in the sky. There were bets on who would tire first. Every advance of the light in space was like a new incitement to the journey, softening in the sweetness of the sunrise the harshness of the ascent. When the music stopped, we could hear in the masonry of the great pipes, through the vents, the waters of the Carioca river, murmuring poetic complaints like a walled-in naiad.

From time to time we would catch views of the bay, the ocean unfolding, vast, in flames, an extended cataclysm of lava.

On the Plateau of the Hat, we stopped. The headmaster had decided that, at the call to disband, we would assault, at a run, the granite crest rising at the rim of the mountain. The boys cheered the proposal, and with a barbaric battle cry, we hurled ourselves at the peak. At the head of the crowd was Tonico, a nervous little guy from St. Fidelis, unbeaten at races, a runner in practice and principle, who at every exam of Public Instruction fled twice from roll call, figuring that flight is the true expression of strength, and bravery an artificial invention of those who can't run.

Romulo was stupid enough to attempt the crest; he stopped halfway up, inanimate, wheezing on the ground.

We had lunch at ten, each on his own, after the frugal distribution of food. Satiated with landscape, we fell into formation for the descent.

It was painful. Imprudently, we had exhausted ourselves in play. The return march was misery. We were still in formation, but nobody paid attention to proper alignment. Loose belts fell off waists, shirts slipped out of the belts; the feet stumbled, thrown off balance by the irregular pavement, the knees buckled like those of drunkards.

The children marching in front turned their pain-filled eyes toward the headmaster, holding each other up by the shoulders, stumbling forward in clusters, like sheep to slaughter. Aristarco, chipper as on the ascent, encouraged his young charges by joking with compassionate irony.

He decided to resort to music as a stimulant. The musicians, exhausted, had left their instruments in the baggage cart that was still far behind. Neither drums nor trumpets, only Romulo, trailing everyone, was rolling the bass drum along the road like a barrel.

As an added torment, the sun flowed over us like hot lead, kindling unbearable glare on the sandy road, while the day reverberated below us, over the houses, on the gardens wrapped in summer mists, on the mountain vegetation, blooming with the sad purple flowers of passion and hallelujah.

We were returning from a joyful day like defeated soldiers. The order of the march had slowly fallen apart.

When we arrived at the Rio Comprido, we were dragging ourselves along in clusters, panting, the more resilient ones in the vanguard; then in an interminable, disheartened rear, came the weaker ones, ending with those who were left lying on the road as if ill, and collected by the supervisors as if they were lost head of cattle.

At the gate of the Athenaeum, hands on hips and small white teeth showing, Angela waited for us, crisp and strong, receiving with hoots of laughing derision that arrival of the defeated, men and boys.

When, after a while, the great picnic at the Botanical Garden was announced, the memory of that debacle of exhaustion was certainly no cause for objections. We had lunched on the mountain; now we would dine in the garden. We were ready!

At noon the Athenaeum disembarked from the special trams that had taken the students to the gates of the great park. We walked through them singing one of the school anthems to the high vault of royal palm trees. By the lake at the end of the avenue, we disbanded.

In the bamboo grove, to the left, long tables had been set up for the banquet to be served at four. Thanks to the good will of the parents, who had been warned in good time, the boards, on their trestles, sagged under the weight of the Rabelaisian abundance of delicacies. To the sides, in baskets, on the ground, there were heaps of fruit, boxes and flasks of sweets.

It was one of these capricious days, likely any time of the year, more frequent in the summer, when rain squalls alternated with healthier stretches of sun, delicious and treacherous, seeming to accord with the unpredictable alternation, in the female soul, of smiles and tears.

It had rained once as we left, again during the trip; in the garden there was much wetness on the grass and on the fallen leaves; in the shadier paths one saw the sand recently pocked with small holes dug from dripping branches. But the stretches of good weather were so clear, in the intervals between the clouds, that no apprehension of a cloudburst could dampen the open joy to which we were looking forward.

The boys dispersed over the lawn toward the mountain, toward the sugarcane clumps and the gated orchards. Some, having provided themselves with fishing rods, crouched beside the reservoir, like frogs, waiting for the long shot of catching a fish.

Those whose mind was at rest looked for solitary spots, and walked immersed in their silent thoughts; the sentimental ones, with the instinct of landscape photographers, described, compared, praised the best views or simply, two by two, intimately, strolled into the distance, their arms around each other, murmuring slow dialogues. The little ones ran, creating animated games, chasing butterflies, and followed the courses of the canals through the park after a floating twig, fearful and unreachable in the quick evasion of the waters. In the darker recesses of the woods, precisely where a Greek artist would post a satyr, one might be able to surprise, on a shirt, the trusting and bucolic abandon of some of the other boys.

From time to time, the trumpet sounded, announcing the distribution of delicacies. Many did not attend.

At four, the band marked, with the national anthem, the great moment of the outdoor party. From all points of the garden there arrived the hurrying swarms of white uniforms. With great energy, the aides organized their placement.

Along the table a threatening wall of teeth closed in.

At the center of the table, in a line, were the plates, countless, cold, with no gravy, but appetizing, browned, exhaling tempting aromas.

Forks stood eagerly at attention, like enemy troops, and knives were being sharpened by the servant staff.

Forced into the stoic sobriety of philosophers, after the definitive trial of the ovens, neither the turkeys nor the suckling pigs nor the timid chickens seemed aware of their danger.

The chickens, their legs tied, lying on their backs, heads hidden under their wings, seemed to sleep, dreaming of their vain sufferings; the plump piglets, in their shining brown armor of toasted crackling, used their olive eyes not to see the lying seduction of life, eager to teach men how to bring to a proper conclusion the culinary toothpick torture enhanced by the acid of lemon slices; the turkeys, lofty to the last, and less philosophic, made do openly with the lack of their heads, proud only of the expanse of their chests, vanity under full sail, distended with stuffing.

Standing guard around the roasts were ranks of uncorked black bottles and mountains of apples, pears, and oranges, leaning on the quintessential bananas, which provided a nativist touch. The puddings, marmalades, and compotes filled the gaps on the tablecloth, with the zeal of flexible mediators. Even without counting the roast beef contributed by Aristarco, it was clear that dinner was grand.

When the boys sat, on benches brought from the Athenaeum for that purpose, and a gesture from the headmaster commanded the beginning of the assault, the boards groaned. The severity of the guardians was helpless before their savage good will. Joyful license transgressed its boundaries into cannibalism.

Whole birds jumped from the platters; the pigs slid from here to there, clawed at energetically from both sides of the table. The servants fled. Aristarco walked by, smiled at the spectacle, like a powerful lion tamer who relaxes his hold. The bottles, turned bottom up, discharged rivers of drunkenness into the glasses, spilling their blood on the table. Moderation! Moderation! clamored the guardians, digging into banks of toasted cassava, worthy of Mr. Revy, the unauthorized engineer in the news for building a fictitious road. Some of the boys composed toasts, raising, instead of a glass, a leg of pork. At the end of the last table, one of the younger boys had picked up a trombone and was applying himself, very earnestly, to filling the pipe with roast meat. Maurílio had found a stuffed cabbage and was devouring it amid gales of laughter, stating that it was ammunition for feast days. Cerqueira, the rat, bent over his plate, ate like a full restaurant, ate, ate, ate, like the mange, like a cancer. Sanches, half-drunk, kissed his neighbors, falling on them with pursed lips. Ribas, dyspeptic, was the only undemonstrative one; he sighed from afar, angel that he was, contemplating and condemning the excesses of the bacchanal.

Amid the drunken and festive tumult, there was sudden clapping. At the top of the head table stood Aristarco and the prim and copper-skinned Professor Venancio. It was poetry! Venancio de Lemos was known to improvise, more or less in advance, familiar-sounding stanzas for such rustic events.

Other teachers in attendance dedicated themselves to the coarse task of stuffing themselves. Not him!

For a quarter of an hour he had been walking mysteriously along a bamboo alley, pulling on his scanty beard and his coiled hair, rubbing his forehead, tearing inspiration from his scalp, back and nervously forth, watching furtively for our admiration. Nobody dared approach him, afraid of perturbing the workings of his genius.

Adorably whispering breezes, blowing through the woods, sobbing springs that vainly spill the tears of your sufferings, amiably warbling thrushes, O you lookouts, perched high in the palm fronds of our native literature, never honored by any imperial appropriation, come to me and share the secret of your charm! Seductive turtledoves, grant us some of your tenderness! Bejeweled hummingbirds, come to me! You, who are like animate tropes in the verdant poem of our forests . . . And inspiration came. At first, ceremoniously, from on high, circling spirals of vultures above carrion; then, sudden, pecking eagerly at his muse. The dead ass turned into a hippogriff. The poet collected the stanzas.

They were quatrains in easy participle rhymes, scansion achieved with hammer blows on the high notes.

All along the table the gastronomic frenzy of the boys halted. We listened, in amazement.

The breezes whispered; the springs flowed; the thrushes spoke; palm trees rose like fountains; there were flights of doves, of hummingbirds—all those things that feed ordinary poetry and for the sake of which versifiers starve to death. Suddenly, in the middle of the best of the stanzas, precisely as the poet apostrophized the lovely day and the sun, comparing the gaiety of the students to the meadows' radiance, and the presence of the Master to the highest luminary in the sky, O bane of prepared improvisations! the massed clouds let down a once-in-a-lifetime deluge of a rainstorm, onto the banquet, onto the poet, onto the miserable innocent apostrophe.

Venancio did not flinch. He opened an umbrella so as not to be completely belied by the runoff and went on, under his shelter, versifying enthusiastically about the sun and the clear blue of the sky.

Unwilling to discredit his estimable underling, Aristarco pretended to believe it was all improvised and stood indifferent to the downpour. The rim of his straw hat wilted around his head; the white dress coat was losing its starch and hanging in dripping vertical folds.

For the boys, the rain was a new invitation to mayhem. The poet and his rapturous good-weather inspiration were abandoned; the attack on the platters resumed.

The leafy dome that covered us did not attenuate the violence of the waters; on the contrary, it fattened the drops. No matter. The impermeable posture of the headmaster sheltered us as well. Let it rain! It was the sauce we had missed on the roasts. The newly washed fruit glistened with a fresh glaze that even autumn could not provide. The wine spread on the soaking tablecloth in a solemn generalization of crimson. The opportune drenching of the banquet tempered the dryness of the manioc flour used for stuffing. "Our meal is ending with soup," Nearco noted, "where those of the rabble start."

Who was speaking of an end? Nobody was about to finish. It turned out that, as the seats of their pants were wet, nobody wanted to sit, and there was a scramble around the table; the benches were kicked away. The sweets were shared unequally; latecomers got nothing. João Numa and the Counselor, on the pretext of settling a dispute, appropriated a box of peaches and disappeared.

The rain furnished an excuse for the drinking. The consumption of toasts was unbelievable. Toasts to Aristarco, toasts to the other boys, to Silvino the poet, to the sun, to storms, to the Scandinavian god of thunder. In transports of good will, sworn enemies reconciled; Barbalho saluted me enthusiastically. Romulo, somewhat dizzy, removed from the tables, toasted the servant who had brought him another bottle; then he toasted his fiancée; the servant, drinking as well, touched glasses with him.

As it was getting dark, the headmaster had the trumpet call to fall in.

Under the unceasing downpour, the school fell into line as well as it could. Many, complaining about their delicate health, were excused from this inopportune demand on their balance and went ahead to the covered gate of the garden. Then the rest of us marched in formation, dripping wet. The red ribbon of our caps ran in blood-colored rivulets down our faces.

When we came to the gates, the special trams were waiting for us. On the other side of the street, at the entrance of a well-known restaurant, Aristarco's family turned up, with some of the teachers, who had dined there. Dona Ema, on the arm of Crisóstomo, and Melica, haughtily alone and apart.

At the school we received orders to go up and rest in the dorms, a laudably prudent measure, after the excesses and the storm endured in the course of the day. But resting was just a prolongation of the earlier revelry. To make the racket stop, we were called to study. We descended to the great hall. Aristarco, serious and resuming his Olympian harshness, strode in and asked roughly whether we imagined that from now on life would be a perpetual debauched picnic. Tacitly we denied it, and normal calm was back on track.

We did not know that, at that very time, in secret, the highest tribunal was preparing a web of intrigue that would turn into terror the memories of that great outing.

At suppertime, through the same door where one could find the little school gazette, somber as ever, slow like a requiem, lurid like the Last Judgment, entered the headmaster.

He paused, and a shiver of anticipation ran through the lunch hall: "My soul is sad," he started, cavernously. A line of thunderstorms on the horizon, the remains of the afternoon's tempest, provided a backdrop to his words, like an Aeschylean chorus.

"My soul is sad. Gentlemen! Immorality has gained access to this house! At first I refused to believe it, but have had to bow before the evidence . . ." With all the tenebrous vigor of a tragic scene, he told us the story of a saucy escapade. A comical letter and an assignation at the Botanical Garden. "Ah, but nothing escapes me! I have one hundred eyes. Fool me if you can! In my possession I have a piece of paper, a monstrous piece of evidence! Signed by a woman! There are women at the Athenaeum, gentlemen!"

It was a letter from Candido, signed "Candida."

"This woman, this courtesan, speaks of a safe place, of the quiet in the woods, of solitude together . . . a shameless poem! What I must do is of the greatest gravity. Tomorrow justice will be done! I come before you now, simply to say that I will be inexorable, formidable! And to warn you: anyone involved directly or indirectly in this miserable affair—I have a list of the names—and who refuses to cooperate voluntarily with the proceedings to mete out justice will be considered an accomplice and punished as such."

This invitation was a veritable fishing expedition. Rummaging around in the drawers of conscience and memory, there was nobody, one can truly say, who was not implicated in the school comedy of the sexes, at the very least in the plot of "I heard someone say . . ." Hearing and not telling right away was a crime, and a serious one, according to local jurisprudence. The promised inquest caused general alarm. How to predict the complications of the process? How to guess the tremendous secret of the list?

Aristarco prided himself on his inquisitorial perspicacity. Under the hail of questions, threats, promises, the victim of the interrogation would implicate himself, surrender, and betray the others; during the proceedings in the headmaster's office, facts blossomed in corymbs, ripened into fruit clusters; research into one misdeed uncovered three, not counting the ramifications of accidental complicity.

When the headmaster left, the room was stupefied with terror.

I, in particular, had various reasons to be afraid. The latent war that was already tying me to the headmaster, like a disjunctive conjunction, had been aggravated by a very serious episode, a definitive rupture.

On my way to the library, at the same place where the unfortunate encounter with the huge Romulo had taken place, I had unexpectedly found myself in the presence of Bento Alves.

The affections of that excellent companion had not weakened. During vacation, he had come to see me at my home, meeting my family, who insistently recommended to my friend that he should succor me in the difficulties presented by school life and protect me from the constant danger of pernicious friendships. We did not see one another for the entire month of January. When school started again, I noted a new warmth in his friendship, without the previous effusion, but evidenced when his hand trembled as he shook mine, when he spoke with the embarrassment of a lover in the wrong, when his eyes avoided mine, denouncing the reluctance of secret and impetuous movement. Sometimes even, an alarming flash of madness flitted over his features.

That compressed agony interested me. Strange thing, this friendship that, instead of the frank closeness of friends, could thus produce the uncertainty of unease and a prolonged situation of vexation, as if living in close quarters were a sacrifice and sacrifice a necessity.

During the first days of the term, few of the students having arrived, we would spend whole hours in each other's company. He had brought me a present of books, inscribed to me in colors and beautiful handwriting interlaced with a picture of roses in full shiny color. I also remember a very sweet gilt box holding pastilles and other ridiculous tokens of amiability that he would offer me, shrinking in shame for the insignificance of the favor. I am even confusedly aware of a little note of mine, in my role as make-believe girlfriend, and I took the theatrics of it to the point of flirting, arranging the knot on his tie or smoothing the curl that fell into his eyes; I would whisper indistinct secrets into his ear to see him laugh, despairing from not being able to hear them. One of his sisters had gotten married in Rio Grande; he showed me the picture of the groom, who had a drooping black moustache, with the bride, a pure and correct oval face amid the turbulent fog of the bridal veils. He gave me an orange blossom that they had sent him.

That's how things stood, serenely, when the most astounding change occurred.

I don't know what the devil of an expression I saw in his face, ordinarily so very kind. He looked completely frantic. As soon as he saw me, he leaped at me as Romulo had done, and with the same brutality. We rolled in the dark under the stairs. Knocked over, bruised, beaten, I defended myself. In the half darkness of the corner, I saw a large moldy shoe. Fighting in the dust, under the attacker's heavy knee, I attacked his head, his face, his mouth, with formidable blows of the heel, leveraging the cleated shoe sole with the length of my extremities. Bento Alves left me abruptly.

We had fought in silence, nothing to be heard but the thumps on the floor. In the hallway, however, we saw Aristarco, who was coming as if to help. Bento Alves passed; he fixed him with a sightless gaze, wide-eyed, hideous, as from one who had just committed a homicide, and disappeared, limping, dust-stained, his lips swollen, his hair disordered.

Aristarco came over to me. I was to explain the fight! I was looking very much like my adversary, dusty and dirty as if I had been rolling in the muck.

I answered violently.

"Insolent!" the headmaster roared. With one of his hands he grabbed my shirt, popping the buttons, and with the other around the back of my neck, he lifted me in the air and shook me. "Wretch! Wretch, I will wring your neck! Impudent rat! Confess everything or I will kill you!"

Instead of confessing, I grabbed his vigorous moustache. I was still boiling from the excitement of the first battle; I could not bother with the forms of respect. I kicked my legs, twisted in the tight space like a stepped-on scorpion. The headmaster threw me on the ground. And changing his tone, he said: "Sérgio, you dared touch me!"

"You touched me first!" I replied forcefully.

"Child, you wounded an old man!"

I noticed that there were a few white moustache hairs on the ground.

"I have been vilely injured," I said.

"Ah, my son, wounding a master is like wounding your own father, and parricides are cursed."

The emotional tone of the unexpected conclusion touched me to the depth of my soul. I was defeated. For a moment I was horrified at myself. Recovering from my daze, I found myself alone in the hallway. The dramatic exit of the headmaster increased my remorse. There was a reaction from the moral effort, and I broke nervously into tears; I cried uncontrollably, leaning against a windowsill.

I was counting for certain on an exceptional punishment, some imaginative variation of the celebrated code, based on an article whose minimal degree was a solemn decree of expulsion.

I waited one day, then two, and three: the punishment did not come. I learned that Bento Alves had left the Athenaeum on the very afternoon of his extraordinary madness. I believed for a while that my impunity was a special case of the famous system of moral punishment and that Aristarco had delegated to the vulture of my conscience the task of administering justice and redress. Today I think otherwise: it was not worthwhile losing at a single blow two clients prompt in their payments, just for the sake of one trifling event, certainly unpleasant, but for which there were no witnesses.

The case died in discreet secrecy, and the headmaster and I found ourselves in a bilateral conspiracy of reserve, as if nothing had happened.

But the resentment must have been deep, and the tormenting expectation of the process threatened me like an imminent occasion for retaliation.

It was not possible to sleep in peace.

At breakfast time, as he had promised, Aristarco showed up with all the funereal greatness of someone who would dispense justice. All in black. Magnificently measuring their steps by his, many of the teachers followed him, like an honor guard. At the front door, more teachers, standing, and the beadles, and the gossipy multitude of the servants.

The silence was so complete that one could clearly hear the ticking of the clock in the waiting room, pulsating the anxious seconds.

Aristarco blew twice through his moustache, flooding the room with his all-powerful breath.

And without any introduction:

"Mr. Candido Lima, rise!

"I present to you, gentlemen, Miss Candida," he added with dispirited irony.

"To the middle of the room! And bow to your colleagues."

Candido was a large boy, with thick lips, blond, green-eyed, with a languid manner denoting indolence and tedium. Slowly he crossed the room, bowing his head, covering his face with his sleeve, chastened by all that public curiosity.

"Rise, Mr. Emilio Tourinho."

"This, gentlemen, is the accomplice."

Tourinho was a little older than the other boy, but shorter, stocky, brown-skinned, with wide nostrils, curly eyebrows that formed one continuous bow on his forehead. He did not at all look the leading man, but was in fact the lover.

"Come and kneel with your companion."

"Now the helpers . . ."

Aristarco had been working on the procedure since five in the morning. The interrogation, with the appendix of the allegations by the secret police and the more timid of the boys, had compromised only ten students.

On being called up by the headmaster, they left their places and knelt, joining the main culprits.

"These are the acolytes of shame, the codefendants of silence!"

Candido and Tourinho, arms shielding their eyes, stole glances at each other, taking comfort in the shared disgrace like Francesca and Paolo in Dante's *Inferno*.

The twelve boys, prostrated before Aristarco in the long passage between the heads of the table, looked like participants in an unknown wedding ritual, waiting for the blessing of the couple before them.

But instead of a blessing it was rage that washed over them.

". . . You forget parents and siblings, the future that awaits them and God's ineluctable vigilance! . . . These polluted faces did not accept the saintly kiss of their mothers . . . shame fell on them like a cracked glaze . . . Their countenance deformed, their dignity trampled, they offend nature, forget sacred laws of respect for human individuality . . . And they find companions perverse enough to abet them, suppressing their own revulsion, dodging their duty to make way for the revenge of morality and the restorative work of justice . . ."

I am unable to reignite the fiery rhetoric that ran there about Pentapolis. This is only a sample of the brimstone.

But it was just a beginning. Led by the supervisors, the twelve left like a detachment of convicts for the headmaster's office, where they would be literally abused, in accordance with customary judicial discretion.

It was said that there were severe beatings. The convicts denied it later. In any case, the mere rumor was effective, boosted by the nebulous refraction of hearsay.

The call-up of the accused having been effected, the entire room breathed relief. Off on their break, the boys shouted gaily.

Franco, especially, had never been seen happier. Casually free, since there had not been a reading of the *notes*, he turned the circumstance into payback against Silvino. "So I am the bad one," he repeated, walking in circles. "I am the worthless one, the pest of the school! The evil one, that's me alone!" Gradually, Silvino lost his patience. Eventually he flung himself against Franco, and in desperation threw him to the ground and started trampling him. Some of the boys shouted in protest, and Silvino threatened them. Afire with the exaltation of the previous day's outing, which for a while had been suppressed by the terror of the proceedings, they gathered en masse against Silvino. The supervisor restored his moral authority by taking refuge at the top of the stairs and from there energetically waving notepad and pencil.

In the afternoon, on orders from the headmaster, the instigators of the revolt were called up for their punishment.

I was among them. We were lined up, twenty or so of us in the hallway that led out of the refectory. We thought of ourselves as *political prisoners*, victims of our generous sedition, and as such were not vexed by our penance. Some chatted and joked, others sat on the floor. By my side was a closet where teaching apparatus was kept, its glass door reinforced by a metal mesh. Through the wires, in the last light, I observed the beloved planets glowing vaguely, as if the very night had been made prisoner.

Behind the closet there was a door. On the other side, in the sitting room, Aristarco and the accountant were talking. Some scattered words reached me: "of a good family . . . two, that would be a discredit! They will think . . . Expelling is not the same as correcting . . . That's the least of it; aren't there any scholarship ones? . . . Yes, yes. As for me . . . it is always unpleasant to erase it . . . it blotches the writing . . . In sum . . . youth . . ."

They had just turned on the lights at the Athenaeum.

It was definitely a bad day. From the hallway, we heard an enormous noise coming from the yard. The booing was starting over. Protected by the night, the boys were on a rampage. It was an indescribable tumult, the voices of a populace in revolt, whistles, shouts, insults, in which the high-pitched screams of the younger ones pierced the confused clamor.

The supervisors, terrified, came in, seeking out the head-master, showing their faces, speckled with red warts. I guessed. It was the revolution of the guava paste! An old complaint.

The food at the Athenaeum was not terrible. It was reasonable for a few hundred little idiots. It even had the indispensable condiment of flies, a delight. But the insistent impertinence of certain dishes became a bore. For instance, an epidemic of stewed liver, all year long. Lately, for three months, a mushy guava paste, made with bananas, economically manufactured on orders of the pantry master.

Aristarco paled with umbrage. This cheeky insurrection was aimed directly at him. And that on the same day on which he had provided a spectacle of awe-inspiring justice. However, he did not want to put his prestige on the line. We saw him in the hall, uncertain, bloodless, telling the beadles to calm down.

The yes or no on expulsions was still torturing him. Expel . . . expel . . . mayhap go bankrupt. The code, in gothic script in its black frame, was there, imperious and formal as the Law, prescribing disconnection for the heads of the rebellion as well. Morality, discipline, all at the same time . . . It was too much, too much! . . . Justice was reaching into his pocket like a catastrophe. The best course would be to punch the damned glass, tear up the document, and have the wind carry away the scraps, that stupid gothic nonsense about justice!

When informed of the motive for the row, a weight fell from his heart. "Ah, they had a reason . . . It was just the stupidity of the pantry man. If they stoned him that would still be too little . . . But it was not their fault. It was the secret industry of guava paste made with bananas . . ."

The bell ringing to supper calmed the spirits. The rumor was that Aristarco had surrendered to the revolt and was about to speak.

He appeared at the same door where he had been so formi-dable in the morning, but now he was tame and smooth like meekness and loyalty personified, yet as haughty as submission allowed.

"But why, my friends, did you not convene a delegation? A delegation is a mutiny in its orderly and paper-based form! What need was there to express yourself by means of a rebellion? You are all right . . . I forgive you all . . . But I am as deceived as you were . . . Till today, I was certain that the guava paste was made with guavas. The budget specifies guaranteed guava paste from Campos. In this house there is no skimping. Should anything be amiss, speak up, for I am here to take care of it; I am your Master, your father . . . Guaranteed, pure fruit guava paste from Campos . . . Here are the cans . . . More cans! . . . read the labels. How could I have even suspected?"

While the headmaster spoke, a kitchen servant was heaping up around him all the empty cans to be found in the pantry. Large, round tin boxes, shiny like moons, labeled in large script. Aristarco's frame was mirrored in those gleaming documents of his integrity. "Pure paste! Pure paste, gentlemen!" he assured us, drumming his knuckles on the top of one of the boxes.

The boxes were tumbling noisily on the floor, but the pile rose nevertheless, in a disorderly fashion, gleaming in crumpled reflexes from the gaslights. Aristarco rose above the cans, like the principle of authority rescued from corrosion. His vindication was complete. A few more words, lubricated with tenderness, and all the resentment waned, and we saluted the headmaster, large, before us, as always, above the gleaming Flanders tin.

Chapter 9

The amnesty to the revolutionaries extended to the defendants in the immorality case. The fibers of moral rigor frayed, Aristarco dismissed them from his office, with the penance of a few tens of pages of writing and a three-day reclusion in one of the rooms. The Law was discredited, but many things were preserved, among them the establishment's credit line, since there was no profit in the scandal of a large number of expulsions. As for the locking up of the culprits in their darkened dungeon, there was, impossibly, Franco, by express demand of Silvino, as the first cause of the unmentionable disturbances of the Athenaeum's order.

This resolution pleased me greatly. It would have been a shame, in truth, if, so soon after Bento Alves, and the disastrous conclusion of the sentimental history of our relations, I had lost my friend Egbert as well.

I had acquired him in the transition to the upper classes, where I found him with others of the more advanced boys. Sitting side by side, we understood each other, were in sympathy with each other, as if a secret purposeful necessity had guided the chance of our placement.

For the first time, I knew friendship. The insignificance of daily life at school, filled with boredom, is favorable to the development of inclinations more serious than those of simple boyish convenience. Boredom is an aspect of idleness, and this proverbial mother of all vices also generates the vice of feeling.

The intimacy with Sanches had been most like the agglutinating closeness of a medicinal plaster, a kind of lazy slavery of inexperience and fear; the friendship with Bento Alves had been genuine, but on my part there had been only gratitude, obeisance to strength, the ease of voluntary subjection, the feminine vanity of dominating through weakness—in short, all the elements of a passive form of affection in which the expense of energy is null and sentiment lives on a diet of rest and sleep. But to Egbert I was a true friend. For no better reason than that one does not argue with affection. We improvised on the theme of collaboration; we exchanged meanings; neither owed the other. Nevertheless I experienced the delightful need for dedication. I thought myself strong for being able to love and show it. I burned with the inexplicable ardor of disinterest. Egbert called up in me the tenderness of an older brother.

His face was irregular, and seemed beautiful to me. Of English origin, he had brown hair streaked with blond, an exotic touch in his pronunciation, blue eyes striated in gray, oblique, with negligent lids almost closed, which, however, opened in conversation in a wide and graceful line.

We were neighbors in the dorm as well, and I, lying in my bed, waited for him to fall asleep so I could watch him sleeping, and woke early so I could watch him wake. We owned everything in common. For myself, I positively adored him, and thought him perfect. He was elegant, skillful, hardworking, generous. I admired him, from his heart to the color of his skin and the harmony of his form. He swam like a porpoise. The blue water opened before him murmuring, or rose to his shoulders, bathing the whiteness of his body with a sheen as of polished ivory. He repeated his lessons calmly, sometimes with difficulty, hampered by the anxious breathing of asphyxia. I prized him more when he had his fits of anguish caused by illness. I dreamed that he had died, that he had suddenly left the Athenaeum; the dream jolted me awake, and with relief I saw him, lying peacefully in the bed beside mine, one of his hands under his cheek, breathing regularly, with a slight wheeze. At recess we were inseparable, complementary, like two reciprocal conditions of existence. I regretted that no terrible event loomed, threatening my friend, so I could show the courage of my sacrifice, as I traded places with him facing the danger, losing myself for the sake of a person from whom I wanted absolutely nothing. I remembered examples of friendship in history, and compared myself favorably against them.

Afternoons, we walked together endlessly around the athletics field, talking about nothing, in scattered sentences, alighting like butterflies on the sweetness of a mutual well-being, inexpressible. We spoke in low voices, kindly, as if fearing to chase away, with a louder, harsher intonation, the protection of a benign genie that had spread over us the invisible canopy of his wings. *Amor unus erat.*

We walked into the grassy area. How far away, the happy buzz of our companions! The two of us, alone! We sat on the grass. I rested my head on his knees, or his on mine. In silence, we would pull at the grass seeds. The meadow was huge, its borders disappearing into the early dusk. We looked up, into the sky. What transparency. What light! High up, there was still, in a golden streak, a memory of the sun. The deep dome extended toward the mountains, in the vast, tenuous dilution of a rainbow. Soft glimmers of flame, and then the beautiful silken blue, and the degeneration of tints toward the melancholy of night, presaged by a last band of painful purple. If only we could be the birds we espied on high, friendly, lowering their flight toward the sunset, the happy destination of light, in full day still, while on earth all became wrapped in shadows.

Other times we climbed on the double trapeze. We swung slowly at first, facing the quick caress of the air. Little by little we increased the arc and risked crazy flips, startling the Athenaeum, carried along by vertigo, arms extended, feet forward, heads down, hair blown by the wind, drunk with the danger, happy should the ropes break and we end there, as with one life, on the same surge.

We read a lot in each other's company. Pages that did not end, delicate readings, fertile in dreams: *Robinson Crusoe*, solitude and human industry; *Paul and Virginia*, solitude and sentiment. We thought up lovely hypotheses: what would either of us do, if caught in the plight of finding ourselves on a desert island?

"As for me, I would immediately initiate a furious advertising campaign for immigration and go cry it out on the beaches till the world heard me."

"I would do better: I would preventively decree marriage to be obligatory and wait for time to pass."

Bernardin de Saint-Pierre's pastoral was our main source of delight. The Bay of the Tomb, with its deep and somber waters, greeted for a few hours only, every day, by the sun at its zenith, always softly sad; in the distance, through the opening of a gorge, the sight of a white façade, the rustic church of Pamplemousses.

We visualized, vaguely but completely, in the wordless meditation of feeling, with pictures in washes of color and blurred outlines, the scenes we read in that simple narrative, of souls that met, slender palm trees growing tall together, raising little by little the plume of their fringed fronds, in the warmth of happiness and of the tropics. We understood the young lovers, one year old, entwined in their cradle, in their sleep, in their innocence.

We lived through the entire idyll, instinctive and pure. "Virginie, elle sera heureuse! . . ." We were excited to follow the children as they ran free in the wild and enjoyed that topography bearing names witnessing their history: "Discovery of Friendship," "Dried Tears," or alluding to the distant homeland. We heard the beating of wings in a flight of birds that, around Virginia, fought for their share of crumbs. Without thinking, we understood the sensual philosophy of their dainty conversation.

"Is it for your intelligence? But our mothers have more than the two of us. Is it for your caresses? But they kiss me more often than you do . . . I think it is because of your kindness . . . But first, relax on my bosom and I will be rested . . . You ask why you love me. But any two that are raised together love each other. Look at the birds raised in the same nest, they love each other as we do; they are always together as we are. Listen how they call and answer each other from one tree to the next."

It distressed us, however, as we turned the pages, to find the cruel obstacles imposed by fortune and class, the separation of the sister souls when the palm trees could remain together. And the constricting imminence of the south wind, of the catastrophe, the brutal moon of presages in an iron sky.

And we put away the book, luminous song of love over the dark drumbeat of despair in colonial slavery, which appeared as a reminder, composed of sorrow, magic, admiration. What power in the poet: over the accursed soil, where coffee bloomed as did the snowy cotton and the light green corn, showered with blood, to raise the fantastical image of kindness. Virginia crowned; like the omnipotent caprice of the sun, shaping into a glory of vaporous strands the fumes from dungheaps, rising in golden spokes.

With Egbert I did my first, secret experiments with verse. Collaboratively, we sketched out a novel, with excessively tragic medieval episodes, filled with moonlight, surrounded by ogives, where the most notable event was a combat scene, duly organized, with shooting and cannon, anticipating to such an extent Schwartz's invention that forever, in literature, we were safe from the reproach that we had not discovered gunpowder.

When I heard his name, at the roll call of those compromised in the process, I suffered as if from a surprise blow. I was crushed by not being able to find a way to share in his shame.

What kind of complicity was being attributed to him? I did not want to know. Were he the vilest of defendants, he was my friend: anything he suffered, however guilty, was, to my mind, a trial imposed by fatality. And I trembled at the idea that they would ill-treat so gentle a creature, so complacent, so amiable, made of sensibility and mildness, against whom evil would always be but injustice, whom I loved with all his defects, all his imperfections, with the easy pardon of sentimental blindness, that strange preference that accepts all in the loved one, the clear language of the eyes as well as the acrid, even impure smell of the flesh.

When we saw each other again, neither of us had a word to say to the other; we sat on a bench, side by side, in expansive silence. And never afterward, not even by a distant allusion, did we refer to the case. It was an instinctive coincidence of mutual respect, and perhaps distaste for an ominous memory.

Since July of the previous year, I had been taking beginning language courses, pleased to be acquiring a foreign vocabulary, the ability to use the languages of the great nations, as if I were tasting civilization in drafts, as if I were drinking the reality of human activity in remote countries depicted in cosmoramas in which we vaguely believed, as one believes in romances.

There followed the nuisance of endless writing assignments.

In the higher classes, the acquired knowledge eased the work. Pages of literature smiled at me with the familiar expression of well-known objects.

The teachers were good, and moderate. The French teacher, M. Delille, a poet's name attached to a bear, an honorable bear, inoffensive and benevolent, nostalgic for the Third Empire, the fall of which had deported him to a life of adventure overseas, bearded like a horsehair mattress, with a vigorous growth of dense, luxuriant hair, burned red around his mouth, black elsewhere, through which expressive breaths of Halbout's grammar and strong drink would reach us. The English teacher, Dr. Old Jr., with his contradictory name, was the best of men, careful, clear in his explanations, never angry, bald as bald, but what an object he was for our esteem and affection!

Egbert's company completed the delight, and studying was a pleasure.

Master Venancio also taught English; I escaped from his claws, fortunately. He was a beast: submissive toward the headmaster, terrible toward the students. He once threw a gas gauge at one of them, breaking the boy's teeth. Manlio, in addition to teaching first letters, occupied the special chair in Portuguese.

Thanks to another year of study, I achieved passable competence in the vernacular, guaranteed by an official certificate. I am also thankful for the smattering of Latin, into which I was initiated by the priest and master Brother Ambrosio, respectable, his nose always stuffy, gesticulating with the grammar book, reciting the primer with the hollow and deep intonation of sung Masses, consuming enough snuff for an entire monastery, which is responsible for the fact that to this day the magnificent language of *qui, quae, quod* smells to me like the brand he used, and the mere mention of Sallust makes me sneeze.

It was a custom at the Athenaeum to relax the house regulations in the case of a student of a certain standing about to take an exam. One could go out to the garden with one's books and enjoy the comfort of working at one's ease. Always together, Egbert and I took full advantage of this customary privilege. Before the memorable date of the French exam, we took Chateaubriand, Corneille, Racine, Molière for extended walks along the shady alleys. Classical theater lent itself to great effects of recitation. Ah, the great tragedies lost on dry leaves! The noble gestures wasted! The superb speeches entrusted to the frivolous passing breezes!

One of us was Augustus, and the other, Cinna; one Nearchus, the other Polyeucte; one Horatio and one Coriatio; Don Diego and El Cid, Joas and Joad, Nero and Burrus, Philinte and

Alceste, Tartuffe and Cléante. The woods served as exquisite scenery. We dialogued in the full force of our dramatic incarnations, knightly bravery, Roman civic virtue, the heroism of faith, the squabbles of misanthropy, the slickness of the hypocrites. The statue of an anonymous goddess, in chipped china, green with age, was our audience, an audience that paid unstinting attention, but moderate in its reaction, with no excesses in applause or reproof, but constant and tireless.

There were difficulties in casting the female roles; each of us wanted the more energetic parts with the long speeches. We cast lots, and as dictated by chance, one or the other dressed up unceremoniously in any lady's skirts and was perfect in the clothes of sentiment, Chimène's engagement, Camilla's despair, Pauline's mourning, Agrippina's ambition, Esther's domination, Elmira's cunning, Célimène's ambivalence. Another role difficult to cast was that of Burrus, honest and very appealing. But nobody wanted to be Nero's virtuous advisor.

Better still than the privilege of free study was a kind of prize, never listed in the by-laws, with which Aristarco would kindly favor the ones who had distinguished themselves. He would have them to supper at his house—what an honor! at the same tablecloth as the Princess Melica, she of the large eyes.

Good fortune willed that we, the two friends, received the highly prized top grade, to be inscribed forever, vetted by Master Courroux, the awe-inspiring Cato of the black balls, the universal terror of the first-year students.

The headmaster received me, as we arrived from the school hall, with a forced but civil embrace; I noticed that the boil of resentment was still suppurating. Egbert having been invited, so, perforce, was I, and I was there, with an ill will, by obligation. It was up to me to forge a pretext for refusal, but I was curious about a number of points, as for instance, to see how Melica would eat, a thing of high interest to me.

I do remember that there were flowers on the table, that the soup was burning hot; I did not even notice whether the headmaster's daughter was there.

One thing only absorbed my entire attention. Dona Ema recognized me: I was that little boy with the long locks! She talked to me a lot. A white speck of lint sat on the shoulder of my uniform; the good lady finally took it between her fingers, let it float down, and showed me, smiling, the weightless thread falling slowly in the still air . . . I had grown so much! How different from two years before. She seemed to remember having spoken to me briefly, on the day of the art exhibit . . .

"A little scoundrel," Aristarco interrupted, between pointed and condescending, from a window embrasure, where he was talking with Master Crisóstomo.

I wanted to come up with a riposte that was not rude, but the lady was holding my hand in hers, maternally, lightly, in a way that also held back my liveliness, held me back completely, as if I existed only in that hand she held. After Aristarco's interruption, I remember nothing more of that afternoon.

A seductive mirage in white, thick black hair upswept with infinite grace, a rose in her hair, red as lips and hearts are red, red like a shout of triumph. Flowers on the table, a burning hot broth, and always the adorable obsession of white with a red rose.

She was by my side, very close, gorgeous in her snowy dress. I was served a number of dishes and many caresses; I devoured the caresses. I did not dare raise my eyes. I tried at one point. I saw two troubling eyes fixed on me, shedding night. It seemed to me, though I am not sure, that from the other side, behind the flowers, Master Crisóstomo watched me as well.

In his great pride, operative even in his own house, Aristarco presided, but from so high up and so far away that it was as if he were absent.

Back at the Athenaeum, I felt large. I had the vague feeling that my chest had grown, as if I were becoming a man by dilation. I felt elevated, twenty years tall, a miracle. I checked my shoes, to see whether my heels had grown. No strange symptoms. Only one thing: I now looked on Egbert as on a memory, something from yesterday.

From that day on, a coldness settled on the glow of our brotherly friendship.

Chapter 10

The previous evening's delicious exaltation was quite different from the terrified languor I felt the next morning, at the Department of Public Instruction. The mortal expectation of being called on fell on me; academic terror—a trifle, but we were anxious and depressed as if it were the most serious thing. And I was not a newcomer to French exams.

The beginning of the first examination brought on a fever. Three days before, I started suffering from palpitations; my appetite disappeared, then sleep; on the morning of the act, the most elementary notions about the subject went the way of appetite and sleep. *Memoria in albis.*

Master Manlio encouraged us, and his encouragement, reminding me of the danger, increased my fear. In anticipation, I was crushed by the enormous weight of that Bastille of Goldsmith Street, and the ferocious courts from whose judgment there was no appeal; by the terrible opening bell that marked the start of the proceedings; the leaden, thick, green curtains bearing the imperial arms; the formidable walls of centuries-old masonry. It was barbaric, that whole conspiracy against me, of all those uncouth profiles in a row, Matoso, Neves Leão, the commissions, each more powerful and crankier than the other; the Education Council, at heart an unknown, mythological thing, glimpsed like the religious frescoes on dark vaults, where at times the voices in the nave swell in resonance, lending moral force to the justice of commissions, with the prestige of elevation and inaccessibility; higher still than that, the Ministry of the Empire, the Executive, the State, the Social Order, a huge apparatus arrayed against a child.

One entered the tiled lobby from Assembly Street.

I spent I know not how long there, like a condemned man in chapel. Around me other unfortunates died of paleness, waiting to be called. One of them, the oldest of us all, gaunt and with a Christlike air, had a close-cut beard, very black, that looked like an ebony chin attached to a face made of old ivory.

Suddenly a door opened. From inside, from the dark, a voice issued, a list of names: one, then another and another . . . not mine yet . . . Finally! There wasn't even time to faint. They pushed me; the door closed; unaware of my own steps, I found myself in a large, silent, somber room, with a low ceiling of painted beams, that made one instinctively duck one's head. An entire wall of glass made opaque by smoke, the color of parchment, filtered a tired yellowish dusk into the room, attaching jaundiced masks to the faces present.

Between the window and the seats prepared for the students stood the table for the examiners: on the right, a bald old man, short, his baldness framed in blondish wisps of hair, his beard the color of his hair, leaned back in his upholstered chair and read a small volume with the effort of the nearsighted, rubbing the pages against his face. On the left, a man of about thirty, a straggly beard covering his entire face, including the eyelids, dark glasses, curly dry hair. The light coming in behind him darkened his features in a confusing way. The third, president of the commission, could not be seen well, as he was sitting behind a green urn fringed in yellow.

The stamped exam sheets were handed out. One of the examiners rose, gathered a handful of "points," or questions, and threw them into the urn. The tin urn sang, ironically, as the numbers fell in, sonorous.

The question was chosen—one more moment of anguish . . .

Then—a stanza from *The Lusiads*. The wait had ended. I was no longer worried about the difficulty of the question.

After dictation, as if to relax my spirit, I forgot the natural inventory of knowledge that the exam demanded. I started to think about the first readings of Camões, of Sanches, of bathing in the pool, of how Angela laughed, of the murdered servant, of the murderer's trial, which had taken place a short while before. Three touches on my heel called me back from my reverie. I turned: it was the student at the table behind me, the ebony chin, asking for help. "I am lost; please help, I can't remember the direct order of a sentence!" The noise of that whispered question hissed loudly enough to attract the attention of the board. I threw him the main clause, but was afraid of giving him full help. In addition, I also had to take care of my own interests. I left the poor ivory Christ to his despair about his blank page. From time to time the unfortunate soul poked me with his pen.

I went into the oral exam feeling better. The grade on the written one was encouraging.

The oral exams were held in the rooms on the upper floor. One entered from Goldsmith Street. The students were, in general, calmer. In addition to these, the lobby at the stairs was filled with the crowd of assistants, a confusion of uniforms, threadbare cutaways, overcoats, every age, all the schools represented, in addition to independent students who had private lessons, mixed in with whom were some looking suspiciously like ragamuffins, dropouts.

The Athenaeum was the object of envy. Victims of their uniforms, Aristarco's disciples wandered among groups of rival schools, suffering their catcalls with the patience recommended by good breeding.

Some were smoking. In the lightless atmosphere there hung a fog of bad breath and an intolerable smell of smoke; the walls were stained with dark spit. Walking around, people scraped their shoes in the sand covering the floor tiles; loud, ship chandlers' laughs resounded around the room, and jokes laced with obscenities. Some young men, with slack smiles, expressionless, ill-mannered, pushed up their dirty straw hats with the backs of their hands, and went by, swaying their hips. The more distinguished class gave them way, pulling their mouths down in disdain, showing off their elegance.

An extraordinary commotion passed through the multitude. Someone had just found, scribbled into the graffiti- and epigram-covered plaster, a new and very witty inscription: satirical doggerel about Master Courroux, one of the French examiners, all the verses rhyming with the last sound of his name, in *oo*, always in *oo*, from top to bottom, with an astonishing wealth of epithets.

As if on cue, at the same moment, the feared teacher entered and came precipitously down the stairs. "Don't you know him? There he goes!" said one of the students closest to me.

I did not know him . . .

I saw him, thin, angular, unattractive, gazing on us with unabated ferocity; one could not know who was the object of his gaze because he was cross-eyed. My improvised informant started on him, and realizing that I was behind in my information, never left me: "If you invest, you'll make it; if not, byebye. Fish market! Sometimes the fish is expensive, but there is always some fish to be had. Look at Meireles, philosophy examiner, the tall one with the long Russian beard; the investment is little Rita from Pernambuco at the Arches Street; for Simas, at the geography table, with his large belly that got him nicknamed Terrestrial Sphere, just let him have a couple of fighting cocks . . . Barros Andrade, well, buy your grades from him; that devil in rhetoric, who flunked me a couple of days ago, praise his verses, and you won't find more amiable sideburns. Your headmaster understands them. When he comes in, he's a veritable jaguar, even the white ceiling pales, they rise and salute the sovereign! Now, there are some respectable men: old Moreira, nice Ramiro with his patriarchal smile . . ."

From the top of the stairs they shouted into the lobby that the call-up for those to be examined in Portuguese was about to begin.

As I climbed the stairs, I saw a large crowd of boys on the street: a rumble! Whistles blew. Students were exchanging blows with the wagoners, according to the wonderful custom of the time.

Exams were held in a large hall with many windows, narrow casements in thick old glass, badly made, uneven, with a greenish cast at the denser points. An iron grille divided the hall into two parts, the larger of which was for the assistants. In the other there were two examination tables: mathematics close to the entrance, Portuguese farther on, and so close to each other that the answers to the one got all mixed up with the questions of the other, resulting in admirable effects of the application of exact sciences to philology.

Before the ceremony, there was talk in low voices. One person came in, dropping his walking stick. All looked at him. "Don't you know him?" asked my officious companion.

A man in his sixties, gray-haired and helicoidal, with the bland face of a priest, hair curling over stooped shoulders, endless overcoat scratching the ground at every step. "Counselor Vilela, or, rather, Counselor Tee Aitch, an institution! He is presiding over the math exams. He presides over anything, according to need. Incorruptible! Cato and Brutus combined . . . At an English exam, some years ago, he flunked everyone . . . Of course! he would say, they err scandalously when attempting the 'tee aitch'! A while later they caught him consulting the *Tautphoeus*: what the heck, Baron, is this famous 'tee aitch' that so many people get wrong?"

When, on the day of the dinner, I went up to the dorm with Egbert, the image of Ema (it was pleasant to suppress the "Dona") danced in my mind, miniaturized, small as a golden bee, vibrant and unaccountable.

I dreamed: She sat on the bed, and I knelt on the lacquered floor. She showed me her hand, cut of pure jasper, rosy nails, like inset petals. I strove to pick up her hand and kiss it, but the hand escaped me—it would approach then flee upward; sink again and escape farther away, toward the ceiling, toward the sky, and I saw it, unattainable up high, clear and open like a star.

She laughed at my pain, showed me her bare foot, inviting me to dress it, but no more than cover it with the ermine that lay there, the small, white, bloodless shoe, sole up, missing the warm comfort of the foot that wore it and gave it life. Envying the ermine, I bent over the weave of the silk stocking, that miracle of industry, product of the accumulated days and effort of this industrial century, its living fibers filtering the tender transparency of the blood, subtly wrapping the lovely knee, the leg, the ankle that had gloriously and irremediably despoiled pagan statuary. Oh, if only I were able to dress it! But I made her writhe, as I tried, with pain, in a burning torture of kisses, as I breathed out my soul all aflame.

What a different creature I was, as I woke! The enchanting apparition had vanished, but I suffered the tenebrous reaction that follows on such dazzling visions.

I continued to be cordial to Egbert. However, now his friendship seemed a weaker thing, as if there were in me a savage love in chains.

At times Egbert seemed an intruder. Walking with him was so different now from before—it was as if he were a third person. I preferred to be alone.

I don't know what demands of accommodation had me transferred to the older boys' dorm. It was a change that distanced me even more from Egbert; we now met only in the afternoons, in the field.

After classes I would go up to the dormitory, taking advantage of the slack policing of the hall.

The supervisor responsible for it was Silvino. Afraid of reprisals from the older boys, the prudent beadle let things slip by.

I would lie down, lazily, listening to the shouting from the yard as if it had nothing at all to do with my life. I counted the boards in the ceiling, a series of parallel lines that lost themselves in a glimmer of paint. Sometimes I read stories by Dumas that did not hold my attention. In other beds, lying down as I was, face up, feet crossed in their boots, other boys smoked, slowly blowing columns of smoke that rose, vertical, and curled, blue. In one corner, at the end of the room, three boys played cards, yawning, calling the rolls of the dice without enthusiasm, in a game of sleepwalkers. More than once, in the heavy afternoon drowsiness, my back warm against the mattress, I felt my eyes closing against the glare of the sun that I imagined burning outside, and fell asleep. When it was time for class or supper, a companion would pull me awake.

These intervals of dreamless drowsiness, my mind empty of ideas and of thought, were restful. Thinking made me impatient. What did I desire? There was always the despair of reclusion in the school, and of my age. I had nervous fits of activity, when I crisscrossed the yard in frantic steps, eagerly speeding up again and again, as if I were trying to overtake time. I was not even interested in the intrigues bubbling in the hall. And what intrigues! Specifically, the substance of the renowned mystery of the older boys' "chalet."

At one of the ends of the long hall, there stood Silvino's screen, a large pine box, halfway up to the ceiling, with a door and a window about ten inches square, from which emanated an odor of sweaty clothes and various other, indecipherable, unclean smells; from it emanated also, at night, increasing and decreasing, the loud, choking snores of some big-nosed creature.

The boys used drills to make peepholes, and had built up the legend of Silvino. After that, there was the special demographics of the third form, the distribution by regular families, or by eventual approximation, according to character, under the common device of "nothing there" or, as others understood it, "nothing to see." They praised examples of faithfulness, discussed betrayals, condemned attempts at seduction, improvised a theory of home and bed, sang a bacchic anthem to random caprice and passing enthusiasm. They called me "Alves's Sérgio." They judged the new arrivals from a perspective entirely their own. They bet on who would be first, demanded vows of silence before they passed on a story that they had, in turn, sworn not to tell anyone. They offered themselves up to hearty laughter, and exchanged crass anecdotes, accurate or not, according to demand and occasion. The entire obscure chronicle of the Athenaeum was composed right there, in strong and explicit terms, expurgating the fripperies of modesty, of untruth, and the scruples of investigative commissions. Get out, Silvino! He had nothing to do with the conversation of the boys. One of the best maxims at the chalet was this one, characteristic: "The headmaster is hereby revoked."

Everything that was extraordinary for the first and second grade levels was there normal and current. All ages, from Candido to Sanches.

In the lower grades there were some who tried to move to the third. Into the turbid atmosphere of intrigue entered the silent movement of fictions, the seriocomic drama of instincts, in conventional and coarse illusions. And the older boys adopted various characters with conviction, exploring the ephemeral moment of sensation, the tender novelty of an expression as elements of artifice, delighting in artifice, taking to heart the caricature of sensuality.

There were those who affected moderation in their caprices, knowing that they deviated from the rule, like the thief who knows to be honest in his thievery, with the serious, skittish air of the *femmes qui sortent*. There were the naive ones, perpetually childlike, who did it without evil intent, laughing aloud, in on the secret of preserving their innocence intact all though these extremes; there were those who embraced the profession enthusiastically, aware, frank, impetuous, showing off with pleasure, who did not forgive nature the original mistake of their orientation: ah, not to be a woman so as to be more of a woman!

Those formed a group apart, publicly known and happy about it, protected by general favor and understanding, unconfessed but evident, the perverse approval and amiable tolerance that always favors corruption, as a form of applause. There they were, the beautiful ephebes! Models of youthful grace and noble form. Sometimes they wore bracelets; at bathing time, they triumphed, nude, taking their time posing as nymphs by the water, showing up the others—fleshless skeletons, shapeless bodies, in their knit loincloths. There were the corrupted ones, miserable objects of honest contempt, at times used up before even being used, tormented by propensity on one side and repulsion on the other, almsless beggars for compassion, reduced to the extreme of resigning themselves deplorably to solitude.

In contrast, there were those who paraded male pride, hairy, tanned, with knotted muscles, large bones, as well as others shrunken with malice, insatiable, their voices shaking and their avid nostrils quivering like goats'; and the plump ones, their red lips loose, exhibiting superiority for never having cared about the ripeness of their blubber.

Angela dominated them all; she vanquished them.

The windows that opened on the headmaster's yard were strongly barred with wooden rods; through the spaces between them, we gaped.

Angela acted girlish, playing and running with a cat's liveliness. She rolled on the ground, wrapping her face in her dry, loose hair. She jumped, shaking her clothes in the air; she picked flowers and threw them, giving them out equally to all, since she loved all. When there were not too many at the railing from the hall, she became careless, showed herself in a corset and white skirt, loosening the cord over her bosom, showing her arm from the shoulder down, stretching with both hands at the back of the neck and elbows pointing up, telling the window endless stories, while among the folds of her chemise golden curls escaped from her armpits. Always in the sun! Always cheerful! Wild daughter of the light, indomitable fauna of hot climes, braving the heat like a lioness, impervious and proud.

She sang.

Only in song was she sad: nostalgic songs, suffused with the feel of distant things, a friendly home with parents, an adolescent's heart, known once, before it moved on forever, songs of the island where one heard the murmur of a calm ocean and of well-traveled breezes and the anguished scream of the seagulls and the distant noise of sailors at their work, background to an insistent refrain about love, the roguish love of the poor by the seashore, love made up of fish, of sad leisure and heat.

Sometimes she was coarse, exchanging rapid-fire, foul-mouthed repartee with anyone willing to engage; suddenly she would lose patience and disappear, throwing off a curse of carefully calibrated turpitude. She joked: she too had a school where she received boarders, off-campus students, half-pensioners. She tapped her belly.

And with her coarseness, with her mockery, with the sentimental refrains, the laxness about her corset, the flowers, the turbulence of an ill-bred child, Angela was the queen of attention and curiosity: the chalet was inflamed with conflagrations of enthusiasm. If any time went by without her appearing, they would glue themselves to the window bars, scanning the shadows under the trees in the yard, countless little faces, haggard with longing.

And she enjoyed watching the caged ardor of her boys, amusing herself by driving them desperate, like someone stirring up a fire to see the eruption of sparks, the eddies of flaming rubies, with a pleasure between the pride of the lady wooed by a hundred knights and the throbbing expectation of the feast of red meat in a lion's cage.

In time, I found out that a gang of clever boys had managed to loosen some of the bars in a window three or four beds beyond mine, and spent the night, after silence had fallen, taking the fresh air in the headmaster's garden. They preferred the dark nights, which held more stars and more secrets, and the rainy nights, which in matters of fresh air are more decisive. They descended by a rope made of braided sheets and sometimes came back drenched but always refreshed. For the sake of prudence, they did not go out in groups of more than two a night, one standing guard during the other's absence.

I said that the general preoccupations and intrigues of the great hall did not interest me; I was not being precise, and I don't know how I can be about this without resorting to the modalities of expression—actually or virtually—that an unjust anachronism has condemned. I did not care about facts; the spirit of the thing seduced me. Perhaps that was why I discovered the gang's sophistry, the banquet in the small hours, which felt like a theft against me, against the other boys, lost in the illusions of sleep, an odious betrayal of our careless foolishness. One night I was beset by the violent temptation to spread the news of the secret among all, demoralize the smarties, lead Silvino to the window to show him the loosened bars, and serve the traitors a well-deserved dose of betrayal in return. I considered the objections: apart from the ugly voluntary snitching, it could turn out to be a stupid move. Maybe it was already general knowledge and I had been left out, simply because I was only at the third grade level. I tried. I stayed awake till the proper hour, with the patience and effort of a seasoned hunter in his ambush. At the right moment, I rose in bed, rubbing my eyes, feigning surprise. They could not avoid initiating me. The two boys whose night it was told me. Malheiro was the leader of the joke, a joke involving nine, all very discreet and very skillful—also, whoever told would be beaten up.

My irritation against the sophism abated without disappearing. Any time that, by chance, one of the boys surprised the expeditionaries, he would immediately be enticed into the conspiracy, with a combination of privileges and threats. Malheiro's fabulous punch was the punishment.

I did not want the advantages, even without the punch. Not that I did not burn in the late hours, at the chalet! Ah, for a free walk in the garden, the open door to the forced cage. But a hesitation held me back, as of old promises to myself, promises to walk the straight and narrow—I don't quite know how to say it, old reasons of vertebrate vanity; aversion to subterfuges, or perhaps a fear that occurred to me at the last, unfounded: I might go some one time and, on trying to return, not find the rope by which to climb back.

Another sign that I had not escaped the common psychology of the chalet was the fit of rage I had to repress one day when they spoke of Dona Ema before me. What did I care about Dona Ema? A good lady, nothing more, who had paid excessive attention to me out of complacency, still always within the limits dictated by hospitality to many amiable people. She had left a simple memory of gratitude, which was beginning to fade.

The boys repeated the murmurings of Master Crisóstomo, petty nonsense. Through the barred windows they pointed, near the pool wall, to the shutters of the infirmary and sang the praises of the nurse, a careful little nurse with an incomparable way of dealing with the more serious matters of the heart. And there came the stories of students who fell very ill with imaginary ailments . . . All of that pained me, as if they were wounding the most sainted scruples of sentiment. These statements without proof were the highest infamy.

In the middle of this season of discontent, I had one day of pleasure, evil but perfect. The famous Romulo slept in the chalet. He occupied the whole iron cot with his ample flesh, snoring at the other end of the dorm, with the same intensity as Silvino; that demon spoke softly and snored loud. He was one of Malheiro's gang.

When it was his turn, they would reinforce the sheets and take out two more bars.

One night when I saw him descend, I had the idea of playing a trick on him. A very risky trick, as will become clear, but I counted, in the aftermath, on everyone's help, considering the need to hush up the whole business.

You will remember the unfounded fear I mentioned earlier. The comrade in charge of replacing the bars was on watch, till a signal from the yard asked for the rope. I offered to replace him. The comrade went to sleep.

With the cold blood of the best feats of revenge, and at complete leisure, I called back to mind the affront Romulo had offered me. It was fair. Bit by bit I pulled back the sheet rope, replaced the bars firmly, and went to sleep. It was raining hard; all the better: that injury, which blood would not have been able to wash, could well be washed away by torrential rain.

I was avenged!

The next day the tub of lard turned up shivering, sniffling, furious, in slippers without socks, pants and shirt as if salvaged from a shipwreck, miserable, surrounded by the surprise and mockery of all.

He had spent the night under the window, asking for mercy from the impassive slat till, at the break of day, Aristarco had found him in that pitiful state.

The bride had not seen him: she woke late. The father-in-law was smart enough to fathom the adventure. He pretended ignorance.

"Why, that boy!" he exclaimed with great intimate satisfaction.

And only found it strange that his good son-in-law had let himself be caught like an idiot.

Chapter 11

Master Claudio began a series of lectures on Saturdays, imitating Aristarco's Thursday ones, about moral commonplaces. Philosophy, science, literature, political economy, pedagogy, biography, even politics and hygiene, all of them were at some point proper subjects: highly interesting, not weighed down with details. After the headmaster's astronomy, I had not found anything else worthy of so many minutes of my attention.

He told us about life. The plutonian feasts of movement, of ignition; the genesis of rocks; the infernal fecundity of the primal fire, of granite, of porphyry, firstborn from the fire; the great millenary sleep of sediments rocked by titanic upheavals.

He spoke of anthracite and coal, mourning turned to stone, tragic memory of the many proud eras of the planet, monument of the prehistory of trees, black and devastated by the industry of men. He described the staircase of soils where the impressed footprint of the genius of metamorphoses rises from the forest vegetation of ancient ferns to Quaternary man. He spoke to us of Cuvier and the procession of resurgent monsters on their way to museums: the powerful slow megatherium, swaying as he paced, dirty, scraping grit, and the dry hard pieces of the diluvian wolf, solemn, conscious of the load of centuries he carries with him.

Then came the modern alluvial zones, the fertile arable soil. And the master went on to describe humid life in seeds, the evolution of the forest, the universal joy of chlorophyll in the light. He spoke to us about the kernel, the generous tree, the trunk that bleeds in Dante, which in the seas sustains commerce, British Neptune with a golden trident. He spoke to us of the obscure poetry of marine vegetation in the abysses and of the broom bush, isolated in the high snows, flower of desolate places, in the eternal exile of the inaccessible.

Then, the history of the brutes, the great male roaring in the virgin regions, the dramas of egoism in the jungle, the rude egoism of the force that can, blind, formidable, sacred as fatality. And he ran by us the entire series of classifications, showing life in the infinitesimal, the invisibly microbial; the omnipotence of numbers, in that unconscious society of monads, solidary unto death and the immortal reconstruction of the Earth.

Finally, man: womb, heart, and brain; politics, poems, thought; the soul, universe of the universe, God's image; immense reflector, anthropocentric, of light, of colors, which the Sun inflames, which the Sun does not feel.

One time, he spoke about education.

He addressed the question of boarding schools. He disagreed with the general opinion that disparaged them.

Is it an imperfect organization, teaching corruption, promoting contact among individuals of all origins? Is the teacher the personification of tyranny, injustice, terror? Does merit count for nothing, do sinuous lines of indignity snake through it, is spying approved, as well as flattery and humiliation? Does intrigue reign, does gossip, calumny, oppress the privileged of favoritism? Do the older and stronger boys bully, is there an abundance of perverse seduction, and does the audacity of the undeserving triumph? Does reclusion exacerbate inbred tendencies?

So much the better: the school schools for the larger society.

It is not enough to enlighten the spirit; tempering character is all. There has to come a day that shatters the illusion of domestic tenderness. The sooner that happens, the better.

Education does not form souls; it exercises them. And moral exercise does not come from beautiful words about virtue, but from friction against circumstances.

The energy to confront them is a heritage of the blood of those capable of morality, happy winners in destiny's lottery. The disinherited shall go to the slaughter.

Having tried it all out in the microcosm of the boarding school, there will be no more surprises in the large world outside, where all kinds of acquaintanceships will have to be suffered, all airs will have to be breathed; where the reasons of the strongest are the general dialectic and the evolution of all that crawls and all that bites will be all around us, because down-to-earth perfidy is one of the most efficacious processes of victorious vulgarity; where debasement is almost always the condition imposed by success, as if there were such a thing as a downward rise; where power is a leaden cupola weighing down higher aspirations; where the city is open to the Babylonian dissolutions of instinct; where whatever is worthless floats and comes to light, just as in the ocean the submerged pearls are ignored and what rises to the surface are foam and dead algae.

The boarding school is useful; life shakes it up like a prospector's sieve, separating what is worth something from what is worth nothing.

Every youth represents one direction. There will be disguises, hypocrisy, suggestions of ability, of intellectual enlightenment, but deep down the direction of character is immutable. A compass points in one direction only; we all have one necessary North; each one of us has stamped on his back the address to his predetermined fate. School does not deal in illusions: character shows itself with absolute frankness. What has to be is already. And most precisely, the encounter and confusion of classes and

fortunes levels all, eliminating those mistakes caused
by trappings that make certain aspects of life outside so
complicated, but that in the boarding school are erased
in the socialism of the rules.

And let it not be said that it is a hatchery of bad germs,
a nefarious seminary of bad principles that will flower
later. The boarding school does not create society, but
reflects it. The corruption that flowers in it comes from
the outside. The characters that triumph there bring
their passport to success with them, just as those who lose
bring with them the mark of their condemnation.

A day school is a false middle term as far as moral education goes. It is not impressed by life outside, because
the family continues to exert its influence; neither does
it live socially to encourage observation, because it is not
a world apart, as is provided only by the great boarding
schools. These, with the sum of their possible defects,
convey the practical education in virtue, the schooling
of the smith at the forge, the training of the fighter as he
engages in the fight. The weak are sacrificed; they do not
prevail: gyms are for those privileged with health. Rheu-
matism is a terrible acrobat. It is a serious error to fight
the institution of the boarding school.

It is necessary for it to become established, to grow,
to flourish and multiply, for it offers a positive education
in social conflict with its bad educators and dangerous
company, in the corrupting communion, in the tedium
of the cloister, the inaction of the prison. It is necessary
that the generous ardor of the primitive and naive soul
be disciplined through crude and premature disillusion;
it is never too early to feel that the future consists of
more than strolling at ease, hands at one's back, eyes
on the clouds, in the unobstructed plazas of Plato's
republic.

During the talk, I thought about Franco, onerously applying every one of the teacher's opinions to that poor boy, chosen by misfortunc, paying his rent to disdain, every trimester,
abandoned in that house. I remembered the judge from Mato
Grosso and the letter I had read, and the sister who had been
abducted, the extravagant revenge of the glass shards, the low
timidity of his manners, the mute concentration of hatred, the
incomplete movements of rebellion, the final submission of
the shunned, resigned to his fate. I pitied him.

After the talk I went to visit him.

He was in bed in the Green Room, on the right, close to the
windows. He had been unwell since the last time he had gone
to the prison.

Under the house. One entered by way of the cement-floored
hall to the lavatories; one could feel the impact of absolute
darkness. Toward the sides, in the distance, there glimmered,
like white eyes, some barred breathing vents in that huge
cellar. The ground was pounded earth, not quite dry. Immediately one noticed a dank smell of crushed mushrooms. As
one's sight became accustomed to the half-light of the breathing holes, one could discern in the middle of the room a kind
of cage or thicket of strong pine bars. Inside the cage there
were a bench and a plank nailed in as a table. On the table
stood an earthenware inkpot. That was the dungeon.

The condemned would be caged there in the amiable company of remorse and execration; on top of that, he would be
given a task of writing pages, the most difficult part of which
was to find enough light. From time to time, a rat would rush
through the darkness; sometimes some of the repugnant little animals from murky places climbed up the boy's legs. Released, the prisoner emerged, pale as a ghost, dazed by the
clear air, unable to believe in it. Some found ways to return
truly downcast.

Franco came back ill.

Some of his fellows showed an interest in him. He replied with harshness; there was nothing wrong with him! All were guilty; he would fall ill; he would fall gravely ill so they would be sorry, full of remorse, they themselves, Silvino, Aristarco, all his tormentors! He reasoned like old-school victims, who let themselves die, trusting their ghosts would return. And he hid his suffering.

For weeks he was devoured by a slight but impertinent fever. On purpose, he exposed himself to the hot sun and to the dew.

One day he was unable to rise.

A slight headache, he explained. He felt nauseous, and ran to the window. Under it there was a magnolia, thick as a whole copse; in the intervals between fits he would entertain himself by aligning the viscous thread of his vomit with the large white flowers.

I found him in bad shape.

His head buried in his pillow, covered with a number of blankets his neighbors had relinquished to him, he affected the childish carelessness, the horrifying, supreme indifference of those who are not going far. I was surprised and terrified.

Called in by Aristarco, the doctor had come twice. He rejected the idea of moving him, recommended being careful about opening windows, diagnosed some harmless fever, and wrote a prescription, departing both times with the hermetic discretion that signals the importance of the class.

I asked Franco how he was doing. He slowly moved his eyelids and smiled. I had never seen such a beautiful smile on him, the smile of a dying child. It was eight o'clock in the evening. The attenuated gaslight created saddening effluvia of clarity. I left without looking at the other dormitories whose windows would have reflected my shadow as I passed. I sought out the headmaster and communicated my fears to him.

The next day, a sunny Sunday, Franco was dead.

The agent turned up in person for the indispensable arrangements. The body was transferred to the chapel, where the bier had been set up. Aristarco cried, but the cortège was modest; it was not appropriate for the school to engage in a grand burial, which might have advertised it as insalubrious.

I did not see anything; when I returned to the Green Room, everything was over with. Some inquisitive boys were rummaging in the spoils his death had left in his drawer: a frayed toothbrush dyed red by some Chinese powder, an old belt without its buckle, a fat photo of a woman uncovering her breasts, random letters, and a considerable packet of "good grades," collected who knows how, with forged teachers' signatures and Franco's name, a fraudulent proof of success with which the poor boy intended to amaze the magistrate from Cuiabá.

As the bed was stripped, a card fell from the sheets: a print showing St. Rosalie! My missing patron saint. Perhaps he had died kissing her, the pariah.

Soon after, the Athenaeum put on its festive garb.

It was the preparation for the biennial distribution of prizes. The donors were hungry for crowns. Classes were suspended. It was necessary to start preparing way ahead because the plans were for things never seen before. Some of the students had forewarned the headmaster that they had a surprise in store for him: the dedication of a bronze bust! Aristarco was preparing for the surprise with all his soul. A bust! That was the due reward for all his priceless efforts, the longed-for statue. It was arriving in pieces. They started with the head; later they would offer him the abdomen, a beautiful metallic belly and the magnificent navel of a corpulent bonzo—or hypocrite, aggressive as a punch; then the rest of the body, in slices, gradually. Ah, when they finally presented him with the boots! Then more would be needed: the pedestal, which he would offer himself, to expedite the process. And he would screw together the accumulated pieces of his pride, the heap of his desires, the statue! Produced little by little from the slow sincerity of the oblations, the difficult glory ready for the long scrutiny of the centuries.

It would have to be a ceremony the likes of which could not be found in the memory of the celebrations of triumphant pedagogy—an obelisk of expenses, of luxury, of splendor, from the top of which, as from the eruption of a crater, there would jump out the surprise, rewarding his high qualities, and a supreme retort to his rivals' challenges.

There was no room in the Athenaeum big enough to accommodate such a gala, not even the covered yard. It was decided that the central yard would be covered with a canvas sheet, held by great masts conveniently planted. An incalculable tent, the biggest tent ever conceived by human imagination, one that would keep four thousand guests in the shade, with cloth borrowed from all available awnings, the sails of an entire fleet. Under it, the stands, and in the middle, a large arena reserved for the laureates. Through the adjutant-general of the Navy, who had two sons in the establishment, it was easy to obtain all that canvas.

For several days, large shipments of cloth arrived at the Athenaeum. The bolts were laid out in the yard, along the walls. Then the lumber and the carpenters turned up, a whole crowd of carpenters.

The students moved among the workers, helping, interfering, running, jumping, shouting, anticipating the joy of the solemn day. Aristarco approved of the tumult; he wanted to see them happy. Franco's death had created a shadow of panic; some of the boys had even gone home, afraid of the fever.

The bustle of the preparations reanimated the Athenaeum. In a few days the yard became cluttered with poles and girders, planks and sawhorses, like a huge shipyard. Hammers hammered everywhere with the continuous crackle of artillery. The ground disappeared under the sawdust generated by the activity. Aristarco oversaw the operations like a foreman, making his rounds, silent, grave, happily breathing in the emanations of the fresh sawdust, a workshop smell of industry, listening to the scrape of the saws like the noise of a factory, like the breaths of steam moving the powerful up-and-down of pistons. There was a special pleasure in that, in the forest of beams and rafters, and in the efforts of so many active and busy men to honor him, the planks singing under the blows of the mallets, the ladders and stands unfolding like a call to glorification, while he looked forward at the total effect, when all would be velveteen and fine cotton cloth, and the gathered populace would invade and take over, in an earthquake of acclamations for the bust, itself haughty and gleaming.

No greater or nobler pride was that of the monarchs of the pyramids, colossal and macabre idiots, useless architects of tombs.

The carpenters left, and the riggers presented themselves, and covered the timbering with the awnings and the sails, like a canvas sky. The windows on the yard now opened on the amphitheater like tribunes.

The riggers lavished on the valances all the pride of their talent. Everything—in the combination of brilliant colors, the flowing flounces of gauzy cotton, the painted lambrequins of the bandstand, the cardboard columns—that could create an effect of pomp, all that could be done with the spectacular combination of stagecraft and batten, was profusely set up in that yard.

In the central arena a brown rug with light-colored flowers spread itself out. In parts of the stands, conveniently placed, chairs were lined up. Students and the lesser attendees were to be seated on the hard boards. The openings in the construction, which could not be left in that state, were covered in velvet held with gold and crimson braid. Above the seats there was a line of balusters spiraled with ribbons. On each baluster, a shield with the name of a famous pedagogue. Tactfully, they had included Aristarco's name several times. Aristarco did not let on he had noticed.

One of the sides of the carpet rose in waves over four steps toward a long platform, fronting the entrance of the amphitheater, supported by the wall of the large study hall. On it there was a throne, under a canopy, for the Princess Regent. From time to time, tired of moving around, Aristarco climbed to the throne and sat. He liked having the canopy over him. And from there he gave orders to the riggers, like a prudent sovereign dictating the splendor of his coronation.

The originators of the subscription for the bust had finished their task. There were two of them: Climaco, a scholarship student, and the drawing teacher. Climaco, a young man with a practical turn, did not take long to come up with a brilliant idea. What if we offered a bust to our director? At first he thought of soliciting the nonpaying students, but rejected the idea immediately as impracticable. Gratitude could be subscribed to by everyone—that made it considerably cheaper. He started his campaign. The first ones he asked were left cold by the idea. Hell! They were not about to be grateful like that, from one moment to the next. Let him consult fellow students, and if the idea caught on, they would certainly be in on it. The more timid ones signed on right away; some among the younger ones signed without knowing exactly what was involved. In a few minutes, the existence of the subscription was in the public domain. And after that, there was the irresistible pressure of the fact. What stinginess! How could anyone hesitate about ten *mil-réis*? Who would dare be absent from the list of the public proof of gratitude that the offer of the bust meant? It would be an insult to the headmaster! The first signatories were in fierce contention with each other at coercing the rest, as if they did not want to be the only ones to have been bled.

The initiators' efforts were no longer necessary. The idea spread by itself: within two days the subscription was completed. Many paid up immediately; those who did not have the money went to search for some at the office, and in secret the accountant debited the amount, among miscellaneous expenses, on the trimester's bill. Given the ease of obtaining the money, Climaco decided, sensibly, to do away with the discounts to the nonpaying students; they had joined with sincere intention. Reasonable. When the preparations for the solemnities began, the bust, the work of a zealous artist, was already cast.

On November 13, at nine in the morning, people began to arrive. The amphitheater in the yard was still closed. On arrival, the guests greeted the headmaster and then dispersed in groups throughout the garden, or they walked through the rooms of the establishment, examining the teaching equipment, the charts on the walls, the wise maxims, meditating on the seriousness with which teaching was taken in that house. The crowd grew. The invitations had been widely distributed throughout the city. At eleven it was hard to move in the Athenaeum.

The ceremony would begin at two. At noon the amphitheater was opened.

It was as if the bosom of Abraham had been thrown open. The workers' last touches had been as good as their first efforts. High up, around the entire rank of stands, crisscrossing, braided draperies swayed pink, like children's smiles, graced by an orange strip like sunrise; immediately after that came a zone of vivid scarlet, drawing as from its veins the blood of the highest jubilation; straight rose the columns with the escutcheons, and under those, eight superb ranks of stands trimmed in velvet and gold. By the throne a platform rose for the faculty; on the opposite side, symmetrically, stood another platform for the band and the choir. The canvas ceiling was no longer visible; under it, enormous garlands of branches and flowers formed a gracefully disordered tangle, hanging like a spring shower ready to rain down. Between the dark green of the festoons hanging from the ceiling and the brown carpet reigned the obscure serenity of cathedrals and forests, a penetrating mist of contemplation. As they entered, the guests fell silent. All one heard were low voices, whispers as if at Mass, as if muted in velvet, pillowed, as if the carpet were speaking. The valances in the cornice vibrated, out of tune with the religious melancholy of the place. Some strips of canvas above the foliage presented a further contrast, open to the irruption of the light of day.

The students entered in uniform, climbed to their places, and sat, on the left, shaking the whole carpentered construction. Aristarco stood at the door. A huge red curtain with large tassels opened above him as if to show him off. He wore black trousers and a tailcoat, his chest covered with medals as with armor, a dignitary's ribbon around his neck, throttling him with nobility. Marvel! The supreme correctness, the imposing scale of his form, the dominating majesty of his presence, all fused in one, his belly pushed out with conceit. The students looked at him with the pleasure of the soldier proud of his commandant. There he was, the enviable Master, standing straight, brilliant for the celebration, as if he had swallowed an iron rod.

Around Aristarco stood his adjutants and, hurrying past, the members of a reception committee made up of the best-looking teachers and students similarly blessed. With the headmaster they put on an interesting ceremonial of hospitality. A multitude of guests crowded at the entrance of the amphitheater. Aristarco and his helpers checked, sniffed, found the parents, the families of higher social standing, and fished them out for preferred access, over those standing closer to admission. The chosen ones were taken to the stands with the chairs. If the officials found in those special places anyone they had not taken there, they would gently invite them to rise, since the family of the Viscount of Three Stars could not possibly be seated on naked planks. The rigor with which they had to follow etiquette made the committee sweat, embarrassed amid the mass of competitors. Aristarco would also take advantage of the situation to retaliate against those who were slower at paying tuition. Finally, the fishing for the select few became obvious. There were mutterings, quivers of incipient rebellion: the invitations had all been the same! And taking advantage of the crowd, many began to sneak in without waiting for the courtesy committee.

The amphitheater filled up in a tumult.

Her Royal Highness, with her august spouse, arrived punctually at two, answering the invitation she had received before anyone else.

At three minutes past two, Aristarco walked up to the tribune. I do not need to say that the old rattletrap had suffered another of the great upheavals of its ill-fated existence. There it was, square and patient, exercising its job as a rhetoric-bearer. It stood to the right of the princess's throne and supported the choir.

Aristarco bowed slightly to the Gracious Lady. He let his eye wander over the amphitheater. He could not say a word. For the first time in his life, he felt anxious before an audience. The mass of attendees crowded, curious, along the line of stands, in a horseshoe curve. The black of dress coats and suit coats hung in space as a bewildering darkness; he was frightened by the vast, gloomy semicircle. The mass of the public made it impossible for him to recognize a friendly face that would encourage him. But it was urgent that he should improvise something to preface the scribbled eloquence he was carrying with him on strips of paper. Then his gaze met an object that recalled him to himself. In front of the tribune there rose a pedestal in burnished wood; on the pedestal, an indeterminate form, mysteriously wrapped in a cloak of green

wool. The surprise! It was him, there, cloaked in the expectation of his opportunity; he, fearless in bronze, his effigy, his
stimulus, his example: more himself than he, who was shaking, because bronze was the truth of his character, which one
absurd moment of weakness was disfiguring and diminish-
ing. He remembered that the vast tent, the flower garlands,
the timbering, the velveteen, the architecture of the stands,
the pinned-up trim, all the valances, the gaze of his disciples,
the presence of the public, the bust under its green cape, all
of it was his triumph and there for the sake of his triumph,
and his embarrassment dissipated. Inspiration boiled up in his
throat and choked him, vibrated like electricity on his tongue,
and he spoke. He spoke as he never had before; he forgot the
useless tome he had brought with him, he improvised like De-
mosthenes, he flooded the arena, the steps to the throne, all
the ranks of the stands up to the eighth, with the most astonishing barrage of eloquence ever to have flooded the earth.

Easy to guess the subject. Thanks; then the account of his
sufferings as an apostle. He opened the tailcoat and showed.
Under the medals he had the scars. The arrows that had pierced
his soul could not be seen clearly because of his vest. One
could gauge by the description: it must have been horrible.
After the suffering, the service.

The educator is like the music of the future, which one
encounters one day but only understands on the next: only
posterity could judge. As for his past, let us not talk about it! It
was out of modesty that he did not look back, so he would not
turn into a monument, like Lot's wife. With the Athenaeum
he was content; it was a reasonable seedbed; it was not shy
about growing tall. Hearts like the purple earth where coffee
grew into fortunes, where the seeds of virtue grew so well. As
soon as the seed fell on it, virtue popped up. Marvelous, that
fecund garden! Before anyone spoke ill of the farmer, let the
slanderers and the envious consider the cabbages he grew,

weigh the turnips and the thick-stemmed kale, curly, modest, obliging, the innocent lettuces, the sensitive onions, with their tears as easy as they were sincere, the knowledgeable potatoes, the delicate squashes that everyone always intends to plant but does not; the garlic family, eternal types, sometimes in the form of leeks whose liveliness profited all; not counting the goose-pimpled gherkins, the congested eggplants, or the unspeakable wormseed, the bitter cress, the insignificant spinach, or on the other hand, the Malabar spinach, the okra, and the white and blue dayflower by the pool, which has a pretty bloom but in the end is a weed. Edenic garden he was proud of cultivating! The award ceremony would show that.

To conclude, he went back to flog the dead horse some more by demurring about self-praise; he preferred a simple rhetorical firecracker, knowing that Venancio, the master flunky, would speak as well and would once more prove himself a dedicated page, who always fought him for the privilege of helping to carry the cloak of his glory, if only by a little corner.

Then there were some pieces by the Athenaeum band and the school anthems.

It was said that Aristarco had ordered the inclusion of a drum solo in the instrumental portion of the program so he could show off his son-in-law. Mockery.

The award distribution part was, as it should be, exuberant. Aristarco read a report on the literary movement of the last two years. He recited the names of all the students who had won gold and silver medals since the founding of the institution, and invited the secretary to evoke the new recipients, in order of their merit. The list was extensive. At each name a student would walk down, white with emotion, stumbling, and then cross the arena.

To the left of the throne there was a long table at which were seated His Excellency, the minister of the empire, and various luminaries from Public Education.

Before them, piled up and hiding them, there rose one green pyramid of crowns made of oak, paper, and wire, and another of gold and the same. Gold for the medal recipients, oak for the rest, in vast quantities.

On the platform, close by, towers of luxuriously bound books. The prizewinner would receive three, two, or one of those volumes, the medal, the honorable mention, and a friendly little sermon from the minister, and leave, dazed.

On his way out, from behind him, treacherously, an inspector would push a paper crown on his head, all the way to his eyes when it was too big, and worse still when it was too small because then the miserable laureate had to balance it all the way to the stands.

The public clapped, maybe for the prize, or maybe for his luck.

Ribas, Little Hunchback Mata, Nearco, Saulo the prominent, and another received gold medals. Romulo, Malheiro, Climaco, Sanches, Maurílio, Barreto, and about fifteen others got silver. I, Egbert, Cruz the doctrine expert, the ginger-haired Barbalho, Little Almeida, Negrão, and numerous others, a simple honorable mention. Nonrecipients had the satisfaction of uttering low jeers about the justice of the selection and distribution.

Among the mass of guests—several hundred representatives of good society—there were some truly notable persons: titleholders of solid greatness, moneyed men with the most solid titles, political figures of handsome appearance and sonorous traditions, some displaying on their brows the thoughtful snow of the hibernal Senate, others the youthful energy of the time-limited Chamber, doctors made famous by surgical exploits or simply through the reciprocal vivisection of illnesses on public display.

There were journalists, authors, composers, and among the ladies, gathered mainly in the special stands, one could recognize haughty queenly profiles in the full flowering of their beauty, which the soft light of the room enveloped in an ideal mist. There were impressive displays of jewelry and garments; there was youth with unnerving or ravishing eyes and lips, brunettes magically invoking the torpor of the sensual siesta with the oppressive caress of a small, victorious foot, and blondes inviting an embrace to transport one to the clouds, higher still! to the eternal retreat where love and double stars reside . . . None of that was the great attraction; none could rise for us by a single span in the general perspective of the crowd: our great preoccupation was the poet. "The poet!" whispered the school, some searching, some pointing. That was him, hand on hip, flashy on the teachers' platform, pouring out toward the persons closest to him an astonishing profusion of sideburns.

From between the sideburns, like birdsong from the woods, there issued a handsome nose, an alexandrine with two hemistichs, artistically long, hiding the bridge in the caesura, precisely as called forth by fashion on Parnassus. At the root of the poetic appendix there flashed two very bright eyes, round, owl-like, like those of Minerva. So bright were they, deep in their sockets, that one could see in them how brightly the depth of the stanza must shine. The great Dr. Icarus de Nascimento! He had come to the Athenaeum especially to declaim a famous poem that had become obligatory at all school festivities in Rio: *The Educator*. Immediately after the prizes, he spoke.

For half an hour a strange thing happened: an anguished convulsion of whiskers in space. Expanding. The poet disappeared; the platform disappeared; the amphitheater filled up; gone was the throne together with Her Imperial Highness, the long table with Aristarco and His Imperial Excellency; the stands fell into a tangle, and all disappeared in an incalculable expansion of sideburns, a jubilee of chins. No one could see anything in this stormy chaos of hair, through which passed a voice like thunder, a tremendous charge of squadrons cutting through the thick darkness, tramping verses, horse kicks, smashing their way to the front.

Eventually the nose became visible again. Slowly the whiskers calmed down, receding like a flood. The poem had come to its end. Nobody had understood a word of the delivery, but the impression was formidable.

After a part of a concert that felt like rest and restoration, there came the presentation of the bust. Master Venancio had the word.

Aristarco, at the long table, suffered the second convulsion of terror at the ceremony. He made an effort, prepared himself. Sometimes one needs as much fortitude to face a frontal attack of praise as to survive one of aggression. Even vanity becomes a coward. Venancio was about to speak: courage! The oscillation of the censer can make one nauseous. He was afraid of something that might be the migraine of the gods: dizziness from too much incense. He loved praise intensely. But Venancio was too much. And before all these people! No matter. Long live heroism.

It was proper to take on a posture severe and Olympian, to match Venancio's celebration. Done!

The orator patiently gathered all the glorifying epithets, from the rare metal of sincerity to the vibrating, ductile copper of adulation. He fused the mixture in a fire of warm emphases and hit on that mass like a Cyclops, for a long time, till he had shaped the monumental image of the headmaster.

After his earlier fears, Aristarco forgot himself in the delight of a metamorphosis. Venancio was his sculptor.

The statue was no longer an aspiration: it was forged right there. He felt his flesh turning into metal as Venancio spoke. He was experiencing the reverse of the pleasure of the transmutation of brute matter when penetrated and animated by the artistic soul: an iron coldness was freezing his limbs; on his skin, his hands, his face, he saw or guessed unknown glimmers of polish. The folds in his clothing were as if welded into a fixed mold. Inside, he felt strangely massive, as if he had drunk plaster. His blood slowed in his compressed arteries. He was losing the feeling of his clothes; he was turning to stone, mineralized. He was not a human being, but an inorganic body, an inert rock, a metal block, foundry slag, bronze shape, living the external life of sculptures, without consciousness, without individuality, dead on his chair, O glory! turned into a statue.

"Let us crown him!" suddenly shouted Venancio.

At that moment Climaco, strategically positioned, pulled on a cord. From the torn green cape emerged the surprise: the offering—the bust. A ray from the low afternoon sun made its way through the canvas, as if on cue, shattering against the new metal.

"Let us crown him!" repeated Venancio, amid a windstorm of acclamation. And taking from the tribune a splendid crown of laurel, which no one had seen, placed it on the sculpture.

Aristarco came to his senses. Venancio's entire encomiastic oration had referred to the bust. Nothing for him in those beautiful phrases! He was jealous. The pleasure of the metamorphosis was a hallucination. It was the bust that had been acclaimed; it was the bust that had been deified. As for him, he was still poor Aristarco, of mortal flesh and blood. Even Venancio, the faithful Venancio, had abandoned him. And all because of that, of that paltry thing on the pedestal, that piece of Aristarco that was not even a person.

As soon as the teacher stopped speaking, one could see Aristarco rising, frantically crossing the carpeted space and tearing the laurel crown from the bust.

All lauded the magnitude of his modesty.

But the day had become insipid to the headmaster. In confusion, he ruminated the sadness of that new rivalry—the invincible bronze.

Why don't great men use pedestals instead of armchairs?

What is the good of a statue, if it is not us? The use of pedestals as part of the furniture would at least have the advantage of making it easier to enjoy the taste of glory, practical glory, actual glory, effective glory.

In a corner, over there, was the pillar. When the need arose, nothing easier than to climb the height, take the pose, wait motionless till the spasm passed. But . . . maybe not! It was necessary to accept the bitter truth.

The monument does not need the hero, does not know him, discharges him and replaces him, crushes him, annuls him.

The devil! Why should immortality, in the end, be like that: a piece of marble over a dead body?!

At dusk the guests began to leave, the families, the confused multitude of joys and resentments. Mothers bestowed warm caresses on the sons who had not received any prizes; their fathers hated the headmaster and looked like the vanquished at those who went by contented, the other parents, the son's classmates, less pleased with their own victory than with the humiliation of the others.

Humble, in one corner, on the margin of the current of those who left, just outside the entrance of the amphitheater, they showed me a family in mourning—Franco's family. The judge, hat in hand, forgetting to cover his head: a short man, with a sad face, a long gray beard, bald, with small eyes and puffy lids.

He had come from Mato Grosso one year later than he had planned. The agent had sent him the news.

Now he was showing Rio de Janeiro to his family. He had come to the school feast, to the son's school to entertain his daughter, the one who had been abducted, and who was there with her mother and two younger sisters, very pale, thin, in a somber idiocy of incurable melancholy and silence, her lashes down, her gaze on the ground, as if expecting to find something.

Chapter 12

Strange music, at the hottest hour. Must have been Gottschalk. That agonizing effort of sound, slow, plangent, the delicious anguish of extreme pleasure for which one could give one's life because its conclusion was triumphant. Grave notes, one and then another, pauses of silence and darkness to which the instrument succumbs, and then a bright day of rebirth that lights up the world like the fantastic instant of a bolt of lightning immediately felled again by darkness . . .

Some memories of sound remain forever, like an echo of the past. At times I remember the piano, and that date rises in my memory.

From the deep rest of convalescence, in the extenuated serenity in which we are left by a fever, infantilized by weakness as if we were starting life again, helpless against sensation through a morbid refinement of sensibility—I breathed in the music like the exquisitely sweet intoxication of a baneful perfume: music enveloped me in a contagion of vibrations as if the air had nerves. The distant notes grew in my soul, resonating as in a cistern; I suffered, as with the strong palpitations of the heart when feeling is exacerbated, the dissolving sensuality of sound.

Slack, on top of the sheets, in the ideal comfort of the tomb, since the will was dead, I allowed the charm to martyr me. Imagination grew wings and, loosened, escaped.

I recognized ancient visions, on the ceiling of the infirmary, on the pale pink wallpaper—an appropriate color, sickly and faint . . . That white face, hair like that of a water sprite, flowing loose, very dark and wavy, to both sides of a face I had adored when I was seven and who had had for me a stanza (parody of one in an almanac, if I am to tell the truth, and given to her, painful mockery! by none other than her fiancé); another face, just as white, small, dead, whom I had loved so much, whose existence in the world had been like the flight of diaphanous garments in dreams, carried away, like the fugitive song from an angel choir absorbed by the blueness of the sky . . . Other confused memories, precipitous, soft, tireless mutations of the clouds, carrying one joyfully away in the giddiness of heights; smooth escapades on a tilt of flight, oscillations of a prodigious aerostat, serene in the air.

Complete landscapes, a departure, hugs, tears, the black steamer on the quiet and bottomless emerald waters, the small white rope railing around the poop, the lifeboats like large flat necklaces, lines lost to sight upward along the masts, currents dissolving in the vitreous thickness of the sea; the golden chamber, low, suffocating, the hubbub of those who get settled for their stay, of those hurrying to go down to the lifeboats . . .

A window. Below, the large grassy surface where clothes were bleached; farther on, mango trees rounding their somber crowns against the clear canvas of the sky; beyond the mangoes, cumuli visibly rising like globes, a colossal silver forest; on the other side, tree-covered mountains exposing here and there rusty pectorals like old armor. On the grass, spread out under the sun, there were clothes, iridescent from soap, long stockings with red borders rolled out, longing for the absent legs, large sheets, dresses wrinkled with moisture; above the bleaching area, ropes, and hanging from the ropes, transparent chemises, cut out, bordered with lace, sleeveless, slowly dripping tears from the wash as if they were sweating in the sun the sweat of much toil, white skirts dancing in the breeze the choreographic memories of the latest evening ball.

When the wind was stronger, it puffed up the hanging clothes, filling the shirts and skirts with women's bellies. Angela turned up. Always in her own sunbeam, like the fairies in moonbeams. She greeted me at the window with an exclamation like that of a surprised boy. Coatless, carrying over her hands, piled up, two heaps of rinsed clothes. She helped the washerwoman, to pass the time. She would speak looking up, braving the day without shading her eyes.

She was bored, feeling lazy; she wanted to lie on someone's lap! and she started one of her infinite stories, told slowly, as if melting on her hot lips, retold from when she was a little girl, immigration adventures, the houses where she had worked. She told the origins of the drama from the past year . . . she had tried to accommodate both men to see if things would turn out well; bad luck would not have it. Now, to tell the truth, she liked the one who had died better than the other. The murderer was very nasty, demanded things from her as if she were a slave; he was brutish, very brutish. But he was from Spain, a travel companion, and a handsome man! vigorous—I had seen him. But he mistreated her, hit her, pushed her: look she still had the marks, and innocently she lifted her dress to show, on her knee, on her thigh, scars, old bruises that I did not see at all, and neither did she.

The music would stop.

The open shutters let in the light. With it came an imperceptible murmur of trees, distant voices, muted birdsong, indistinct human cries attenuated by the immense distance, tiny hammer blows from building sites, the tremor of cars on the streets, extreme miniatures of thunder, tiny particles of life floating like dust in the light.

The door to the infirmary opened slowly, and in her morning attire of elegant and loose muslin there appeared the amiable lady. She had come to see if I was sleeping, to know how I was doing now.

Her presence was enough to reanimate me in my bed. So good, so good and tender a nurse, a mother.

Close to the bed, a modest night table and a chair. Dona Ema sat. She rested her elbows on the edge of the mattress, and her eyes on mine—that unforgettable look, black, deep as an abyss, bordered by all the seductions of vertigo. I could not resist; I closed my eyes; I could still feel on my lids the velvet breath, the caress of that attention.

After some time, the lady rested her small, cool, fine hand on my forehead, to see if I was still feverish, and it felt delicious as a crown of happiness.

I became lost in a nameless drowsiness that none of the sweetest vapors of Eastern narcotics would ever be able to reproduce.

Under that bracing therapeutic, my health returned quickly.

Soon after the physical education ceremony, which took place after the great solemnity of the prizes, I had fallen ill. Chicken pox, no less. Because of my sufferings, my father had taken off for Europe with the family. I had been left at the Athenaeum, under the care of the headmaster as if he had been an agent.

Half a dozen boys were my companions. How terribly lonely was the deserted Athenaeum. In the yard, silence slept in the sun, like a lizard. We drifted, yawning, through the school-rooms where the desks had been piled up in one corner; on the walls, a few nails still stuck in the plaster, holding up charts and leftover framed maxims, for the sake of the greatest possible insipidity, those with the most stubborn moral counsel. In the dorms, the unmade beds showed their white-painted iron skeletons, the crisscrossing slabs. There began the vast job of washing, varnishing, plastering; painters arrived to redo those parts of the building that have to be renovated every year.

Sad vacation recluses, we felt, amid all that general restoration, like antiques, left over from the year past, with the deplorable disadvantage of not being eligible for repainting or replastering.

In that situation, as if from the excess brilliance of the walls under the sun, reflecting light onto the tepid melancholy of the surrounding hills, my eyes began to hurt till they shed tears, my tongue was coated with an unpleasant taste of raw chestnuts. Was that the taste of boredom? My head felt heavy, and so did my body, as if I were being encased in lead.

I spent a few days like that, without complaining. One morning, I saw on my body an anthill of little red dots. Aristarco had me taken to the infirmary, an extension of his residence on the side of the pool. The doctor came, the same who had treated Franco; he did not kill me. Dona Ema was my true rescuer. She knew how to nurse the sick, how to encourage and caress, so that even the pain of the treatment she provided became a kind of resurrection.

The infirmary was just a wing of the house, a kind of lateral pavilion, with an independent entrance from the farmstead, communicating with the other rooms from inside.

The lady never left the infirmary. She watched over me as I slept, as I raved, like a sister of charity.

Aristarco turned up at times, solemnly, and did not stay. Angela never came—she had been forbidden to enter.

By the bed, Dona Ema was touched by my pallor and prostration whenever I reopened my eyes after one of those periods of fevered sleep, which look so much like death. Then she would take my hand in hers for a long time; her eyes shone as if with tears. It was she who brought the food I was allowed to eat. Sometimes, with tender playfulness, she offered to feed me herself, tasting the sago on the little spoon with an adorable pursing of the lips as if for a kiss. If she had to walk around the room, to change a flask or open the window, she did so like a shadow on a down-covered floor.

I felt deliciously small in that cozy circle, as in a nest.

When I entered into convalescence, the graceful nurse became cheery. Behind the doctor's back, she inebriated me with her medicine of laughter, an inimitable laugh as of tumbling pearls, burbling up on any pretext. She chattered, moved around like an imprisoned bird. She sang, sometimes, to make me sleep, unknown songs, so finely done, so subtly, that the sounds almost died on her lips, soft like the flutter of an expiring butterfly. When she thought me asleep, she would arrange the quilt round my shoulders and smooth it over my body; once she kissed my temple. And then she would leave, imperceptibly, evaporating.

Because of some quirk of the acoustics of the various parts of the house, one could hear quite well, but softened, the sound of the piano in the living room. The gentle lady, in order to still send over to me, in her absence, something that would caress me, that would be pleasant to me, translated onto the piano, with the same feeling softness, the songs she knew to sing. No violence in the execution. Only feeling, the melodic succession of deep sounds, distinct like the November ringing of the bronze bells; then a brilliant sequence of tears, collected in a sea of repose, final, serene, comforting . . . moving musical effects as Schopenhauer describes them: form without matter, a crowd of airy spirits.

The first time I got up, still shaky and weak, Ema helped me walk to the window. Ten o'clock. The earth still kept its morning freshness. Before us, the verdant garden, constellated with daisies; then, the ivied wall, bamboo to its right; a patch of grasses in front, the houses, towers, more houses, roofs in the distance, the city. Everything looked strange to me, renewed. A curious splendor lay on that spectacle. For the first time, I was delighted with those gradations of green: the blackish, shiny, stoneware green of the ivy; the lighter, flowing green of the bamboo; the very light green of the field visible over the wall, in all the splendor of the morning. Roofs! what novelty! What novelty, the profile of a chimney inscribed in space! Ema gave herself up, as I did, to the pleasure of vision. She held me in a light embrace; she touched me with her hip as she rested on it.

Absorbed in the contemplation of the morning, suffused with tenderness, I bent my head on Ema's shoulder, like a son, half closing my eyes, looking, as if through a vibrating cloth of gold and light, at the field, the red roofs infinitely far away, like things dreamed.

From that time on, I conceived a desperate need for the company of the good lady. No! I had never loved my mother in the same way. She was now away, traveling through remote lands, as if she no longer lived for me. I did not miss her. I did not think of her . . . My memories of her were darkened by that black, beautiful, powerful gaze, the way lines, shapes, profiles, colors disappear at night, in the uniform annihilation of darkness. Very little remained, a frayed remainder of longing, in that overwhelming, intense inertia.

Only one thing frightened me, the eternal fear of those who are happy, the irremediable bitterness of the finest days: that the state of affairs would suddenly collapse. My convalescence proceeded apace. It was heartbreaking.

The small infirmary room enclosed the world for me. My past consisted of the memories of the previous day, a special caress from Ema, a seductive attitude engraved on my memory as on an ever-present screen, the two dimples she would leave on the mattress with her elbows—before leaving, after the last visit at night when she stayed, waiting for me to fall asleep and holding her head in her hands, with her arms on the bed, imposing on me the lethargy of her last, vast, glance—and that I would kiss.

My future was the early wakening, the anxious hope for the first visit. I jumped out of bed, imprudently opened the window and the shutters. Still dark. A light ahead, far away, shining in solitude, thickening the darkness by contrast. Everywhere, the clean sky. The most complete silence. One could almost hear, in the blue silence of on high, the crackle of the burning stars.

I returned to the bed. I waited. I did not sleep. After a long time, the first blush of dawn entered the infirmary, moved onto the sheets, slowly, like spilled milk spreading. The trees outside moved with an increasing bustle of waking leaves. The tender light, fearful, spread sweetly over the floor and up the walls.

On the wall there was a large picture of a landscape, with snow-covered mountains in the background and, toward the front, a ramshackle house, an indigo waterfall, and spectral pines, twisted and hoary from a century's worth of storms. Dawn climbed up the picture as if it were morning among the pines as well. And I waited. The morning advanced.

The vegetation dressed up in the colors of day. The first dialogue between birds could be heard. And I waited. And she came . . . like dawn.

Once she brought me a letter, from Paris, from my father.

. . . *Save the present moment. The moral rule is the same as that of activity. Nothing left for tomorrow that could be done today; save the present. Let nothing else preoccupy you. The future is corrupting; the past is a solvent; only the present is strong. Longing is cowardice, apprehension another form of cowardice. Tomorrow is transient; the past is saddening, and sadness weakens.*

Longing, apprehension, hope are vain phantoms, inane projections of a mirage; only the present moment is actual and transitory. And save it! You will save the shipwreck of time.

As for a line of conduct: move forward. It is the honest logic of action.

Forward, in the line of duty, is the same as upward. In general, the expense of heroism is null. Think about that. For a lie to prevail, it is necessary that there be a complete system of lies harmonizing. Not to lie is easy.

. . . *I am in a big, interesting, busy city. The houses are taller than over there; in compensation, the ceilings are lower. It is as if the upper stories were crushing us. And as everyone has, above his head, a poorer neighbor, it seems that oppression, over here, means misery weighing upon the rich.*

Agitation is not good for me.

I open the window onto the boulevard: an effervescence of animation, of noise, of people, the lit-up feast of business, of attempts, of fortunes . . . But all come toward me, pass before me, move away from me, disappear. What a spectacle for a sick person. It is as if life were fleeing.

I give you my blessing . . .

The present moment . . . I still felt on my face the hand that had given me the letter; on my face, on my lips, happily, ardently, as if that were the moment, as if I were drinking from the beautiful shell of that hand the immortal delight of the living truth.

"Ah, you still have a father," said Ema, "a dear mother, brothers who love you . . . I have nothing; they are all dead . . . Sometimes they come to me in the night . . . shadows. There is no one for me. In this house I do not count. Let us leave these things aside.

"You don't know what it is to have a lonely heart like mine. All lie. Those who come closest are the greater traitors."

The daily contact in the solitude of that room had established the deep-seated familiarity of married couples.

Ema affected no longer having toward me the parsimony of small things. "Sérgio, my son." She greeted me in the morning. She left, returned refreshed, with the great vernal smile still moistened with the dew of the first wash. She laughed without reason—at the happy light of the morning, at seeing me strong, almost well.

She bent over me, expansive, shining her beauty on me, in the opening of her robe, like flowers spilling from a cornucopia.

She took my head in her hands, touched it to her own, moved back a little, and looked at me from close up, right in my eyes, in an inebriating meeting of gazes. She held her face close to mine and, lips against lips, told lovely little wordless tales, where the flushed liveliness of her mouth spoke more clearly than the imperceptible cooing that sang confusedly in her throat like a necklace of sound.

She thought me tiny, tiny. She sat on the chair. She took me on her lap, rocked me, pressed me to her bosom as if I were a newborn, flooding me with the warm radiation of motherhood, of love. She would loosen her hair and with a slight movement of her shoulders drop a dark tent over me. From above, from her cheeks there came to me the warm touch of her breath. I saw, in the depth of the tent, uncertain as in a dream, the sidereal fulguration of two eyes.

And it would be necessary to know how to bruise a heart and write in blood, with one's own life, a page that could do justice to the next few days, the last days . . .

And it all came to an end like the abrupt conclusion of a bad novel . . .

A sudden shout made me shudder in my bed: "Fire! Fire!" I threw the window open. The Athenaeum was burning.

The flames rose above the chalet in the direction of the main building. A huge ball of smoke contorted itself upward, sable on the upper reaches that seemed to touch the sky, and lit below with a copper-colored gleam.

Aristarco's house was completely silent.

The doors were open; everyone had left. I hurtled out of the infirmary.

Among the vacation recluses there was a recently matriculated boy, Americo. He came from the countryside. He seemed vexed from the first day. Aristarco tried to soften him—impossible; every day he seemed angrier. He never spoke to anyone. He was rather tall and seemed unusually robust. All looked upon him as upon a wild beast that should be respected. Suddenly, he disappeared. After a while three people brought him back: his father, the agent, and a servant. The boy, yellow, with red, moving splotches on his face, bit his lips till they bled. The father asked that he be treated with great severity. Aristarco, who thought highly of his ability to break in such boys, and of his irresistible method that combined energy with love, reassured the landowner: "I have seen worse."

Looking at him severely, with all the intensity of his moral force, he held the student tightly by the arm and made him sit down: "You shall stay here, my son!" The boy answered simply, his head bowed, with sudden complacency: "I shall stay." They said the father had treated him cruelly when he turned up at home, a fugitive from school.

With the celebration of the prizes so close, the case of the deserter was forgotten; for his part, he had given the most extreme example of discretion of any student ever.

In fact, the Athenaeum was burning. I sprinted through the door that connected Aristarco's house to the school.

The serious work of extinguishing the flames had not yet started. The greater part of the servants were always dismissed during school vacations; the few who remained were running around like mad people, unsure what to do, crying, "Fire!"

I found Aristarco on the side porch, agitated, shouting for the pumps, shouting that he was lost, that this was a complete disaster for him! Around him, neighbors who had run up were working to save the office before the flames got to it.

The fire had started in the wash hall.

Adding to the catastrophe, in the yard, a large pile of the wood left from the stands was in flames as well, heating the walls next to it, drying out the beams, favoring the spread of the fire.

I had been so surprised and shocked that I was not really conscious of the moment. I forgot myself watching the golden dragons flying over the Athenaeum, the huge smoky salamanders rising into the sky, writhing monstrously, and diving into the shadows half a mile above us.

The garden was invaded by a multitude; they vociferated, lamented themselves, clamored for help. Above the confusion of voices one could hear the whistle of the police in alarm mode, cutting, electric, and the plangent tolling of a bell, in the distance, like a discouraged cripple who would have liked to come.

The fire grew with bursts of enthusiasm, as if gladdened by its own flashes, challenging the night with the whip of its flames.

Over the patio, the garden, the entire neighborhood rained the sparks, contrasting the tameness of their fall with the tempestuous audacity of the fire. Incinerated cinders were dropping everywhere as the burning air projected them away from itself like dry leaves from a huge shaken tree.

When the water tanks turned up, the collapse of the buildings had already started. From moment to moment, loud booms sounded, like cannon shots, though muffled at times, shaking the ground like underground explosions. At times, as the flames revived, the burning column rose high, and one saw the terrified trees, motionless, the closest ones singed by the waves of torrid air sent out by the fire. The alleys, suddenly all lit up, multiplied the livid faces of those watching. On the street one could hear the hurrying wheeze of a steam-propelled fire truck; hoses, like endless serpents, crawled on the ground, squeezed against the walls, disappeared through a window. In the eaves, silhouetted against the terrible colors of the fire, the firemen moved.

The main part of the building was completely destroyed: entrance hall, chapel, all the dorms of the first and second forms. One salvage platoon tried to isolate the refectory and the rooms next to it, engaging in a complete job of vandalism, breaking down the roof, cutting the beams, destroying the furniture.

Toward the side porch, where Aristarco stood, impassive under the searing rain of sparks, there was a continuous flow of the miserable ruins of the rescue effort: broken cupboards, equipment, teaching posters, a thousand unrecognizable fragments of scorched pedagogy.

The façade of the Athenaeum looked terrifying. From various points on the roof, like twisted columns, there were thick, spiraling eruptions of smoke, and from the upper windows the smoke also rose in immense arms that seemed to hold up the incalculable mass of vapor above. In the absence of any wind, the clouds, heaped and compressed, seemed to consolidate into vaporous and restless rocks. Flames appeared in the windows of the second floor, darkening the ledges and blackening the lintels. Licked by the fire, the glass shattered in the windows. In the tempest one could tell the crystalline sound of the glass on the stone balconies, like lost toasts in that saturnalia of devastation.

Where the flames had not yet reached, firemen and other dedicated helpers were throwing out iron bedsteads, various belongings, night tables, which shattered in the garden with loud crushing noises. The images in the chapel had been rescued at the start of the fire. They were standing in the dew, beside a grassy area, turned toward the building, as if diverted by the sight. The Virgin of the Immaculate Conception cried. St. Anthony, carrying the child Jesus, was the least attentive, balancing with effort a disproportionate crown and offering, before the terrors confronting him, the example of the impassiveness of the foolish smile that a rascally image-maker had given him.

The work of the fire trucks, in that time of legendary limitations, was shameful. Fires ended when they had exhausted themselves. The mere presence of the fire chief irritated the flames as if it were a combustible impertinence. It became clear that a fire would be controlled more easily without the efforts of the professionals of the hose.

In the disaster of the Athenaeum the thing was obvious. After the arrival of the firefighters, the violence of the flames reached its peak. From inside the building, as from the entrails of a dying animal, there issued a muffled and vast roar. Through the windows, jambless, casementless, glassless, burst, carbonized, one could see the ceilings burn; the roof was collapsing, opening gaping holes to the sky. The rafters, above invisible braziers, twisted up in terrible contortions, as if animated by pain, and disappeared in the furnace.

Among the people, the fire was being discussed, explained, defined.

"How lucky that this disaster happened during the vacations!" "They say it was arson! . . ." Someone said that the fire had started in one room where mattresses were piled up, put aside so the house could be washed. They said that it had started all at once from various points, a gas line near the floor having been broken. Some suspected Aristarco and ventured considerations about the financial circumstances of the establishment and the headmaster's luxuries.

The news of the fire had spread through a good part of the city, despite the hour. In the side streets there was a festive atmosphere. A large number of students had gathered to witness the proceedings. Some were bravely helping the firefighters. Others surrounded the headmaster, either in silence, or exclaiming at random and manifesting symptoms of the most dangerous desolation.

Aristarco, in despair at the start, reflected that despair was incompatible with dignity. Calmly, he received the important people searching him out, authorities, friends, who tried to lessen his pain with soothing offers of support. He faced adversity in a manner sovereign, contemplating the annihilation of his fortune with the tranquility of the great victims.

He accepted the rigors of fortune.

> *Et comme il voit en nous des âmes peu communes*
> *Hors de l'ordre commun il nous fait des fortunes.*

After a few hours of sleep, I went back to the school. The fire had abated. Part of the house had escaped. Dining hall, kitchen, pantry, one or two of the rooms. The independent pavilions in the yard had been spared. The pumps were still working, cooling the burned rubble and the walls. From all sides, as from an extensive field of volcanic vents, there rose threads of smoke, spreading a dark fog and a strong smell of burned wood. The main walls held, pierced by windows as if broken into at regular intervals, blackened as if by the work of long ages of ruination.

Upon the remaining internal walls bits of rafters balanced, covered by a light mold of ashes. In the luminous atmosphere of the morning there floated the funereal quiet that comes on the day following the spectacle of a great disaster.

They told me extraordinary things. The fire had been set on purpose by Americo, who, with that intention, had broken up the gas pipes in the lavatory hall. He had disappeared after the assault.

The headmaster's lady had also disappeared during the fire.

I went to the marble terrace. There was Aristarco, who had not slept, the poor man. In the garden the multitude of gawkers was still around.

Some families were strolling by, all done up in their morning attire. Around the headmaster many disciples had stayed since the day before, immovable and compassionate. There he was, in the chair where he had spent the night, motionless, oblivious, covered with ashes like a penitent, his right foot on a huge heap of coal, his elbow stuck on his thigh, the great hairy hand holding his chin, fingers lost in the white moustache, brows knitted.

They were talking about the firebug. He did not move! They said that the lady could not be found. Motionless! The very lady on whom he had counted to run the kindergarten. Venerable grief! Supreme indifference of exceptional suffering! Inert majesty of the felled oak! His was the monopoly of sorrow. The Athenaeum devastated! His work lost, the incalculable conquest due to his effort! In peace! . . .

What we saw was not a man, but a *de profundis.*

There he was: around him, in heaps, toasted geometric shapes, broken cosmography instruments, huge wall posters in shreds, burned, tarnished, scattered guts from anatomy lessons, broken prints of sacred history in pictures, chronologies of national history, zoological illustrations, moral precepts on the tiles, like lost teachings, wounded terrestrial globes, split celestial globes. Dregs and soot over everything—black spoils of life, of history, of traditional beliefs, of the vegetation from past times, splinters of calcined continents, ejected planets from a dead astronomy, golden suns dethroned and incinerated.

And he, like an unlucky god, sad, hovering over the universal destruction of his work.

And here I end this chronicle of nostalgia. True nostalgia? Pure memories, nostalgia perhaps, if we ponder that time is the passing occasion of facts but more important, the eternal funeral of the hours.

I am indebted to Zenir Campos Reis, who wrote the introduction and notes to the 1979 Brazilian edition of *O Ateneu,* published by Editora Ática, for some of the information contained in these notes.

5   *the Brazilian empire*   Brazil was an empire until 1889, when it became a republic; at that point, "provinces" became "states."

9   *murals by Kaulbach*   Wilhelm von Kaulbach (1805–1874) was a German painter then famous as a muralist; he decorated many public buildings, mostly in Munich.

28   *Thersites*   A character in the *Iliad,* Thersites was a foul-mouthed commoner in the Greek army who was beaten for insulting Agamemnon.

31   *a few cambucá trees*   "Cambucá" is the name (of Indian origin) of a fruit tree native to the Atlantic forest near Rio and São Paulo, now rare. It is said to produce an extraordinarily delicious fruit that tastes like mango and papaya; its scientific name is *Plinia edulis.*

32   *Flos Sanctorum*   An illustrated medieval compendium of the lives of the saints.

41   *like Fénelon's benevolent Minerva*   Reference to *Les aventures de Télémaque (The Adventures of Telemachus, Son of Ulysses* [1693–94]), by François Fénelon (1651–1715), in which Minerva, Roman incarnation of the Greek goddess Athena, patroness of learning and war, helps the hero. The book was a best seller in its time, seen as a model for the education of young men.

42   *with Father Anchieta*   Father José de Anchieta (1535–1597) was a Jesuit missionary to the Portuguese colony of Brazil. A poet and playwright, he is credited with founding the city of São Paulo.

42   *Rocio Square*   Historic Largo do Rocio, now renamed in honor of Tiradentes, hero and martyr of Brazilian independence. At its center stands an equestrian statue of (then prince) Dom Pedro I, who, on the banks of the Ipiranga brook, declared Brazil independent of Portugal on September 7, 1822. A famous painting represents him proclaiming independence on a rearing horse, sword drawn.

43   *coffee plant*   Coffee is said to have been smuggled into Brazil from French Guyana with the help of the border state's governor's wife.

43   *Antonio Salema*   Governor of Rio de Janeiro in the late 1500s.

43   *Vidigal*   Probably a reference to Miguel Nunes Vidigal, member of an incipient police force in colonial Rio, notorious for his cruelty to vagrants, idlers, and runaway slaves.

43   *João VI*   King of Portugal, who fled the Napoleonic invasion of the Iberian Peninsula by transferring the court to Rio (1808). His son declared Brazilian independence.

43   *Mem de Sá*   Third governor-general of colonial Brazil, he expelled the French who had tried to establish a colony in the Bay of Guanabara (1567). The founding of Rio de Janeiro (1565) was part of the effort to deny the French access to the land.

43   *Maurice of Nassau*   The first governor of the colony the Dutch tried to establish in northeastern Brazil, in what is now the state of Pernambuco (1581–1654).

43   *the hero from Minas*   Canonical representation of Tiradentes as he was led to the gallows.

43   *Roquette*   Author of a number of works defending absolutist rule.

48   *The Lusiads*   One of the great epic poems of the Renaissance, published in 1572. Written by the Portuguese poet Luis Vaz de Camões and modeled on Virgil's *Aeneid*, it recounts the Portuguese voyages of discovery to Africa and India in 1497–98.

52   *the Southern Cross*   A constellation visible in the Southern Hemisphere; its longest leg points south.

56   *gospel injunction*   A reference to Matt. 5:39 (New International Version): "But I tell you, do not resist an evil person. If anyone slaps you on the right cheek, turn to them the other cheek also."

59   *so many Ladislau Nettos*   Ladislau de Souza Mello Netto (1838–1894), named director of the National Museum by Emperor Pedro II, wanted to make the museum into a center of exhibits and education. Netto was for a time the most influential scientist in the country; eventually he turned to physical anthropology and promoted racist theories supposedly based on Darwin. He lost support with the fall of the monarchy in 1889 (Maria Margareth Lopes, *O Brasil descobre a pesquisa científica: Os museus e as ciências naturais no século XIX* [São Paulo: Hucitec, 1997], 206).

62   *Gautier's later poetry*   A French Romantic poet in his youth, Théophile Gautier (1811–1872) lived long enough to inspire the modernists.

64   *Mount Horeb*   The mountain where Moses received the Tablets of the Law.

67   *Mato Grosso*   A sparsely populated western state, mostly agricultural and forested, on the border with Bolivia. Its capital is about 1,200 miles from Rio—seat of the Imperial Court—over difficult roads.

69   *ad majorem gloriam*   The full Latin expression is *ad majorem dei gloriam*: for the greater glory of God.

77   *Alexandre Herculano*   An important Portuguese poet, novelist, and historian, and the author of one of the best-known historical novels of the period, *Eurico, o presbítero,* Herculano lived from 1810 to 1877. Pictures show him with a very high forehead and a grim expression.

77   *New Forest*   The full title in Portuguese is *Nova floresta ou Sylva de varios apophthegmas e ditos sentenciosos, espirituaes e moraes com reflexoens, em que o util da doutrina se acompanha com o vario da erudição, assim divina, como humana* ("New Forest, or Forest of various apothegms and sayings, spiritual and moral, with reflections in which useful points of doctrine are accompanied by diverse comments of divine as well as human erudition). The work was written by Reverend Manuel Bernardes, in Lisbon, between 1726 and 1728. It consists of a series of anecdotes and popular tales, with a moral or exemplary point, followed by commentary that extracts edifying lessons from them.

78   *five loaves of bread*   Reference to the miracle of the fish and five loaves that fed a multitude, reported in all four canonical Gospels (Matt. 14:13–21; Mark 6:31–44; Luke 9:10–17, and John 6:5–15).

79   *a two-hundred réis coin*   The coin at the time was the *real,* plural *réis.*

80   *clearinghouse*   In English in the original.

80   *Fox's theory*   The reference may be to Sir Charles James Fox (1749–1806), a British statesman active at the time of the American and French Revolutions. There may also be a reference to contemporary arguments about monetary policy: Brazil was the first country in the Americas to abandon the gold standard for a financial system based entirely on paper currency.

83   *"bird's eye"*   Strong, fine Virginia tobacco, prepared by cutting the whole leaf, including the veins. In English in the original.

83   *the maté gourd*   In Rio Grande do Sul, the southernmost Brazilian state, it is customary for the gaucho cattlemen to sit, of an evening, by a fire, and pass around a communal gourd filled with hot maté tea.

85   *closed . . . on the days of Janus's peace*   The temple of the two-faced Roman god Janus closed only during times of peace.

90   *"Morió"*   This is the author's spelling. The correct form in Spanish is *murió*, meaning "he died."

91   *the skin of Ceres*   Ceres (Roman) or Demeter (Greek) was the goddess of agriculture and of the earth. Her beautiful face is said to have wrinkled up in despair when her daughter was kidnapped by the god of the underworld, Pluto (Hades in the Greek pantheon).

91   *sabbath*   Believed by some to be an assembly of witches and warlocks presided over by Satan, and conducted on Saturday at midnight.

93   *Pernambuco*   One of the states in the Brazilian northeast.

94   *Blondin*   Charles Blondin (1824–1897) was a French gymnast and acrobat who gave public shows from the age of five. One of his exploits was walking on a tightrope across the Niagara Gorge.

97   *the daredevil from the Rubicon*   Pompey, a Roman senator, formed the first Roman triumvirate, with Crassus and Julius Caesar. Julius Caesar wrote, of his military campaign in Gaul, that he "came, saw, and conquered." Returning from the campaign, he crossed the Rubicon creek with his army, which was considered an act of insurrection, as he took sole charge of the government, breaking up the triumvirate; the expression "crossing the Rubicon" came to mean "passing a point of no return."

98   *Believer's Harp*   Volume of poetry by Alexandre Herculano.

98   *O Guarani*   Well-known novel by José de Alencar, with an indigenous hero, Pery.

98   *Aimbiré*   Variant of the name of a group of indigenous tribes in Brazil.

98   *Cilla and Marius, Titus and Nero*   Roman political leaders in the years roughly contemporary with the life of Julius Caesar.

98   *Plutarch and the Boeotians*   Born in the Greek region of Boeotia, Plutarch (A.D. 46–120) was a Greek historian, biographer, and essayist who became a Roman citizen.

99   *Quintilian*   Quintilian (c. 35–c. 100) was a Roman orator and lawyer, born in Hispania. The author of a classic treatise on rhetoric, he was an admirer of Cicero and an opponent of Seneca, whose oratory he considered too attractive.

101   *Simon of Nantua*   A collection of didactic tales by Laurent Pierre de Jussieu (1792–1886), *Simon de Nantua* was widely read through the nineteenth century.

101   *Bernardes*   Manuel Bernardes (1644–1710), author of the five-volume *Nova Floresta*.

101   *Bertoldo*   Possibly a reference to *Le sottilissime astutie di Bertoldo*, by Giulio Cesare Croce, the first of a collection of three tales narrating, first, the adventures of the wily peasant Bertoldo, who becomes an advisor to the king; and then of his son, Bertoldino; and, finally, of his grandson Carcasenno. The work, published in 1620, was based on material that had been circulating since the Middle Ages.

101   *The Rooster's Will*   A satirical folk poem of Portuguese origin performed at the time of Carnival, in which a rooster about to die leaves various parts of himself to the villagers.

103   *Rio Grande do Sul*   Southernmost Brazilian state.

104   *Professor Hartt*   Charles Frederick Hartt (1848–1878), a Canadian-American geologist, paleontologist, naturalist, and ethnographer. He was a student assistant to Louis Agassiz and went with him to Brazil in 1868; in all, he participated in four expeditions to Brazil between 1870 and 1878, dying in Rio de Janeiro, of yellow fever.

105   *a critique of Brazilian literature*   Dr. Claudio presents a roster of prominent Brazilian writers (with some notable omissions), from colonial times on.

107   *five letters expressing the energy of the people*   French *merde*, Portuguese *merda*; literally "shit" or, more loosely, "go to hell!" Some sources say that when the British called on Pierre Cambronne, one of Napoleon's army commanders, to surrender at Waterloo, he replied: "Merde!"

116   *dies irae*   Latin, "days of wrath"; by implication, the Last Judgment.

117   *Rome in flames*   In July of A.D. 64, under Emperor Nero, Rome caught fire; Nero was accused of setting the blaze. As for aesthetics, Nero thought himself a poet and is said to have exclaimed, as he committed suicide: "Ah, what an artist the world is about to lose!"

122   *Mallets and Guillots*   Reference unclear; may refer to family crest cards or stamps the students collected and traded.

125   *a true Capanema*   In 1852, Dr. G. Schüch de Capanema, professor of physics in Rio, installed a telegraph line from the country residence of the emperor to the military headquarters. It became known as the Capanema telegraph (Victor Maximilian Berthold, *History of the Telephone and Telegraph in Brazil, 1851–1921* [New York, 1922]).

126   *O, Havas*   Havas, the first French news agency, was founded in 1835.

128   *kakós kaì ruparós*   Greek: "bad and dirty."

129   *Froebel's methods*   Friedrich Wilhelm August Froebel (1782–1852), a German pedagogue and a student of Pestalozzi's, laid the foundation for modern pedagogical theories; he created the concept of the kindergarten.

129   *Crescite!*   Latin imperative: "grow!"

130   *Ceará*   A state in the Brazilian northeast that is poor and subject to catastrophic droughts.

140   *most respectable Veronica*   According to legend, a pious woman of Jerusalem known in tradition as Veronica (apparently from *vera icon,* or "true image"), offered Jesus, on his way to Calvary, a cloth with which to wipe his face; the cloth then bore the imprint of the face and was said to perform miracles.

141   *Primus inter pares*   Latin: "first among equals."

143   *the Two Brothers*   "Dois Irmãos," or "Two Brothers," is a pair of mountains at the end of Leblon Beach, in Rio; the trail to the top of the bigger "brother" takes about an hour and a half to walk.

143   *the Corcovado*   The Corcovado, with the large statue of Christ at the top, is widely recognized as the symbol of Rio.

143   *the Praia Vermelha*   The "Red Beach," a small and lovely beach in Rio, where several military installations were and are located, whence, presumably, the continuation of the military simile.

148   *Mr. Revy*   In the *Annaes do Parlamento Brazileiro, Câmara dos Sres. Deputados* (*Annals of the Brazilian Parliament, Chamber of Deputies,* April 15–June 2, 1886, vol. 1, p. 111), there is mention of a Mr. Revy, involved in some dubious engineering project in northern Brazil. Presumably that had made the news.

158   *Pentapolis*   The region where Sodom, Gomorrah, and another three cities that were to be destroyed for their sins were located.

164 *Amor unus erat* Latin, "It was an only love."

165 *Paul and Virginia* A widely read 1788 novel by Bernardin de Saint-Pierre, about two children brought up in isolation, on an island in the Antilles, by their mothers. The girl is sent back to France for an education, can't stand it, returns, and drowns as her ship is about to land. The young man dies of a broken heart.

165 *"Virginie, elle sera heureuse!"* "Virginia, she will be happy!"

166 *"Is it for your intelligence? . . ."* In French in the original.

166 *Schwartz's invention* The German monk and alchemist Berthold Schwartz (1310–1384) was long credited with the invention of gunpowder. However, it seems that he merely concocted a form of gunpowder that could be used for more than pyrotechnics.

167 *Halbout's grammar* J. F. Halbout was the author of a French grammar widely used at the time.

168 *mere mention of Sallust* Gallus Sallustius Crispus (c. 86–35 B.C.) was a Roman historian and the author of *The Conspiracy of Catiline*, among other works. The implication is that the students read his work in Latin.

168 *One of us was Augustus . . .* Augustus: Roman emperor. Cinna: member of an important ancient Roman family, connected with Julius Caesar. Nearchus: general under Alexander the Great. Polyeucte: Armenian nobleman, Christian convert, martyred by the Romans. Horatii and Curiatii: two sets of triplets who battled for the fate of Rome, seventh century B.C. El Cid, national hero of Spain, and his son, Don Diego, about whom many epics and plays were written. Joas and Joad: biblical characters, about whom Racine wrote one of his tragedies (and Händel, an oratorio). Nero: Roman emperor. Burrus: one of Nero's advisors, probably poisoned. Philinte and Alceste: characters in Molière's *Misanthrope.* Tartuffe and Cléante: characters in Molière's comedy *Tartuffe.*

169 *Chimène's engagement . . .* Chimène: the main female character in Corneille's play *Le Cid.* Camilla (or Camille): main character in *La Dame aux Camélias* by Alexandre Dumas fils. Agrippina: wife of Emperor Claudius, sister of Emperor Caligula, mother of Emperor Nero. Elmira and Célimène: characters in Molière's *Tartuffe.*

169 *Cato of the black balls* Cato the Elder was a conservative Roman politician who preached the destruction of Carthage. It is not

clear that he engaged in the use of black spheres to exclude people from organizations, a practice that became known as "blackballing," which seems to have started in the eighteenth century.

172   *Memoria in albis*   Latin: "memory was a blank."

176   *'tee aitch'*   The sound represented by the English letter combination *th* is notoriously difficult for Portuguese speakers to pronounce.

176   *Tautphoeus*   The German-born Baron Tautphoeus became a teacher at the Pedro II College in Rio.

179   *femmes qui sortent*   French: "women who go out" (connoting looseness).

186   *Cuvier*   Baron Georges Cuvier (1769–1832) was a French zoologist who established the fields of comparative anatomy and paleontology; he is the author of *The Animal Kingdom.*

192   *Cuiabá*   Capital of Franco's home state of Mato Grosso.

195   *the Princess Regent*   During her father's absences, Princess Isabel, who was the heiress to the throne, acted as regent. On the third of these absences, she signed the law known as the Golden Law or Lei Áurea, ending slavery in Brazil (1888). The emperor was deposed the following year; Isabel spent the rest of her life in exile, in France.

206   *Gottschalk*   Born in New Orleans in 1829, Louis Moreau Gottschalk was an American pianist and composer, thought of as the greatest classical musician in the New World. Arriving in Rio de Janeiro in 1869, he gave numerous concerts, greatly influencing the local musical scene. He contracted malaria and died of the disease or of the treatment in Rio in 1869.

211   *as Schopenhauer describes them*   The highly influential German philosopher Arthur Schopenhauer (1788–1860) is well known for what is labeled as pessimism; he also wrote feelingly about music.

220   *Et comme il voit . . . fait des fortunes.*   From *Horace* by the French dramatist Pierre Corneille (1606–1684): "And since he sees in us uncommon souls / He chooses for us uncommon fortunes."

221   *de profundis*   Opening Latin words of Psalm 130 (129 in the Vulgate, the Latin translation of the Bible): *de profundis clamavi,* "from the depths I cried out."